FIERCE TIDES

THE PURGATORY REIGN SERIES
BOOK 3

BY
LM. PRESTON

CONTENTS

COPYRIGHT

Copyright © 2017 by LM Preston
All rights reserved.
ISBN 978-0-9969195-7-9
ISBN 978-0-9969195-6-2

Editor: Cindy Davis
Proof Reader: Dawn Yacovetta
Cover Design by We've Got You Covered. All Rights Reserved.
Interior Design and Formatting by Stephany Wallace.
All Rights Reserved.

A Phenomenal One Press publication 2017
www.phenomenalonepress.com

SYPNOSIS

In the Purgatory Reign Series Peter Saints understood the reason he was hated and hunted by an evil so twisted he had to brace himself to face it. He didn't mind taking his part of the blame of unleashing it. Now he would destroy it for nothing less than to calm the fear he'd seen simmering in Angel's eyes. The love he had for her was boundless, he'd fight anything to heal it, heal her, and free them. This made it personal. He would finish it.

ALSO BY L.M. PRESTON

PURGATORY REIGN SERIES

Purgatory Reign, Book 1

Deviant Storm, Book 2

Fierce Tides, Book 3

THE PACK SERIES

The Pack, Book 1

Retribution, Book 2

THE BANDITS SERIES

Bandits, Book 1

Wastelands, Book 2

DEDICATION

For my children and my husband, who helped me dream the impossible and gave me the support to achieve it. To my husband who wrote a short story for a class that I dug out of a box, and read to be inspired to create this great adventure.

ACKNOWLEDGMENTS

Thanks to God for giving me this anxious energy to create and tenacious spirit of positivity with an active imagination. To my devoted Beta Readers, Jordan, Missy and my daughter, who helped me create a better story. To my husband, who created the basis and inspiration for this story. To my editor, Cindy Davis, who's been my best support in my art. To my kids and my husband, who continue to give me true and honest feedback for all of my work. I thank you.

CHAPTER 1

"One me, one him." Peter Saints spat on the ground as he tossed a knife at the smiling and deceptive face of Gavin Steele. "I hate you." He glared at the image of Gavin. Behind the man on the poster, Steele Industries company headquarters loomed with slick gold trimmed windows and pale concrete in a cluster of high-rise buildings that consumed a city block. Its slogan 'Bold New Directions' taunted Peter. The poster was tattered and hung on the packed dirt wall by a nail. The smell of earth permeated the place and gave Peter the feeling of being buried alive. A wayward tickle of helplessness scratched at the surface of his neck. A restlessness he'd felt even before he and his friends came to this off-the-grid Sanctuary managed by the Decretum Venia. He fought it. Wrestled it down deep into the depths of his mind.

Peter bent over the cot he shared with Angel to zip the backpack holding his gear. They'd moved two of the battered blue metal-framed makeshift beds together to keep warm and stave off the memories of the hell on earth they'd endured for over two years. But Peter would end this war with Gavin Steele, the demon inside him, and his minions from the Order of the Dragon, even if he died trying. God knows, he'd come close – too close – many times before.

While sliding on the backpack, a rumble above him caused a pounding in his chest. Something was wrong. It was time to get Angel and the others in his crew out of there. They'd lain low too long, yet still didn't have a plan or a way to end Gavin Steele completely. Now though, Peter just had to wing it. The first thing they had to do was get answers. And though that deadly hand had been played before and led to the ruin of humankind, Peter had no choice but to do it again. Only this time would be his last chance; there were no more treasures to be found. The one he was after now would end him – or Gavin. Peter ran toward the arched opening of the room and punched the pale beaded curtains aside. Heart pounding, feet stomping, he ran into the main hall and collided into Remmy who was barreling around the corner.

"Glad I found you, man; the Elders are moving all the kids out of here. Crap's gone wrong with security, and the Order of the Dragon has found our location." His shock of red hair was closely cut, with the exception of the long curly lop that fell to the side of his forehead, making the freckles on his nose stand out on his heated face.

Peter stared down at him and placed his burning brown hand on Remmy's shoulder. "Where's Angel? Kyle and Argia?"

"This way." Remmy led Peter with a wave of a hand. "Rosa and Pastor Finn are briefing the elders of the Decretum Venia."

"About?" Peter hurried beside Remmy and dodged the wave of kids, old and young, running and screaming through the carved-out tunnels.

"The Wall of Ash," Remmy uttered.

Peter tugged at Remmy's shoulder to twist him around. "What about it?"

"If the barrier keeps weakening...Gavin will be free." Remmy shrugged away from Peter's hand to continue down the passageway.

"What are Pastor Finn and Rosa going to do? Did you hear that part?"

"The sentinels of the Decretum Venia have been assassinating the head people in the Extraho of Obscurum to slow Gavin's people's capture of us kids. Other than that, they've got nothing. They can't penetrate Steele Industries' key players in Gavin's inner circle. High security and only well-known membership can enter the buildings. The kids they've captured are well hidden, and Rosa believes they have been drugged heavily to the point where she can't connect to them."

This was worse than Peter thought. He'd hoped Gavin would be trapped longer. Argia and Rosa built a strong shield to keep him there, but it wasn't going to hold. Once it fractured, Gavin would be stronger and more determined to destroy Peter and the others.

"You're kiddin' me! They should know going back is the only way to finish this. We have to destroy the Wall of Ash and Gavin within it."

Remmy took the dirt stairs two at a time; Peter was close behind.

"Well, they got nothin', so it's up to us now, right?"

"Right. Show me to the way out. I'm grabbin' my crew and going it on my own." Peter cleared the last step and entered the main room of the compound. He spied Angel and Argia pointing the younger kids in various directions, while Kyle leaned against the wall, peeling his fingernails.

Remmy elbowed him. "Yeah, up to us. Meet me outside in ten minutes; I'll get a car ready for you." He put his hand to Peter's chest. "On the condition that I get a piece of this. I want into your team."

Peter hesitated a moment; he and Remmy never really got along. Bringing the guy could mean trouble, but he needed the nut-head's brawn.

"Not on my team – but part of the action."

Remmy smirked. "I'll take it."

CHAPTER 2

Gavin's enlarged hand, pale with fingers fashioned like talons, pounded the gray, moving cloud matter of the Wall of Ash. Fire licked his tongue. The pain was intense yet fed his insatiable craving for it.

He was trapped in his creation, a tornado of soot and fire with a black murky tarred substance like acid. It reeked of the rotting flesh of those killed within in it. The tornado of dark matter emitted pulsing smoke that trembled with each blow of his thick fist. It swirled and twisted upward to the heavens and deep to the depths of what some would call hell. It was a portal—a sliver between both worlds. It could not be entered or escaped without Gavin's command. He liked it that way.

Gavin was in control of the most powerful place on Earth, and he hungered for more of it. He maintained his grasp of the authority over his demon master by keeping Balaal tortured inside the special realms of hell that was now Gavin's domain.

Gavin sniffed the air for the residue of those who trapped him within the Wall of Ash. The wall's ability to eat angels and their genetically modified humans hadn't served him the way he'd hoped. It was supposed to be impenetrable for them – not him.

Peter Saints and his psychic gifted followers had imprisoned him within his own masterpiece. Gavin would get out. The witch, his fiancée, would find a way. His brother's job was to make sure of it.

He inhaled. The fragrant smell of sour smoke and the essence of the tortured souls sacrificed for his freedom hung heavy around him. Their passing souls were suctioned into the murky tornado's walls where Gavin could will their trapped beings to the devourer. It kept the demon king sated. Unfortunately, it wasn't working fast enough.

"Kill Peter Saints!" Gavin screamed with each blow of his fist to the barrier.

He knew his demands were heard by Mara. Her psychic ability to connect to his thoughts urged her to sacrifice many young souls to his freedom. The increase of the ambiances of the little ones passed through the barrier of the Wall of Ash. It must've been frightening for her victims to be thrown into what would appear to be a standing tornado of fire, storm clouds, and lightning, to those on the other side. He needed more of the sacrificed. She had to find the spell to deteriorate the structure, or he would be trapped for too long, and the boy, Peter Saints, would find a way to weaken the progress of his loyal subjects.

He slivered out his tongue, its forked tip snapping toward the moving gray matter as a small, eel-like creature with eyes of fire weaved in and out of it. Gavin's clawed feet grazed the ground as he prepared to charge forward yet again.

The floor of dried molten rock, black with flecks of silver, was jagged under his thick bare feet. The cavernous surroundings were the color of midnight, but his eyes clearly focused with each blow of his fist. Although, it appeared a mass of moving smoke, it didn't part easily. It had a slimy wet form that bounced then re-shaped to his fisted blows. The flash of brightness from the light-ning pulsing and raging within its smoky soot seemed to fight against Gavin's attack. The portal covered only acres of land to those on the other side, but within it were unseen dark corridors that could suck one through various entrances into the hellish realm.

"Ahhhhhhh!"

His muscles tensed. Gavin stumbled as Balaal's claws dug deeper into his twisted soul. Their connection was unbreakable. Gavin swallowed back the blood that seeped into his throat as Balaal seemed to force his way up from his stomach and into his esophagus. The agony, though fierce, wasn't effective to wrestle Gavin's reign over Balaal. The torture had become Gavin's drug of choice, which fueled his tenacity to steady his rule over his former puppet master. Ever since the fated day when Peter Saints unknowingly transferred power to Gavin over the demon, Gavin refused to allow any being to have dominion over him. For that small act of retaliation, Gavin respected Peter Saints. It wouldn't save Peter though; the boy would be dead—and soon. Gavin's mouth watered at the thought.

Stumbling back from the Wall of Ash, Gavin whispered a promise, "Peter Saints, I will eat every drop of your flesh for this." Then he raised his chin and yelled, "Witch! Mara get me out of here! Free me."

Gavin hunched his wide shoulders and slashed his talons through the thick gray substance. The demonites—miniature demon souls with razor sharp teeth and eyes of fire—challenged him. A few bit at his talons as he ripped down through its sticky mass to thin it out for his form.

Voices, distinct yet distant, called his name. "Gavin! We have found a way in. The blockade burns us; can you give us a sign that you're alive?" Lucien yelled, his voice riding through the waves of Mara's psychic connection. His voice, her voice, intertwined.

Gavin's eyes slanted into reptilian slits. Brother, his servant Lucien, would pay for this. After all the training, torture, and mind control he'd bestowed on the worthless miscreant, his brother continued to make priceless mistakes. Gavin charged through the burning gray mass, jerked back his shoulders against the slashing bites of the small demons, and balled his talons into fists.

The barricade erected by Peter's collaborators was a clear throbbing wall. It separated Gavin from the Earthly plane and incinerated anyone with the heritage of his kind who dared touch it. The transparent oppressor pressed against the rip he'd created in the astral plane between Earth and Hell, mocking him.

He was getting out. Now. Gavin would not stop beating at it until the barrier tumbled.

"Let – me – out!" Gavin hit it, tore at it, and then growled.

Stepping back just enough for momentum, he charged horns-first into the barrier, over and over again.

The pounding was relentless; the boom sounded like thunder, urging him onward in his continuous onslaught. His huge body ached, but it was euphoric. It fueled him. Fed his desire to feel more of the impact. Again, he rammed his head into it.

Red, slimy, dark blood smeared the opposite side of the obstacle. His towering soot-filled tornado pounded at his back and threatened to knock him down. But Gavin didn't stop. Balaal's piercing claws dug deeper. The demonites were in a frenzy, nipping and slicing at his entire form – leaving no place untouched. Even with his demon-fused body, he bled and was ripped open by the ravaging fight against the Wall of Ash's hunger to keep him within.

The vision of Peter Saints' head at his sacrificial table spurned, fed, and drove him to crash harder into the imposing prison.

The chanting on the other side grew louder, melodious, and strengthened his resolve. Gavin rammed, tore, and beat the imposter. His followers fought just as hard to free him. More blood spattered on it, a small body thrown against it. He would be free. One, then another victim was hurled at the structure, all of which Gavin would devour when he got free.

Crack.

Gavin didn't stop; heat boiled in his blood. Balaal grew stronger, pushing out, breaking ribs, licking at Gavin's bones. But Gavin didn't stop the pounding; he'd deal with Balaal later; he needed this, more pain, more fuel, more...

It shattered. Finally! Gavin burst through, near a second death. Burned, seared, and stabbed through his eyes, chest, stomach then legs. Gavin stumbled, but licked his lips and pounded with every bit of power within him.

"Ahh!" he roared.

Skin ripped from his body in chunks, fire torched his skin, and within his throat, but he didn't stop the onslaught. His charred, broken, and ripped body was soaked in blood. Every part of him was shaken.

"Is he alive?" someone asked.

With the last bit of strength Gavin wrestled, he released a hoarse cry, "Kill Peter Saints!" and collapsed into the darkness of sleep.

CHAPTER 3

Peter zigzagged through the dim passageways of the doomsday-prepper version of the Decretum Venia's. The kids ran to and fro. Peter dodged some of them. Even though they were being attacked, it didn't come as a total surprise. They'd been trained for it. Some of the kids Peter passed on his way through the underground compound actually appeared excited and ready to fight off their attackers. Peter grinned knowing the adults there wouldn't give half of the kids the chance. Everyone seemed to be directed to go to the escape passages.

Peter was glad the tunnel he'd used to get out of the prepper site wasn't well known to the others. Not many kids were going his direction. They were heading to the other corridors that had bulletproof escape vans guarded by some of the strongest fighters in the order.

The kids and elders of the Decretum Venia would get out safely, but only he and his crew knew the more difficult and longest way out of the place. It wasn't in the direction where the others were going—to safety. It went toward the fight.

Peter slipped into what appeared to be an uneven crack in the rock wall of the tunnel. It was the tightest and most uncomfortable of passageways, but it led to the farthest exit from the attack and damage to the compound. Miles of rock had been dug, placing them a safe distance from the intimidation tactics of their enemies.

His flashlight guided the path. Placing it in his mouth, Peter climbed the steep stairwell, only large enough for him to squeeze up. He grasped a few of the steps above to stay balanced, hugging the edges as he ascended. Pushing his head on the wooden door he'd left unlocked the week he decided they would be leaving the safety of the bunker, he grunted against the weight.

The brush and density of the trees around the exit blocked the sun. Small pins of light pierced the grass thick with dead leaves. That was all the illumination Peter needed. He tucked the flashlight into his backpack and jogged to the covered clearing.

Peter slowed his pace and smiled when he found the vehicles Remmy promised would be waiting. The black jeep was beat up, but it would get them there. It was tucked under thick brush, and the grass surrounding it was slightly flattened from its well tread wheels. It was parked next to a gray jeep, not quite in as good of shape, but sturdy and clean with spots of rust under the carriage.

A thunder of firepower agitated the leaves of the thick cover of trees. Even though the surrounding area was under attack, the fighters in the Decretum Venia seemed to be handling the fray efficiently.

Peter dropped his gear into the already packed trunk. Then, he hit the top of the black roof, glad the jeep had a hard roof. They'd need it.

He pivoted around, hearing the wrestle of trees. The others were close. They knew the score. Keep quiet, stay hidden, and get the hell out of dodge when crap hit the fan.

"Damn! It's good to see you." Kyle broke through the thick

bush to the side of the jeep. His blond buzz-cut sported a few loose leaves on top. He shook them off and blinked and then squinted his blue eyes at Peter. "Time to ditch this place."

"What took you so long?" Peter scanned behind Kyle, anxiousness pulsing in his chest while he searched for Angel.

"Peter!" Angel's exasperated response rushed from her lips. She pushed Kyle out of the way. Then, she sprinted towards Peter with arms outstretched. Peter caught her. He held her close when she jumped up and wrapped her legs around his waist.

Kissing Angel hungrily, Peter nipped her full pink bottom lip and brushed a wavy black strand of hair from her pale freckled cheek.

"Glad you made it," Peter uttered; the deep rumble of his voice skipped. He gave Angel one final tight hug before letting her slip from his arms.

"That beast, Remmy, tried to convince us to let him follow us to the next Sanctuary." Sparks lighted from within her green eyes. Angel tossed her bag into the trunk and tucked her white t-shirt into her jeans.

Peter's hand rested on the top of the jeep while he waited for Argia to finish with her bag. Her tiny frame and bobbed blue hair covered her slanted eyes as she struggled to pull the huge duffle bag behind her. The girl's silver mini-skirt flapped against the tops of her slight thighs, just above the elastic of her thick thigh-high tights. Peter shook his head, never understanding the strange girl's aversion to jeans like the rest of them preferred to wear.

"Where is he? And Gil?" Peter asked.

"They are behind us."

"We can skip out on Remmy now." Kyle plopped the duffle bag he'd taken from Argia into the trunk.

Angel snorted. "Remmy has the key to both jeeps so we won't leave them." Angel tucked a gun in the back of her jeans.

"Gil can go with us, but Remmy...well, I'd rather he not. I promised he could work with us though." Peter sighed.

"No freakin' way! That assphat has a serious ego problem. And I can't say I trust him. The fire-ball head always thinks he's running shits." Kyle spat.

Peter lifted an eyebrow. "You've got a nerve, prep school dropout and reformed drug dealer."

"Oh, there it is, ripping me up about my past transgressions. Kick rocks, man, I don't like the guy. He hit on Argia, even though he knew she and I had a thing."

"More than a thing I thought," Argia's singsong voice chided Kyle.

"Yeah, well, the dude knew Argia and I were together. Remmy had the nerve to tell her that I wasn't even a full blood descendent of the Decretum Venia. The shit-breath red-faced bastard told me he could protect Argia better than me...the pond scum."

Peter slapped Kyle on the back. "Think without your heart. We need the guy. He's got skill and pull. He's one of the strongest fighters in the compound. We may need him."

"Damn right you need me!" Remmy burst through the brush, jingling keys in his hand.

Gil followed, his thick bushy black hair, fashioned into a Mohawk. "Don't forget us and my girl; she's on the way, too."

Peter smiled at Gil, knowing he wouldn't go anywhere without Chloe, his longtime girlfriend they'd saved from Gavin's fiendish Order of the Dragon organization.

"Hand over the keys, and I'll tell you where to meet us in a few days. Be there, or be left." Peter snatched the keys from Remmy.

"We will," Remmy answered.

Peter's hand heated up; he lifted his palm, making the burning symbol on it visible to Remmy. "This will hurt." Peter placed his hand on the side of Remmy's face.

Remmy's eyes clashed with Peter's, but the guy never gave in to the need to flinch from the onslaught of images that pounded into his consciousness. Peter willed the gift of locating various safe houses or sanctuaries to pass to Remmy. But with that transfer came all the scars Peter suffered in getting them. Not many others had been able to withstand the transition and passed out from the pressure within their heads and throughout their bodies.

A tear slipped from Remmy's eye.

Peter nodded in silence assurance that Remmy could take it. Swallowing back the essence of vomit caused by remembering the past in order to share the gift, Peter removed his hand. "You did well, man," Peter stated.

Remmy staggered. Argia was there to right him. "Remmy, you must've had a lot of trials in your life to take that so well. Peter doesn't share the gift often; it could kill most." She grasped Remmy on the shoulder. Her nose twitched as she sniffed at him. "I will cover you with a special armor you can use if the demons find you. You have Peter's scent on you now, and that puts you in more danger than before."

"He seems to like danger," Kyle muttered under his breath.

Peter punched Kyle in the arm. "Get over the jealousy, man. She's just helping him so he can help us."

"Whatever." Kyle snatched the keys from Peter and went to the front.

Peter got into the passenger seat of the jeep. "C'mon Kyle, what's with you? Get over it. Argia's gotta touch people when she helps them. I remember when you didn't even like the girl."

Kyle shrugged. "Well, I more than like her now, and it's killing me. I try to keep her safe, and she flies around like a butterfly, never even acting like she's in danger."

"I get that, but Argia is gifted. The girl's even stronger than I am against Gavin and the demons. Remember, Argia was the one who trapped him for us in that place. If it wasn't for her, I would be dead and in Hell within the Wall of Ash."

The girls got into the backseat.

Angel hit the back of Kyle's head. "Take off!"

"About damn time." Peter captured Angel's hand in his.

***

Peter glanced at Kyle's pinched expression. He leaned back in the passenger seat, shaking his head. The guy really loved Argia. Peter couldn't believe it really. Kyle had always taunted and picked at the weaker kids in the previous safe-houses.

"Stop staring at me. I feel it, and it creeps me out." Kyle grunted.

"I can't help myself; your thin lips are poking out like spikes. You big baby, suck it up. Remmy is *not* trying to steal your girl."

"He can't handle her." Kyle frowned.

"But he wants to, which is more than I can say you did. Remember calling her 'spacey' and a 'lunatic' and a 'crazy noodle'. Oh, and that you were afraid to be with her alone." Peter laughed.

Kyle sighed. "Yeah, and I regret saying those things. I just didn't know or couldn't even begin to realize how amazing she is."

Peter's lifted his eyebrow and smirked at that; Kyle had never said that about any other female.

Peter teased, "So is she feelin' what Remmy is offering?"

Argia's blue-haired head leaned forward. "Not even. Kyle's my guy." Then, she pecked Kyle on the cheek and plopped back in her chair, singing some tune playing in her head and not on the radio station they had on.

Kyle grinned. "I guess she only feels what's coming off me." He jabbed Peter with his elbow.

"I'm glad you gave her a chance; she told me she had a feeling you wanted her from the moment you met. I had fun watching you figure it out."

"Well, shut up. I remember you treating Angel like a boy when we first met."

"That's because she was perpetrating a boy. Man, I was just confused." Peter chuckled.

"Still are." Kyle cleared his throat. "Why do you let her do this with you?"

"She's a fighter. She was made for it. Like we all are."

"We hope. But are you sure that finding and opening this last book is a good idea? It's how we started this shit-hole of a mess in the first place."

"No, I am not sure. It's the only option we have. No other person on earth today will know how to destroy the Wall of Ash. Argia nearly died erecting that barrier. If Gavin escapes, he won't fall for the same trick twice. He will hunt us until we are dead."

"How will he know where to find us?"

"He will know." Peter lifted his hand to study the circled brand on the palm. It puckered, and the blood beneath it moved to thicken it and then retracted it into his skin.

"Why did you agree to let Remmy and Gil in on this? They should've gone with Rosa and the others."

"I need them. Remmy's a good fighter—that I know from living with him in the orphanage. He also knows where Sam hides his weapons. I didn't like Remmy, but he was a brute force, and he's not hard to control. He won't put us at risk; we are the closest to friends I've ever known him to have."

"I am not the dude's friend."

Argia sang, "I am."

Peter coughed. "She is."

Kyle punched him in the arm.

CHAPTER 4

Lucien forced down the bile that threatened to bubble up from his stomach. He pushed a nervous hand through ear-length wavy blond hair to gain some composure. A repressed shiver snaked up his spine as he lifted his tanned fist to knock on the door that separated him from the brother—or better yet—the monster who was some hybrid human-demon. He'd wanted that Wall of Ash to devour the abomination that was his brother. It seemed fate was determined to make him its permanent whipping toy.

Many men, women, and children died being sacrificed to the king of evil to free Gavin and his demon-master, Balaal, from the outer door to Hell. Lucien wanted to still himself against the continued deception of calm he exhibited in front of the others in the Extraho of Obscurum. He had to continue this farce until he could kill the thing – the human who'd become more evil than the demon within it.

Shoulders back, smile plastered, Lucien sauntered into the large, ornate room. He didn't offer a greeting to the young child holding the door. If Lucien did, he might reveal sympathy knowing the child was to be sacrificed tonight—along with many others—to heal his brother. Their lives weren't worth it, if it was given to keep this sadistic freak alive.

The four-poster canopy bed draped in black and red scarves sat against the back wall in the middle of the room. The wallpaper was smoky gray. Silver lines were woven artfully through the white dragons and the satirical riding demons imprinted in a whirled design. His brother had demanded Lucien stare at the walls of this room during one of his torturing sessions. In doing so, Lucien realized the design served as a mode to hypnotize, and a huge figure of a horned demon was imbedded within the small ornate drawings. He hated this room and the heaviness that hit him whenever he entered it. However, here he was, faking his homage to the monstrosity he grudgingly served.

Gavin lay stiffly on the bed, now in full human form. Bloody bandages covering the majority of his face, arms, chest, and legs were soaked through to the silk comforters that were in disarray around his large form. He had an audience of members from the Extraho of Obscurum around him. Gavin's fiancée and queen witch's dark hair swayed around her bowed head. Mara, with the other elders of the Extraho of Obscurum, chanted, rocking back and forth, while a young boy softly sang the death song in Latin.

"Lucien, glad you could make it." Mara's eyes narrowed at Lucien as she changed the bandage on his brother's face.

"Gavin needed his rest"—Lucien winked at her—"and so did you." He knew bringing up the innuendo of nights he'd spent seducing her, making her fall in love with him while Gavin was out of the picture, would remind her where her loyalty should lie. He'd paid dearly in his persuasion while she enjoyed brutalizing his body as much as the act of copulating. Blood and pleasure seemed to go hand in hand with both Mara and Gavin.

Mara eyes softened, her desire for him slipping through. It was the one thing Lucien could always count on, the attraction women had to his easy nature, blond good looks and charm. And using Mara to help him destroy her intended mate was just one step in his plan to end Gavin and the Order of the Dragon's reign of terror.

Stepping purposefully to the foot of Gavin's bed, Lucien motioned for the singing boy and the others in the room to leave.

Jack, the dark haired leader of another clan, stood dipping his eyelids at Lucien in a silent doubtfulness of their former agreements. "I'm not leaving. We need to make sure Gavin isn't disturbed and that the interest of the Extraho of Obscurum will be served."

Lucien wanted to smack Jack; his only interest was that he could take Gavin's place. Lucien nodded, affirming to himself that Jack would die also. If he played this right, he could literally kill both birds with the same sword.

Gavin growled, "Brother, you finally made it to my side. What have you been doing to move my agenda forward during my imprisonment?" His broken voice was deep yet demanding.

"We've located and attacked several underground safe houses used by our enemies in the Decretum Venia, focusing on locations we believe are housing the boy Peter Saints." Lucien forced a smug grin forward, typical of his persona portrayed for his brother throughout the years.

"Acceptable, but we will need more of their young warriors. Mara here told me you had to use the blood from the captives we'd stored to free me from their shield."

Lucien hated what he had to do to make his plans come to fruition. "We captured a few. They are stronger now. Draining blood from them should rebuild our collection of their special enzymes. The scientist I have researching their DNA and their blood's potency have seen changes in the consistency. It's as if with your awakening, they've gained almost inhuman strength." Those kids had fought with every bit of their power, but the witch was able to bespell them, weakening them enough for Lucien's men to drug them. In the past, when Lucian captured children of the Decretum Venia, he'd end their lives hoping to save them from the torturous future ahead of them.

"Start collecting their drained blood, but don't kill them this time, Lucien. We may need their skin to cover us if we want to use my creation, Transfero of Lux Lucis, to slip into the heavenly realms for war."

"I won't. I have started to better control my urges, brother," Lucien stated, knowing that his brother considered the killing of the kids they'd had in the torture chambers to be a positive trait for his servant, someone raised in dark magic and fleshy sacrifices.

Gavin struggled slightly to sit up. His piercing blue eyes studied Lucien a moment. "Lucien, did you get the boy? Peter Saints, his friends? Any of them?"

Lucien leaned against the wood frame at the foot of the bed, forcing every muscle in his body to relax. "No, they weren't in the compound we searched. I don't have any leads on where they are. The Decretum Venia seems to be doing a good job at hiding them."

"The girl with him, one of them, she has the gift. There are only a few of them. If we had her, we could guarantee success. We can't let Peter Saints open the final book. If he does, it can circumvent our success. Find him. Kill him. Bring me his head."

"I will, brother." Lucien bowed.

"If you don't, there will be a price to pay. One, I don't know if you are prepared for."

Lucien stood, "There always is a price, my master. Always." Then with a pivot, Lucien willed himself to not run for the door.

CHAPTER 5

Peter examined the main road for any cars. Nothing, and that was a good thing. The moon was high and bright, casting a soft glow on the scarcely lit roadway. Releasing a breath, he confirmed that there was no one lurking ahead. Peter didn't allow himself comfort in the deduction. Anyone or anything could be working for the Extraho of Obscurum, which made being around crowded places unsafe.

"We are out of gas, dude," Kyle's deep voice pricked Peter's thoughts.

"Find a place to hide and camp. It's late, and I think the trunk had a gas can in it. Hadn't had time to check it though." Peter adjusted his seat back a bit to spy on the girls who were staring out the windows at the dense set of trees on either side of the road.

Kyle drove on a few uneventful miles.

"Pull into there." Peter pointed at a covered dirt road. Bushes and low hanging trees hid the place, but it seemed passable with the jeep.

"On it." Kyle jerked the wheel and turned left as the glare from oncoming lights peeked from the dip in the road ahead.

The jeep swerved and jumped on the rocks and debris. Leaves and branches pounded the plastic top.

Peter braced himself by pushing his palm against the ceiling bar and his foot on the dashboard.

"Go as deep in as you can; we need to stay outta sight until we can get communication on the Decretum Venia and come up with clear plan."

Kyle snorted. "Thought the plan was to go to the Stronghold, open the book that may end the world, then kill Gavin and his machine?" He shrugged. "Good plan to me."

"Yeah, well, there are other things at risk here. People too, ya know. I need a night to get a grip on this."

"Understood. And I need a night alone with Argia. The cramped quarters in our old safe-house had us sharing a floor with way too many other kids for me to sleep well."

"It wasn't as bad as the other places we'd been in."

"No, but I'd rather be outside with fresh air and my eyes open." Kyle nodded at the view ahead. "And besides, I have definitely been many more nice places than you."

They broke through to a small clearing in the trees where the trunks were interlinked and wrapped, impeding any growth of grass or weeds.

"True that, rich boy." Peter relaxed in his seat and put his foot down off the dashboard as the jeep came to a stop.

"Not rich anymore. Well, I don't think. If I tried to get my father's money, someone would kill me. I'll wait till we annihilate these asses, and then you guys could crash in my mansion."

"Promises, promises."

The clearing was only big enough for their jeeps and about two tents, but without the headlights, only speckles of moonlight hit the ground between the leaves and branches of the surrounding trees.

"Good eye on spotting these hiding places. I wouldn't have given this a second look." Kyle opened his door.

"I'm good at finding places to hide out since I've been doing it all my life." Peter chuckled.

Peter opened the door and then beat Angel to opening hers. Her black wavy mass of curls was tied back in a bun, which Peter unraveled while he kissed her. His dark fingers teased the sprinkle of freckles over her pale nose.

"I hate that instead of tanning in the sun, I get freckles." Angel rubbed her nose on Peter's t-shirt.

"I think they are delicious on you." He slid his arm around her shoulders. They walked to the back of the jeep while Kyle opened the trunk.

Argia held a flashlight high so they could see in the corners of the trunk.

Kyle grabbed a green vinyl bag. "Only two sleeping sofas and sleeping bags. Guess Remmy knew we'd share."

"Naw, there wasn't much left in supplies that could be taken out when we left. He'd heard the attack and came straight to my room."

Kyle shook his head. "Nope, I'm not buying that. The way this jeep is packed with every little detailed thing we might need, Remmy's been stealing stuff and packing this for a while."

"Yeah, it is meticulous." Peter leaned over and inspected the way the items were packed. They were neatly organized and left little space for more. Small bags were labeled and fit tightly into every corner. The curved spout-like top of a plastic container poked out above the packed nylon bags.

"I don't trust that guy: red hair, chin hair and an earring. Hell, who has all those tattoos at seventeen years old that they drew on themselves? Something's up with him." Kyle closed the trunk.

Angel pushed at Kyle's arm. "Not you, too? It's Peter's job not to trust anyone. You at least gave most people the benefit of the doubt."

"Uh umm, I just pretended to until they screwed up – which they usually did, eventually."

Peter burst out laughing. "I knew I was rubbing off on you. You screw-up."

Angel linked her fingers through Peter's. "I think that spot next to the driver's door is good, in case we have to make a quick exit."

Peter nodded. "I see that. Can you set up for us?" He pointed his thumb at Argia. "And get her to protect the place?"

Angel nodded. "I'm on it." She walked to Argia and whispered in her ear. Peter went back over to Kyle who was taking a laptop out of the backseat.

"Hey, can you route this location?" Peter gave Kyle a torn piece of paper containing the name of a large state park.

Kyle's eyebrows bunched. "A waterfall park? Really? The Decretum Venia definitely made their locations interesting." Kyle rested the laptop on the hood of the car. "Why'd you write it down?"

"I had planned to give it to Pastor Finn; I wanted him to follow us there."

"He never would; the guy doesn't want to take the chance he may lead the enemy to us."

"I guess." Peter released a breath.

Pastor Finn was like his father. Even though the retired cop-turned teacher and bodyguard for orphans in the Decretum Venia complained about his job – he loved them. However, Peter knew that with all the man had done for him, Pastor Finn wanted the role of his father.

"Don't be pitiful about it. The guy left the last hideout after he recovered from his injuries in protecting all of us. He said Gavin tasted his blood, and for some reason, Pastor Finn has felt the demon-man's presence inside his head ever since."

"I know. It's just sometimes I'd like to bounce an idea off him...ya know?"

"No, I don't know. Remember my jackass father hated my guts, told me I was never good enough to be part of his elite family's Decretum Venia because my typical human mom didn't have angelic DNA hidden in her. I would gladly take your Pastor Finn's protection any day."

"Mind checked." Peter nodded. "I get your words of wisdom, and I know he'll reach me when he needs to." Peter studied the Google Earth depiction of the Stronghold he'd dreamed about the last few weeks. That was his signal it was time to move from the underground sanctuary where they were hiding. The dreams of his Caribbean-born mother and his birth father's watery death were not only a haunting of his past but a clue to the direction of his future.

"That's the place." Kyle pointed to the screen. "We should go in the back road, that way no one will see us coming in there."

Peter nodded. "Yeah, but I doubt anyone from the Order of the Dragon could get past the protection there." Peter searched for Argia who was chanting and praying in the circle of the clearing while Angel watched her dripping oil mixed with herbs. The sweet calming smell of the concoction filled the air. Peter sniffed it in, his eyes drifting closed.

"Wake up! Plan at work here." Kyle nudged Peter's leg with his foot.

"Oh! I was spacin' for a minute. The Sanctuary should have the books we need to find the Stronghold. Now that we've got the direction planned, that's a lot of miles to eat up, we have to route a back way so we can't be spotted on the main road."

"The main roads aren't our only problem; the perimeter of this place is surrounded by water. Got any ideas on how we can get a boat?"

"I'll think on it." Peter smacked Kyle on the back. "Good night; we are going to need it. I don't know when we'll get the chance again."

CHAPTER 6

With his sleeping bag under his arm, Peter held Angel's hand as he led her to a spot near the driver side door. There was a curved bush riddled with sweet scented flowers that created a cover for them.

"This is the best I can do for air freshener." Peter bought her hand to his lips and gently kissed it.

"I'll take it after sneaking around in that last Decretum Venia underground. Smelly kids and a girls-only sleeping bag room was no fun."

"Especially when I had to hang around the door waiting for you to sneak out of there." Peter tossed the sleeping bag on the soft thick grass that was sprinkled with petals from the scents wafting through the air around them. Then he slid his hand out of hers as he prepped their bed. "It'll be a close fit for both of us. Do you mind?" He winked at her knowingly, remembering how many nights they'd slept on the dirt floor and cramped corner of the tiny alcove he and Kyle shared.

"Not a bit, as long as I'm next to you." She dived into the bag.

Peter side-stepped her hand as her hand jetted out to grasp the bottom of his jeans. "Patience." He tugged his shirt over his head and tossed it on the ground, then slid into the cool sleeping bag with Angel. Peter's t-shirt was in place and he tugged it down over his hips. His gaze never left hers. She placed her head on his arm, and wrapped her jean clad leg around his. Her shirt sleeves were soft and brushed against his skin.

"About time." She sighed.

Leaning in, Peter kissed her, opening his mouth to the kiss. His heart felt like it would burst out his chest. "I love you," he whispered.

"I love you, too, always."

"Always, even when we were separated, and you stayed with Rob?"

She nodded. "Even then. How many times do I have to tell you that he and I were just friends?"

"I don't know. Forever. I'm insecure since I have mommy issues."

Angel laughed. "And I don't? Besides, your mom was perfect."

"Yeah, she was, till they killed her. That's my issue."

"Mine, too. But we have each other now. Right?"

"Right, only I..." Peter hesitated. Frustration bubbled up in his chest to the point he felt he would choke on it.

"Please talk to me, don't hide it."

"It's just that I don't want this for you. If we'd met like normal kids, not people on the run for as long as we can remember, I'd protect you."

"You have protected me, and all the others who get in your way." She pecked his lips with hers.

Peter shrugged. "Some died because of me. My mistakes have made us all pay a price. I can't make that up to you – or them. Ever."

"That's why I love you. The fact that you admit to your

mistakes; the responsibility you feel for all of us lets me know you are human. We all are, but at least, you are a human that cares for others."

"A stupid one who fell for Gavin's manipulations." Peter groaned. "Then opened the secrets he is using against us to kill everyone he can find in the Decretum Venia," Peter chided, ticked off that even with knowing his mistakes, there was no way out of the mess but to finish the journey.

"It's what evil does. What Gavin does. I know. I have really bad nightmares about my time in his personal dungeons."

"I wish I could leave you out of this. That I could find a safe place for you to stay and live the way you've always wanted. Remember your dream of what we would do after this is all over?"

"That we'd be in a castle somewhere surrounded by trees and mountains, even a beach?"

Angel's finger drew invisible circles on Peter's chest.

"Yeah, that dream. I like it. I want that for us – for you."

"I've lived someplace like that before."

Peter rested his hand on her waist, snuggling closer. "When?"

"It was after my father resigned from Steele Industries. I believe that's when we first went on the run. We stayed there for months. The place was like a fairytale."

"Why'd you leave?"

Angel shook her head. "I don't know. But we left in a hurry."

"I don't remember a place like that being a Decretum Venia Sanctuary."

"I don't think it was. My father was like Argia and Rosa. He could communicate with both the Angels and Demons from the Decretum Venia and the Extraho of Obscurum. Rosa told me during a private therapy session. After we talked, I started remembering things about my father that I never considered important before. Though, I think he got too careless after Gavin seemed to have a sick interest in me."

"Maybe he did one selfish act for his family and put the needs of the Decretum Venia aside?"

She nodded. "I think he did. My mother and he argued about blowing their cover. Then for a long time, it seemed that Gavin had forgotten about us."

"The man embodies evil at a level far beyond what I think even a demon can. He is way too patient." Peter caressed her chin and kissed her. "I don't want you to talk about it anymore. Losing your parents the way you did, it hurts me to think that you had to go through that alone."

"I was alone for only a short time before I found you at that diner." Her hand pressed against Peter's chest before she squeezed it under his arm and around his back.

"Too bad you looked like a boy. If I knew then that you were a girl, I would've sat next to you."

"I bet you would have, player boy."

"You like me this way. If I was a softie, you'd run all over me."

"No I wouldn't, I'd kick butt protecting you – like I do now." She laughed.

"One time! Just one time you saved me, and I'll never live it down." Peter nipped at her neck and tickled her.

Angel covered her mouth to stifle her laugh. "Stop it! We'll wake up Kyle and Argia."

"They're not asleep." Peter stopped and re-adjusted Angel in his arms, "They've taken their relationship to the next level."

Angel blushed. "I guessed."

"How?"

"Uh, we did share a small room with them. No matter how quiet they tried to be, or that Kyle always had to sleep with 'soft' music on, I knew what they were doing."

"Me too. I just don't want you to ever feel like what they are doing, we have to rush to do."

She gave him a sanguine smile. "I don't feel rushed. I want to. I do." Her eyes shuttered closed. She sniffed and when they opened, the moisture from building tears threatened to overflow.

"I can wait for you." Peter caressed her check with his hand.

"I know. It's not that Lucien or Gavin raped me, it was the torture and the threat of it that just freezes me up whenever...you and I get close."

"We don't have to do it, you know. Holding you is enough for me." Peter meant it even though the needs of his body drummed at him constantly while he was around her. So far, he'd hidden it from her. Suppressing it because she meant so much more to him than a fast lay. He'd had those. The time they'd been separated, he'd gorged himself on willing girls only to find that afterwards he felt empty.

"It's not enough for me anymore. Peter, I'm almost eighteen years old, and I want you in ways I never imagined. It just hurts me that whenever I want to express that part of me to you, all I think of is Gavin and what he did to me."

"What he did to us." Peter kissed her deep and long, till the point her body vibrated against his in frustrated need.

She wrenched back from his lips. "I will kill him for this."

Peter believed she could. With the strength she'd gained from her awakening the inherent power of her angelic ancestor, Michael 2—one of the greatest warriors of the battle over the heavens and earth—Angel was stronger than all of them. Not only that, but she had more of a vendetta than Peter.

"We will, dream of what we are going to do after we have our victory." Peter smiled, knowing he would surely enjoy the burden of destroying Gavin and his demon master Balaal.

CHAPTER 7

P eter woke first. Angel was a small distance away with her arm draped over her face. She hadn't had nightmares last night. But he had.

He pushed the zipper downward and rolled onto the grass then used his arms as leverage to hop up. There was just enough room for his 6 foot 2 inch form to stand next to their sleeping bag. Ducking a bit, he pushed a branch out of the way. Then he went to find someplace to relieve himself.

Peter didn't go far, just within the lines of where Argia laid her herbs, and protection. He finished and wiped his hands on the wet leaves from the morning dew. It was still dark, and the sounds of the night creatures' songs still drummed through the air. Peter figured that was a good sign, but not reliable to make sure nothing found them there.

Peter hoped the fight was over. For some reason he felt edgy. It was a small premonition that something was brewing.

Peter felt comfort that they were protected by Argia's tactics for concealing their presence from the demons, but it didn't work well for humans. Peter made a fist, the burning sensation of the brand on his palm made him itch. He stared into the darkness; the nagging itch to never get too comfortable ticked the hairs on his neck. The moon was covered by clouds chasing it away to the dawn. But that didn't bother him as much as the dim, ashen figure a short distance away that seemed to be checking him out just as intently as Peter was watching it.

A demon. One likely sent to hunt them, had caught their scent. Peter didn't know if it was him or Argia that they tracked, but somehow or someway, they always found him when he was out in the open. Anywhere outside a sacred Sanctuary or Stronghold was fair game for the creatures of darkness.

In a flash, the burning yellow lights of fire that licked the ashen lids of the beast hidden in the trees disappeared. Peter knew it was time to get going.

Pivoting, he stumbled at bit after bumping with Argia's small frame. She was standing so close he'd almost knocked her backwards.

"I smelled them you know," Argia mentioned in her sing-song voice.

He nodded. "Not surprised. They smell like rotten trash wrapped in cigarettes. Ugly, too."

Argia's almond eyes widened. "Not all of them. The supreme evil one is quite beautiful, I'm told."

"What?" Peter's heart pounded in his chest.

"I hear them speak, the fallen ones, the demons. We see them as they truly are with their decrepit and twisted souls exposed. But to other humans, they are beautiful beings of light. Some consider them ghosts, angels, or spirit guides. All of them are their victim's reflection of beauty. Quite a talent I'd say."

"Well, I didn't know all that. I am glad I see them for what they are."

"Rosa helped me decipher my confusion. When I was in the

Asylum, I saw such beautiful creatures that told me to do the most hideous things. Sometimes I listened. Other times I made them think I listened, until I started to hear the voices and see the angels whose words and actions aligned to be the same."

"Hah! My mother always said that: 'actions speaks louder than false words.' I guess she was right."

"A smart one she was. Rosa told me I'd done well on my own." Argia's gaze fell to the ground. "But my mistakes caused many others harm. Someone special to me gave his life so I could find Rosa. I found her, but she made no promise to answer my request."

Peter rested his hand on Argia's shoulder. "She will try; Rosa can move mountains." He flexed his hand and scratched at the brand on his palm. It throbbed and burned of fire. A cold numbness spread on his hand as a symbol plumped from his skin. The blood pulsated within the brand.

"It's glowing." She traced the puckered skin.

"Yeah." Peter swallowed back the rising taste of bile in the back of his throat. "The Seer that gave this to me, I regret that I can't make things right between us."

Argia sighed. "She did what she was meant to do."

"No, Hanna did what Gavin's witches tricked her into doing. She was chasing me that day, likely to find peace. She said the only time she didn't hear the voices was when she was with me."

A smile bloomed on Argia's face. "I know what she means. You silence the bad voices unless I decide to seek them out to hear their nefarious plans." She hugged Peter. "Thank you for that."

"Get away from my woman!" Kyle's booming voice teasingly warned Peter.

"You buzz-head, I don't know why she puts up with you."

Kyle draped his sleeping bag over his shoulder. "Because I'm simply irresistible."

"No you're not," Angel piped in from behind Peter.

Kyle pointed at Angel. "You wouldn't know. It's only for her."

Argia giggled. "Silly, willy, you are cute, but we must go." Argia whipped her gaze to the side and froze. Her blue-black bob slapped against her pale chin. Crouching low, she whispered, "Quiet, don't move. They are sniffing about."

Peter's heart pounded in his chest; the brand on his hand grew firmer, harder as he fisted it close to his leg. They froze for what seemed like hours.

Argia crawled on the ground, crouched like a frog, chanting and rocking back and forth. Her chin pushed forward, jerking from side to side as she appeared to be begging some unseen force.

In an instant, she stilled.

Peter stepped forward, ready to fight their way out.

A bloodcurdling scream, louder than thunder, spilled from Argia's lips. Flashes of light poured from her mouth and disappeared into the trees as if they were seeking missiles.

The clouds slipped away and the brightness of daylight speckled around them through the trees.

Argia slumped to the ground, a dribble of blood sliding from her lips.

CHAPTER 8

They stood there stunned for a moment. Every muscle in Peter's body was primed and ready to attack. Birds sang and the sunlight seemed to burst through the trees as though just awakening.

Kyle lovingly lifted a dazed and limp Argia into his arms.

"She's only done that once." Angel's hand lightly touched on Peter's shoulder.

Peter lifted his palm to hers; even with its throbbing pulsing center, he rested it on her hand.

"It was to create the prison that trapped Gavin. Why would she do it now? It couldn't have been more demons than we've handled before."

"Maybe she sensed something we didn't." Angel shook her head. "I did feel a presence."

Peter nodded. "It's gone now."

Kyle opened the door to the jeep. "You drive, and I'll be in the backseat with her."

Peter smirked. "That means I gotta pick up your stuff, too?"

"You got it." Kyle slammed the door.

Angel twisted around Peter, and stood on her tiptoes to give him a kiss. "I'll get their stuff, and you can do ours. *Te amo,*" Angel smiled. She went to Kyle and Argia's heap of covers and food wrappers scattered opposite theirs.

"I love you, too." Peter rolled up their sleeping bag and put on his shirt. The pulsating in his palm had calmed, and the brand sank back within his hand. He started to relax, knowing that whatever Argia had done, he felt safer.

By the time Peter slammed the hatch on the jeep, Angel was in the car with the others. He took one last searching glance around and got in the driver's seat.

"Here." Kyle tossed the keys at Peter.

Easily, Peter caught them. "Now we roll."

"Will we make it there by tonight?" Angel asked.

He wished. "Nope. Callin' this as we go."

"Figures, they never make it easy for us." Angel stretched in her seat. Then she pulled her fingers through her tangled hair.

Peter adjusted the mirrors and spied on Kyle who was rocking and kissing Argia's closed eyes.

"Stop staring at me, man. I can feel it," Kyle mumbled.

Peter grinned. "Ready?"

"Just go before whatever she scared off finds us again," Kyle replied.

Peter gunned the engine then backed from the cover of trees to the road. He took one final peek in his rearview mirror, noted no cars were around, and sped onto the highway. "Next stop – gas."

Angel groaned. "That never works out well for us. There are way too many people for it to be safe now."

"We don't have a choice. Walking is worse."

"Wasn't there gas in the can in the trunk?" Angel asked.

"Yeah, but we are using it now; it won't last the duration of the trip. We'll have to fill the tank and the can on our next stop."

Peter and Angel fell into silence. He wanted to tell her more. To share his fear of failure, his guilt of starting this chain of events that was literally sending the Earth to 'Hell in a hand-basket', but he wouldn't. Bringing up what brought them here wasn't going to solve the problem. He needed to give everyone the vibe that he could do this. That he wasn't leading them to their end.

The road was calm...an untraveled paved two lane highway with nothing in sight for miles. Peter hoped it would stay that way. With Argia asleep, the demons could sneak up on them before they knew it. Whereas Argia was able to hear them for miles she once told him.

"Argia never told me how she met up with you and Kyle. Everything's been hectic since you rescued me from the Sanctuary where the crazy doctor was experimenting on us."

"She followed me. Seems that's how I collect my friends. They stalk me for some reason." He winked at her. "But I think her life was more screwed up than mine. I don't want to even think about what it would be like to be sent to a psychiatric hospital, cornered by demons and angels fighting for my attention, and trying to deal with the abuse of the people running those hospitals."

"Wow, no wonder she doesn't mind being left alone." Angel peeked at Kyle and Argia.

"She doesn't really enjoy being alone as much as she has been 'left alone' by others. People think her mumbling at night, her jerking around or sitting up and staring at something that isn't there, is just damn strange."

"I guess she just gave up on most people."

Peter reached over and grabbed Angel's hand. "You can understand that, right? When something hurts you so bad, you don't feel comfortable telling anyone why you are reacting the way you do?"

"Ah, are you implying the way I acted with you when we first were separated?"

"I think about it."

"That was a bad time. It's like the torture from Gavin and Lucien kept reminding me of how vulnerable I was. Watching my parents die from the hidden place in our ceiling was the worst nightmare I'd had...until I was kidnapped by the Extraho of Obscurum."

"I know. Gavin and Steele Industries' creation of that machine is costing us literal blood loss." Peter locked his jaw against the anger with the Order of Dragon and their blood-draining techniques used.

"They tried to drain my friend Rob after the torture. They told him his blood would mask any assassin in the Extraho of Obscurum from the Decretum Venia's protection."

"It also will allow them to conceal themselves when they use that machine Gavin created to transport them to the Heavenly Realm to do battle." Peter squeezed the steering wheel a bit tighter. "Your old friend Rob...I appreciate him being there for you, but I still don't like how he felt about you."

She kissed Peter's cheek. "He's over that. You realize he has a girlfriend now."

"I know, but I feel like the dude's waiting for me to screw up so he'd have another shot at you."

"I doubt that. No way would his girlfriend let him out of her clutches now; she chased him for two years before I even got to the last sanctuary. You know what they say about redheads."

"Possessive, got attitude, *and* feisty?"

"Hum, yes, but that sounds like...you!" she giggled.

CHAPTER 9

Peter tried to ignore Argia's mumbling, followed by a groan.

"Peter, Gavin's free." Her voice trembled.

His heart dropped to his chest. It literally felt like it pounded down his ribs. Swallowing back the sickness that threatened to spill from his mouth, his hands shook as he rubbed a sweaty palm on his jeans. "How do you know?"

"They spoke of him. The demons that were hunting us. They were arguing about doing his bidding over Balaal, his demon master."

"Is that how the Extraho of Obscurum works? Demon possession?" Kyle asked.

Peter spied Argia snuggling into Kyle's arm and smiled. "Not exactly. The human and demon communicate through hypnosis, dreams, and rituals. The Extraho of Obscurum members' ancestors are said to have been Nephilim, born of the abomination of fallen angels raping men and woman of their day. But those children were decimated secretly by the Decretum Venia that injected them with some type of antibody that made the demonic blood in them dormant. It broke their DNA, making them regular humans and weaker than their forefathers. Although, they are born truly evil, they are still given the chance to live a different type of life, if they so choose."

"So they are half-human, half-demon?" Angel asked.

"Somewhat, but they bred with humans and seriously diluted the ability to be considered demons. By doing so, they increased the potency of the antibody given to their ancestors to weaken the evil out of them. So in order to regain the ability to converse or allow their demon masters to take over their bodies, they have to sacrifice those with psychic abilities through use of rituals or witches."

"Then Gavin had killed people to be able to join with Balaal," Kyle said.

"I'm sure he did," Argia replied. "He would've loved to get his hands on someone like me."

"So, the demons know his name, and they've been whispering it to you?" Angel asked.

"They've been chanting his name and Balaal's, but most of all – they've been chanting 'Peter Saints, get Peter Saints'."

Peter fought the shudder and braced against it. "Not until I kill the bastards that are controlling them. Gavin and his demon, Balaal, will die. That's a promise," Peter hit the gas and sped to the exit off the road.

He had to get them somewhere safe, and fast. It was the only answer. The more time they waited, the more in danger they would be in.

Peter drove to the rest stop gas station and let the car idle a moment. Slowly, he studied the area before cutting the engine. There were only two other guys there. One was finishing up at the pump ahead, and the other was at the cash register, which seemed safe enough.

He shut off the car. And waited.

"Let's make this quick." Kyle kicked the back of Peter's seat.

"I am, just want to make sure there aren't a lot of people around. I'll go pay, you pump."

"Gotcha," Kyle replied.

Peter climbed out of the car as the guy at the pump finished and got in his van. Putting his hand in his pocket, Peter opened the door to the convenience store, and ignored the jingle of the bell above it.

He was glad Remmy had put a bag of cash in the jeep; it would make it easier to stay off the grid. The guy at the counter was thin with large brown eyes that seemed to sit back on his pale skin. Peter waited until the man in front of him got his change, then Peter stepped up to the counter.

"Give me $40 on pump number 2, and keep the change." Peter tossed down the wrinkled money from his pocket.

"Uh, we are only accepting credit or debit at this time."

Peter's heart bumped faster in his chest. Something wasn't right. He narrowed his gaze, then grabbed the guy's wrist as it slowly inched towards a hidden button under the counter.

"Why are you going for the button, man?" Peter twisted the guy's wrist.

"You look suspicious," said the bony, pale guy that looked a minute from the coffin with a lift of his chin.

"And you don't? Look, make this simple, put the gas pump on, now."

The guy's eyebrow lifted. "Fine." He smiled, then said, "Better hurry," and jerked his wrist out of Peter's hand.

Peter pounded his fist on the counter. "What did you do?" His gaze slid to the fallen piece of paper on the floor behind the guy and recognized his face. A *Most Wanted* banner over his head, with a million dollar reward scribbled on the paper in red ink.

The guy smirked. "You'll find out soon enough if you hang around."

Peter dashed through the door. He signaled to Kyle, who was pouring gas into the can.

"Get in the car!" Peter leaped into the driver's seat.

A minute later, Kyle climbed in the backseat and placed the gas can between his legs while tightening the top.

Kyle knocked his fist on the roof of the jeep. Peter sped off just as the lights of several other vehicles poured into the station behind him.

"What the hell happened back there?" Kyle asked.

"A set-up." Peter weaved between the scattered cars on the highway.

"They know we made it out of the bunker," Angel stated.

"Yeah, and they have a bounty on us. Our faces are plastered all over the place like we are criminals."

"Nothing new. They've done it every time we slip out of their traps," Kyle spat.

"It won't matter"—Argia whistled—"their demons can't smell us for miles. They are immobile for few days." Then she sniffed the air and smacked her hands. "They are silent for now."

"Thanks for that," Angel said. "However, that doesn't stop humans."

"Nope, but their demon puppet-masters can't tip them off for a while." Argia giggled. "Crazy things they are."

"Did you get enough gas for about a hundred miles?" Peter asked. His eyes met Kyle's in the rearview mirror.

"I hope. I didn't get to top off the tank since I noticed the way you and that shop clerk were going at it. I took the nozzle out of the jeep and started filling the gas can."

"Good. We should make it without a...problem." In the mirror,

Peter scrutinized the lone car following them, then he relaxed a bit as it backed off, slowing down.

"What's up?" Kyle asked.

"Just want to make sure we aren't being tailed." Peter exhaled when the car turned off on the exit behind him. Somehow the feeling of unease couldn't be shaken.

"Just drive, they'll become obvious soon enough," Kyle grumbled.

Peter tightened his grasp on the steering wheel. "They always do."

CHAPTER 10

Night had fallen, and the road didn't have many cars on it. But Peter still couldn't shake his uneasy feeling that something wasn't right. Angel was asleep beside him, and he reached over to adjust her head so it lay against the headrest.

The thick brush of trees, bushes, and high grass bordered each side of the highway. Oncoming cars' lights pierced the night here and there. But the occasional headlight glares behind him were the ones that made him the most uncomfortable.

"I can't figure it out." Kyle slapped Peter's seat.

"What?"

"The pieces. If Gavin is free and the Wall of Ash is still in operation, what is his next move?"

Argia leaned up and sang, "It had to hurt him."

"Hurt?" Peter said.

"Gavin," Argia whispered. "Our barrier was filled with sacred fire. Rosa and I had figured out how to replicate the barrier that keeps Hell where it's supposed to be. Rosa spent years cataloguing the Decretum Venia's records and was compelled to search for clues regarding it."

"He had to have help," Peter asked.

"Regrets, regrets. Many die to help him. His demon is weaker, too. It will take a while for Gavin to be able to summon more of his demon-master's slaves. The strong ones anyway." Argia snorted.

"So, we haven't even started fighting the warriors yet?" Kyle smacked his lips.

"We did fight the demon warriors on the day we trapped Gavin. But the demons out here now, the slaves, can't fully materialize into flesh because they are the weaker ones. That is why we are the only ones who can see them. Except..." Argia tapped her lower lip with her index finger.

"Tell it all," Peter stated. "Remember, since Kyle isn't a pure blood from the Decretum Venia, he doesn't see everything we see."

"I don't have to see something to know shit ain't right," Kyle snorted.

"The demons that were after us, appeared like ashy human-shaped hybrid beasts. Demons with fire in their eyes, no soul, just evil. Did you see that?" Argia asked.

"No, but I smelled it. I felt it," Kyle replied.

"But you saw the demons we were fighting when we were attacking Gavin?" Argia inquired.

"Yes, I saw them. Still have the nightmares to remind me."

"Those demons are the warriors. They can slice through the portal barrier to appear to humans who aren't psychic, or anointed by the Decretum Venia. But the slave demons...they manipulate the minds of men and women who have no protection, and a small compulsion to do evil things." Argia stretched her arms. "So the excuse of 'the devil made me do it' isn't entirely true, his slave demons present the idea, but it is the person who decides whether to act on it."

"Tell me about it. I fight the urge every day to go to Gavin's businesses, his home, to his followers and just – pow! Blow the bastards up," Kyle spat. "Now...about the warriors."

"They go hunting for people like me, psychically sensitive ones that they can control or devour. They start appearing to us when we are young. Then try to consume us if they can once we become of age. Those, Gavin can send to hunt us now, and they can tear through the barrier separating Hell from Earth to eat us, drag us to hell, or torture us."

"Let's hope Gavin stays out of the game longer. Dealing with the people he has hunting us is bad enough." Peter glanced in the rearview mirror, noting that two cars were keeping pace with him now.

"Yeah, and he's got plenty of money-hungry people after us. I mean putting us on the Most Wanted list in all these states might get us killed instead of just captured."

"We don't want to be captured," Angel spoke up.

"Whatever goes down, we have to live through it. If we don't fight, our entire world will be thrown into hell on earth. And our surviving ancestors would be attacked in Heaven, because we were manipulated by Gavin."

"Getting captured will royally screw us over," Peter said.

"I'll just make sure that doesn't happen," Kyle said.

"You can't make that promise," Angel replied.

Peter grabbed her hand. "I promise you one thing, if this doesn't end well, I will get you free."

Argia rested her head on Peter's seat. "No, I will get us free, silly!"

They fell into silence, and Peter drove holding onto Angel's hand. She'd squeezed it several times.

Peter counted the number of cars behind him multiplying. First one, now another two came on from the highway exit they'd passed. He gunned the engine. His heart raced as he pressed the gas to put some distance between him and the cars.

"You seeing what I'm seeing?" Kyle echoed Peter's thoughts.

"Yep, and I'm trying to test them to keep them off our backs until I get to the exit over there."

Two of the cars were now on his tail. The others hung back as if waiting for something to happen. Peter tensed at the police siren that blasted through the night. He pressed the gas harder as one cop car, then another, sped through the lane of oncoming traffic, to ease up through the other cars tailing Peter.

"Screw it!" Peter hit the gas. Jerking the jeep forward; he eyed the facing traffic in the opposite lane. For some reason, it had grown to even more cars. He had no idea where they were coming from and didn't have time to figure it out.

"Do it!" Angel yelled.

Peter gripped the wheel, hit the speed, and jackknifed the jeep. The cops were gaining ground. The other dark cars behind them had also caught up. Peter tapped his finger on the steering wheel while waiting on a small break in the oncoming traffic.

"Hold on!" He pushed the gas pedal to the floor, whipped the wheel around and drove through the gap between a small compact car and a gas truck. Timing it just right, the two cop cars and black cars closed in on the chase.

The gas truck bumped the back of the jeep, sending it into a tailspin. Angel jerked the wheel, and the jeep skidded to a stop.

Peter didn't hesitate; he pushed the gas hard and sped to the area on the opposite side of the road as one car barely missed hitting the rear of the jeep.

"At least they're not shooting at us." Argia leaned between Angel and Peter.

"Any demon company with them?" Peter asked.

"Nope, they are silent. Their voices are quiet in my head. But..."

Peter barreled the jeep through the brush. The noise of branches slapping against the vehicle didn't drown out the sound of bullets whizzing by.

"There's your bullets, baby," Kyle snorted. "Knew it was too good to be true."

"Shoot back at them. I need to put more space between us. The trees are thinning up," Peter said.

"Yeah, there's another road on the other side," Angel said.

"I've been waiting to fire this instrument." Kyle laughed; he waved his gun in front of Peter's view before the jeep jerked.

"Be careful," Argia sang and rested her head on the seat between Angel and Peter.

Peter sped the jeep through a stream, and up a few small hills where the trees thinned out, revealing a one-lane road ahead. "Almost there. Kyle, how you doing?"

"Shooting man! Just keep driving," Kyle slapped his fist against the frame. "Damn! Dropped the gun. Hit the gas!"

"They're gaining on us!" Angel called.

Peter twisted the wheel, grazed a tree, and the jeep hit the smooth pavement of the one-lane road. He turned the wheel and sped down the road just barely a quarter mile. A barricade of trucks, and two police cars waited for them.

Behind them, the sirens blared as the other cars hit the pavement.

Peter searched for a detour, anything to get them away from the trap. His heart beat wildly in his chest, his blood drummed through his veins; he felt trapped. There was nowhere, no escape.

"We're done," Kyle said.

"No, just stopped. For now." Peter slowed the jeep.

"Go for it, dude," Kyle growled.

Peter nodded and pressed the accelerator. No way was he going out this easy, the engine revved.

CHAPTER 11

Lucien simmered down the excitement within him at seeing the girl, Angel Ramirez again. The small helicopter he was in started its descent on a rented estate he'd acquired once his men notified him that they had a lead on the group. It was no surprise what money could buy. Everyone had a price. He wanted to get to see the captives personally before anyone else from the Extraho of Obscurum found out they were held there.

The order had too many personal agendas going on, and even so, Gavin's plan to use his machine to cross the dimension to create a war was one for which all the Extraho of Obscurum subjects hungered. Their entire organization was built on it. Doing their demon master's bidding meant pushing the evil agenda of the known loser in the equation of good versus evil. It was the mantra they'd learned since birth. For some reason, he was never really on board with the entire campaign. When he could dream, he'd dreamt of escaping, changing his identity, and forgetting Gavin and he shared the same father.

He hated them, despised them both with every fiber of his

being. And he hated himself for having a thread of hope that they'd ever change. When he was young, he was continuously held down by his father. Restrained while his brother beat him with all types of bloody instruments, something he'd never become immune to like expected. He'd chanted, prayed, and begged that part of them would love him, show him some mercy. That they would stop hurting him wearing the sick bliss of pleasure on their faces, the day never came.

Angel. Her name was a whisper within his mind. Lucien remembered her pale faintly freckled face, and riot of black curls that framed her green eyes. The same color eyes as his. Well, his when they changed from blue to green. He'd thought his initial attraction to the girl odd since he wasn't interested in the young people he killed in a personal way. His interest in his youthful victims was more likened to a sympathetic killing he'd give to a wounded animal. However, with Angel, he'd wanted to hurt his brother to save her.

At times, his father and Gavin's mind games disturbed him more than the beatings. They'd changed him. Made him crave deep, dark things that came with being a pain addict, a co-dependent vessel that was so broken he would accept even their abuse since it was laced with his hope for a reconciliation. Even with the killing of the children the Order of the Dragon held for blood draining sacrifices, there did seem to be a compulsion in doing it. Those temptations were fed just by being a member of the Order of the Dragon. It disgusted him.

Maybe, he figured, that some part of himself felt pleasure in 'stealing' those souls from his brother. Since his brother never ate of flesh from the dead victims, preferring to feast on victims barely living or awake for the act. He didn't want that for these kids. Peter had done something to be respected, he'd contained the monster.

His brother got off on watching something living being terrified by the power Gavin wielded over them. Lucien knew, as did the others, that Gavin's hunger for flesh was his own, not a side effect of having a demon master to which he prayed constantly. Gavin had just been born mentally ill, which likely came from the years of inbreeding to create the purest blooded maniac possible to serve demons and lead the Extraho of Obscurum. Gavin's illness wouldn't be fed if Lucien had anything to do with it. His father had taught him a few things. Lie, cheat, and kill until you reach your goal. Lucien smiled—he would do what he was groomed to do.

"Sir, we are descending," the pilot announced.

Lucien locked in his seatbelt. Within moments, they were on the ground. The pilot cut off the helicopter and came around to open the door.

Lucien hopped out unassisted, modeled his expression into bland indifference, and followed the pilot to the front door that was guarded by two heavily armed men. The estate was inviting, a brick home on a few acres of privately wooded land. One of the men opened the door.

"The packages are chained to the wall in the area under the basement. When you see the painted lady, slide the picture slightly and the entrance to the crawlspace will be revealed." The man nodded in the direction of the hall.

"Thank you. Keep this quiet and you and your family will be well compensated." Lucien patted the man's shoulder. "And free." Lucien proceeded down the hall.

That was the ultimate desire of the underlings within the Order, eventually. They realized money and notoriety came with a heavy price. One they didn't realize was an uneven exchange until it was way too late.

He counted his steps. It was what he'd done since he was a child. Doing it helped him remember specifically where he'd been taken when it was torturing time. Now the head of security, he was privy to many operations. The job served him well. It allowed him to manipulate the organization's resources so he could research ways to stop their madness.

With Angel Ramirez, he'd realized something: meeting her changed the focus of his research and discoveries. She gave him hope that he could seriously destroy what his father and brother built. Finding out that his birth mother, who was raped in hopes of producing a servant child for Gavin's father, was already pregnant with another man's child, freed part of him to believe his biological father wasn't a sadistic bastard who hated him. Maybe the guy was someone who could've loved what Lucien had the potential to become. That was enough salvation for him.

Lucien slowly walked down the basement steps. Soft classical music filled the space from hidden speakers. The area was furnished with antique couches, rich rugs both on the walls and on the floor. A thick rug in the middle of the room was framed by the ornate furniture. The main room was large, but comfortable with a television decorated like pictures in frames on the wall.

There was indeed a reason he was anxious to see Angel Ramirez. She was his salvation, the reason he'd searched for a different reality to his morbid existence. She confirmed that there was good in him, that the Order of the Dragon didn't create him. His research had revealed that the man, a Decretum Venia spy, was actually Lucien's birth father and was in some way genetically linked to Angel Ramirez.

Many paintings of various sizes and shapes covered the walls. All had men or boys in them with the exception of a small ornately framed painting of a mocha-colored woman in a gold and white headdress. Her expression was solemn and her dress was white and pressed like that of a servant in early times.

Lucien smiled. "One step closer." He slid the picture to the side. Creaking sounded behind him, and he circled around.

The long, plush runner laid on the back of the couch lifted. Lucien went over to it, raised the door, and walked down the stairs into the darkness.

His steps echoed. It made him frown since the echo reminded him of the emptiness within his heart. The one person he'd allowed himself to fall in love with, Gavin had killed. These kids wouldn't realize they had an ally in him. But they did. Lucien would make sure Peter Saints got what he wanted, even if he had to push Gavin off the cliff himself.

Chains rattled, and Lucien reached for his lighter in his suit pocket. He flicked it on, and smiled at the vision before him. A tall, angry faced young man stared at him. The boy's ruddy brown features appeared vibrant, healthy, and strong.

He walked around the expanse of the room and lit the enclosed torches to illuminate the room. The flickering glow scattered the rodents and roaches that littered the floor.

"You, Peter Saints, have caused us more trouble than you know. Over ten of my men were injured near death taking you. I'm stunned that your wounds are few, considering the condition of your vehicle." Lucien's regard caressed the girl beside Peter. Angel, his cousin by blood, seemed larger and more muscled than before. "You and you friends will recover here in our humble abode until I figure out what to do with you."

"Take me to Gavin!" Peter struggled against his bonds.

Lucien smirked. "You'd like that, wouldn't you? Well, not just yet. I have my own plans on ways to play with you to get the answers I seek. Then, I'll give you to Gavin."

Whispering and the snapping of biting teeth came from the

tiny Asian girl next to Angel. Lucien stared at her, recognizing her as another wayward Decretum Venia child he'd attempted to put out of her misery by killing.

"You, slimy one. They know you," the girl sang, "I know you," she whispered.

The boy next to her with a shock of white-blond hair in a buzz cut that framed angular strong features growled, "You touch the girls – I'll kill you. Then let Peter have the pieces."

"Oh, I'm so scared." Lucien lifted his finger to his mouth and bit down until the blood flowed. "I'd like to see you try – boy." He wiped the remains of the blood on the boy's face.

"What do you want?" Angel asked, her voice wounded, frightened. It was nothing like Lucien remembered.

"You to tell me what the books you opened revealed about the thousand year war. I need to know if you kids have revealed a method to defeat Gavin."

Peter Saints charged at him, as far as he could go. "You don't ask her a damn thing, you sicko!"

Lucien caressed Angel's face, and then kissed her shivering forehead. "Answer my question or I will unlock her and do what I've wanted to do to her since I first laid eyes on her."

"You would kill her," the petite one hissed. "Sickness, evil, betrayer!"

"We have not! But there will be other ways," Peter yelled. "Let us go and we will finish the search. With each step we take – Gavin will get stronger, he'd have a chance."

"We will have a chance," the Asian girl echoed, then made a wind sound through her pursed lips.

"Just let us go; let them go Lucien," Angel responded. "Take me if you want, but let them free."

"Sorry, but I can't let you go. I need to speak to that girl there – alone." Lucien reached for the small one. With her he had a history. He knew her small size was controllable. Tugging on the handkerchief in his suit, he stuffed it in the girl's mouth.

"Argia! Fight him." Peter jerked and yanked against the chains.

"She'd lose." Lucien smacked Peter with the back of his fist. "And so will you. Now, if you want her to live through what I'm about to do to her – you'll keep your mouth quiet and wait." He leaned down and kissed the girl's forehead.

Lucien grasped one then the other of the girl's wrists in one hand. With the other, he dug in his pocket for handcuffs. Using his fingers to adjust them, he proceeded to place them on her wrist. Tugging her forward, he unlocked the chained cuffs. He secured his hand at the base of her neck and pushed her forward. "Go, and watch your step tiny one, we are going upstairs."

The girl didn't whimper, cry, or complain. She complied easily, but Lucien wasn't fooled. The last time he'd held Argia like this, she played possum before she stabbed him with a scalpel.

And she would be a perfect decoy for him. Lucien smiled.

He'd left the door open and picked her up before she'd reached the last step. "Now, play nice with me, and I'll play nice with you," Lucien whispered and turned the girl around. He looped her arms over the slim back of a nearby chair.

Lucien bent and lifted her chin so she could see him. "Argia. You remember me, don't you?"

The girl shrugged and her eyes dropped, studying him from head to toe.

"Your friends won't survive if you attempt to escape. I plan to have my guards come for you, down these basement stairs, from the guard post at the front door and surrounding the back – just to see me drain you and your friends dry of every drop of blood within you."

The girl narrowed her eyes at him. She spewed off a dozen or so muted curses around the rag he'd stuffed in her mouth.

Lucien waved a finger at her. "Uh-uh." He jabbed the linen deeper, until she coughed against it.

Lucien hoped she was daring enough to fight for her freedom. Their work wasn't done, and in order for him to destroy Gavin and Balaal, he needed everything revealed to them. They had to live.

"Don't even think about getting out of here or making it to the woods. I will find you. Gavin will find you." Lucien leaned closer to Argia, touching his nose to hers. "Demons. The one Balaal controls, will hunt you and tell him where you are."

She grunted; her slanted eyes filled with a fiery protest unsaid.

"Nod if you understand."

The girl didn't nod, but her lips pressed down on the handkerchief stuffed in her mouth.

"This old house has lots of hidden exits"—Lucien stood and placed his hands in his pockets—"for the guards even the servants. They aren't safe though. Finding one could get you killed if you don't know the clues. One wrong turn in this place and the penalty is a slice off of a head, a finger, or arm. So, don't get any ideas about escaping like you did before, my little bird."

He cracked his fingers and then slid his pinky between her wrist and the handcuffs.

"It was believed that the owner of this home enjoyed torturing and killing young slave girls, then drinking their blood to enhance her beauty. She'd keep her victims captive in that cellar. Her slaves were forced into secrecy and had to clean the stench of her torture daily." Lucien grinned at her, having fun with telling his tale, but not being fooled by the dead spark in her eyes.

The girl blinked.

"Imagine being trapped there until I get the chance to repeat her ritual. I tried to kill you once. Next time, I promise you, I will finish the job – for your own sake, and mine." He smoothed back a straight blue strand of her hair and tucked it behind her ear.

Lucien sauntered to the steps leading upstairs. "Think about what's waiting for you when I return. I bet your blood will be bitter. Just the way I like it." Placing his finger to his lips, he winked and left her there with one final warning without looking back. "Run little bird, run, before the cat catches and eats you." He laughed.

CHAPTER 12

Peter was so furious he yanked on the chains, over and over again. They wouldn't break because of some strange locking mechanism his fingers couldn't reach. Everything went south, and horribly so, when they'd run over the men after them. Another car rammed them from behind, and someone hit him, knocking him out cold before he could even climb out of the car. He woke up in chains in the dungeon with the others. Peter shook his head to clear his thoughts and the ache from a vaguely remembered injury.

"You may as well give up, man. These chains won't give," Kyle said.

"I-I can't believe he took Argia in my place. The things he will do to her. Why didn't he take me instead?"

"We will get her. They have to come down here for one of us next. When they do, fake calm, and then fight with all you've got. Take their guns, anything you can get your hands on. The guards can't be as bad as Lucien," Peter said, swallowing the putrid thick air that stuck in his throat.

"He's known to kill the kids captured by the Extraho of Obscurum. I should know. He tried to kill me." Angel's whisper echoed off the walls.

"What? And he has Argia now!" Kyle lamented and twisted himself in his chains, jerking his body forward. "We've got to get out of here."

The creaking of the door echoed through the dampness of the room.

Peter stilled. So did the others.

Since his eyes were adjusted to the dim light from the oil-lit torches surrounding them, the outline of petite feet in torn tennis shoes came into view.

"Damn, can't be," he whispered.

Argia jumped down the side of the steps and crouched on the floor. "I'm back!" She grinned.

Peter smiled back at her. "How'd you get away?"

"Talk later, I am busting everyone out." Argia giggled. "Time is flying; we have to move." She slid the mechanism that locked the chained cuffs to Peter's wrist.

Then she opened Kyle's. "Hey, babe." He hugged her.

Peter hurriedly unlocked Angel and gave her a hug and kiss. He jogged to the steps.

Argia called, "No! We need to see if there is a trick exit."

"Why? There's a perfectly good exit above. And killing a few guards wouldn't be a bad thing," Peter added.

"Yes, yes, it would." Argia moved her hands on the walls behind them.

Angel pulled on the base of the chains while Kyle slid his fingers along the crevices of the walls.

Peter went over to the flickering light of the torches. "Lucien didn't light all of them."

"What do you mean?" Angel asked.

"The torches; he left one out." Peter frowned. "He couldn't have made it that easy for us."

"If he did, it's probably a trap," Angel said.

Argia jumped and tried to reach the base of the unlit torch. "I don't care; we need to get out." She sighed. "Before..."

"I'll get that for you." Kyle went behind her, kissed the top of her head.

A thundering of feet shook the ceiling above them.

Searching around, Peter grabbed a metal chair from the corner. He sprinted up the stairs and braced the chair against the latch of the door. Fisted banging began almost immediately.

"C'mon Peter!" Angel called.

Peter jumped down the side of the stairs and headed towards the jagged opening in the wall below the torch.

Running towards the opening, Peter hit the torch to put it back in place, and then slid through the closing door.

The odor in the dark tunnel made Peter gag. The heavy smell of death stood the hairs on his neck on end.

A light flickered ahead. Argia said, "The lighter, I picked it from Lucien's pocket."

Peter respected the girl. She was tough, even if a little off in the sanity department.

"How'd you know this place was here?" Peter moved between the others to get closer to Argia.

"Lucien. He's chatty." Argia handed Peter the lighter. "And not what he seems."

"Hell if he isn't," Peter stated.

"Well, he is bad. Too be sure. He has evil intent. But it wars with the good, like it did his ancestor."

Peter lifted the lighter higher; the glow in front of them didn't reveal a way out yet.

"Smells rotten," Kyle said.

"It's from years of them dragging the bodies out this way, I'm sure," Argia answered.

Peter could believe it. The place felt like death hovered around. Like a fiendish spirit was admiring its work, bragging so with each step, the smell, the oppressive air made one feel trapped.

"You know that how?" Peter asked, uncomfortable with Argia's directions.

"Lucien may have felt it. His essence was difficult to read, but my angelic visitor came when I called. Allowed me to see more clearly," Argia hummed. "He would've killed me if I didn't leave."

"No doubt," Peter asked, more accustomed to the smell now, and he didn't slow his breathing like before.

It seemed as if they'd walked over three miles in that dark tunnel. The humidity pressed on them like an invisible force. The brand on his hand itched, zinged, and throbbed. He wondered at why it was itching now.

"There!" Kyle slapped his hand on Peter's shoulder. "An exit."

Peter rushed in front of them, licked the palm of his hand, and fiddled with the lock on the thick wood door.

"Let me." Angel stepped up next to him and slid a hairpin out of her thick hair. Some of it slipped from the sloppy bun at the nape of her neck. Her delicate fingers maneuvered the pin into the lock until it clicked.

Peter smiled at her. "Thanks, babe." He pushed at the wooden door. It was heavy, and he used his shoulder to press hard at it. As it slid away, grass and dirt were caught in the base. Warm night air seeped into the tunnel, and Peter took a deep breath.

"Run!" Argia whispered. "Don't stop."

The knocking of multiple feet was a soft echo on the walls behind them. Each second the sound grew closer. Peter grabbed Angel by the hand and nearly dragged her as he ran. He pounded the thick grass-covered ground and pushed his feet hard toward the thick copse of trees ahead. Within those trees, he felt a darkness. The brand on his hand burned, knowing that something waited for them there.

"Peter! They are hitting the barriers!" Argia called. "The demons are trying to cut through."

"I'll take them over men any day. Let's get ready to play!" Peter yelled.

They broke into the wall of foliage and closely packed trees.

And were thrown into total darkness.

CHAPTER 13

Gavin paced the large office. Waiting for Lucien always angered him. To say he was disappointed was an understatement. Lucien wasn't himself. The years of growing up and training his brother to become his willing servant hadn't worked as well as he'd expected. It would prove Gavin's failure. And Gavin never failed.

Gavin hadn't become the head of the Extraho of Obscurum without meticulous planning and manipulation. From studying the ancient scrolls planted all over the world, to beating his brother into submission from the first day his father laid infant Lucien at his feet, to killing his father in order to succeed to his position. Gavin was groomed for greatness.

He teased at the power bestowed upon him by the demon master trapped within him. Forcing his mind to pinpoint the time and space that connected him to the hell-bound plane that held the most powerful demons physically captive.

"You." Gavin pointed at one of the servants placing wine and bread on the table in front of one of the regional leaders in the Extraho of Obscurums.

"Sir?" The man stood straighter with a faint blush darkening his upper check.

"Get out. Tell Mara to join us." Gavin tapped his finger on the wood desk.

"Lucien should be here shortly; my daughter saw his helicopter landing. His ride was waiting for him."

Gavin flexed his fingers; they were long, pale, and smooth. The burns and gashes completely healed thanks to the witch's constant bathing him in sacrificial blood and casting her spells. With his demon-hybrid body, he would've healed eventually, but her help sped up the process.

"Jack," he said to the servant, "the Order of the Dragon's council meeting is at the end of the month. Do you have everything in place for the ceremony?" Gavin studied the man's slight shaking as he laid his napkin on his lap.

"We are close. I just have one problem."

"Problem?"

"My youngest daughter isn't ready to be the sacrifice. We will have to find another family to give a psychic child in her place."

Gavin narrowed his eyes. "She's fourteen, more than ready to be given to the Master Balaal so I may gain victory to the Extraho of Obscurum."

The insolent man raised his chin. "She is not untouched. Her sacrifice is ruined."

Gavin sauntered over to Jack. "You were to keep her close, locked in the cell beneath your home until the ceremony. Who defiled my sacrifice?"

Jack swallowed, his pupils jumping around within the sockets.

The door opened.

Jack stood. "Lucien! You made it." He wiped his hands on his slacks before shaking Lucien's hand and giving him a small hug. "You bring good news?"

Gavin grunted; he would make Jack pay for the carelessness.

Lucien's gaze met his deep bluish green to Gavin's pale blue. Anger rose up in Gavin's chest, a small flutter that always threatened his control when his brother presented even a small bit of defiance.

"We're waiting, brother," Gavin stated. He narrowed his eyes and willed Balaal's talon to push through his index fingers. Nothing could be heard in the room but the crackling of his forefinger as the bone broke, reformed, then sliced through the skin of his finger. Blood dripped on the smooth wood table.

Lucien cleared his throat. "There's been a mistake."

Gavin bent his forefinger, slicing through the top of the table and making Jack take a slight step backwards. Gavin bit back Balaal's clawing within him. Stepping forward, he said, "There is never room for mistakes. Explain yourself."

Lucien crossed his arms in front of him. "I got a call from one of my trusted advisors. The boy, Peter Saints was captured with a few others and is being held at one of the rented mansions."

"And..." Gavin balled his untransformed fist while scratching his talon-shaped finger on the wood top of the desk.

"I traveled to the site as quickly as possible. There, I called for backup so the young people could be transported. However, the girl was there."

Gavin's blood was on fire; his gums tingled, his teeth lengthened, and he stopped scratching the desk. "Her name?"

"Argia Yong. The girl with double-sight."

Jack gasped. "She's alive? And with Peter Saints."

Gavin's throat felt as it if was filled with shards of glass. "The girl we were able to use as a portal. You said Argia was dead."

"I thought she was. Believe me, it wasn't for my lack of trying. The urges, brother." Lucien walked over to the large painting of their father who was golden like them. Standing there in judgment of the pair he'd born.

"You seem to kill them all when no one's watching, brother. I may need to appoint another to deal with this matter. Having that girl would alleviate the need of another psychic sacrifice. I could use her. It would be my revenge since she was the one who trapped me within the Wall of Ash."

"We'll see, brother, there is the issue. Argia Yong escaped and took Peter Saints and the others with her," Lucien commented, calmly.

Gavin's fury burst forth from his chest. The demon within him clawed through his stomach, up his throat, and a blinding red bloody tinge filled his sight. Gavin's bones bent and reshaped, and without restraint, he ripped and gouged at Lucien's back. Bending, Gavin licked at his brother's wounds knowing the intensity of the torture would be unbearable. Then he reared back and grabbed Lucien by the head. Gavin's mouth stretched open as sharp teeth protruded to rest on Lucien's head.

"Mara!" Jack screamed for the witch. "He'll kill Lucien!"

Grasping Lucien around the neck and lifting him higher, Gavin growled, "Yes. Yes, I will kill him and feed him piece by living piece to my demon master!" Gavin gurgled, his forked tongue slithering out of his mouth to lap at his brother's blood. Then he heaved him forward.

Lucien sagged against the wall, his blood-smeared head resting on the frame of the painting of their father.

Gavin laughed. "Where you have failed, brother, my demon slaves will be victorious!" Gavin backhanded Lucien's limp body, and Lucien flew through the air to hit the table, then flop to the floor.

"Mara, glad you made it. Start the ceremony of the damned; my demons are going hunting

CHAPTER 14

"Quiet!" Peter held up a hand to Kyle to stop his heavy breathing. Flickers of fire from bullets sparked the dense forest. Peter crouched low, pushing Angel's shoulder down to let her know to do the same.

The crunch of multiple feet, and repeated calls from the security force that protected the house were some distance behind. The rapid beat of Peter's heart let him know the men were still too close.

His eyes, although adjusted to the darkness, couldn't see anything but random shapes. Taking a deep breath, he held his hand out in front of him to grope his way through the crowd of trees.

Angel's fingers snaked through Peter's and she gave him a squeeze. He would've smiled, but now he only fought back the bitterness deep in his throat.

The forest smelled fresh, sweet, and welcoming despite the men closing in. Pale glows of their flashlights lit the foliage behind them. Peter kept moving.

The brand on his palm was at peace. It lay flat as if it was a scar that had long healed. Peter felt comfort in it. Although, he didn't want to be shot, or sliced by Gavin's men, he'd rather deal with them than the demons Gavin controlled.

Angel squeezed his hand, and then stopped him. Peter slid his thumb back and forth on the top of her hand. "What?"

"Dogs," she whispered.

"Shit!" Kyle bumped into Peter, his elbow jabbing the middle of Peter's back.

"Use the light from your angelic weapons; humans can't see it," Peter told them; all but Kyle could light their path.

"I don't have any, remember? But cue me and we can run like hell!" Kyle said.

"Hold my hand," Argia told Kyle.

Peter willed the brand on his palm to heat. Hot pulses of energy flowed through his veins, fighting to get to the surface. A red glow appeared on his hand. He flicked his fingers, and the tip of a glowing white sword pushed out of his hand, inch by inch. The pleasure of revealing the weapons felt as if he released a breath he'd been holding.

Next to him, spikes of glowing knives had materialized on Angel's arms and down her back.

"They're closer," Angel whispered, crouched low.

"Not for long. Follow me!" Peter picked up his stride, lopping off small branches and trees to quicken their pace. His chest heaved, his skin tingled, but he moved onward.

Peter pushed on hoping the others could keep up because he wasn't stopping. "Water! We'll have to swim across."

"Good. Hurry, they aren't stopping," Kyle called.

The trees had become less dense. Small animals scurried about, getting out of their way.

Peter sprinted towards the water. Swiping his hand downward, the glowing sword retracted back into his hand. "Follow me.

Quietly. Go underwater and don't stop till you get to the other side."

Peter dove for the lake, his body slicing into the water and barely making a splash. His arms pumped, pulling him as he tilted his head to the side. He grabbed a breath and went back under. Peter forced himself to breathe easy, and to swim as fast as he could. The calmness of the water gave him some comfort, loosened his muscles, and held him up while he pushed on.

His muscles ached a bit; it seemed like he'd been swimming forever, but he'd counted—kept time—and figured it had only been about forty minutes. Just a few more powerful strokes and the tip of his tennis shoe connected with the soft cushion of the muddy bottom.

He stood, feeling the chill of the breeze as water ran down his face and his body. His jeans stuck to his legs, but he didn't care. He searched the moonlit lake for the others.

No flicker of flashlights; no barking dogs. Peter let out a deep breath, relieved they'd gotten the small break they needed to get away – for now.

He took off his shirt and wrung out the water. Peter wished he'd held onto Angel's hand, but when her knives come out, she didn't like to be touched.

The trust she'd given him in sharing her pain that created the cuts on her body where her knives were revealed, he'd never forget. No one had ever let him that far into their soul. If he were honest, he'd been too busy battling the scars within himself to want to get to know someone else's journey. With Angel, that changed – he'd changed.

Her dark hair broke the surface of the water. It was lopped to the side of her pale freckled face, framing her green eyes as she frantically searched for him.

"Here!" Peter stepped forward. He lifted her slim form into his arms and kissed her. Deep, drowning, never-ending and shattering. Peter hugged her close, kissing down her jaw to her neck.

"Love you." She dug her fingers in his thick curly hair.

"I love you too, baby." Peter kissed her lips once more. "Sorry I left you back there."

Angel shook her head. "You know I can't be touched like that. It's just too...too much."

"I get it." He released her, and Angel landed on her feet in a soft thump.

"Damn, I forgot to ask. Kyle and Argia can swim, right?" Peter asked.

"I think so. Argia? I don't think there's anything that girl can't do."

"Right on that."

"But Kyle, I don't know. He wouldn't say anything even if he didn't know how to swim."

Within minutes, Argia appeared, blue hair plastered to the sides of her face. She yanked at the t-shirt sliding off of Kyle's back. She struggled a bit dragging him.

"Kyle!" Peter dove in the water to help Argia.

Kyle stumbled to stand and started a series of rapid coughs.

Peter slapped his back. "Thought you could swim."

"Bastard. You didn't ask." Kyle coughed loudly than spat to the side. "I can but not that damn good. Cramp in my leg."

Peter lifted him, slid his arm under Kyle's shoulder while Argia smacked Kyle's back. Peter smiled when Kyle winced.

"Enough girl; you're stronger than you look." Kyle cleared his throat.

"I've got him. Your lighter work?"

Argia shook her head. "But the moon is shining brightly." Her head jerked left then right. "We need to keep going," she whispered. "The bad ones are hunting us now."

Peter nodded and lifted Kyle higher then followed Angel and Argia through the trees bordering the lake's edge.

"I'm good now." Kyle straightened.

Peter crossed his arms. "About time. You big baby." Peter elbowed Kyle.

"Well, it's been a long time since I've had the luxury of working on my swimming skills. And by the way, where'd you learn?"

Peter shrugged. "The city pool. When I snuck out of the orphanage, I'd go and jump in – with my clothes on."

"What? They didn't kick you out?"

"Nah! Lots of the kids only had shorts to wear. Apparently, the park where we lived under was surrounded by a ghetto. At least on three sides."

Peter walked in silence awhile, enjoying the breeze over his damp clothes. The chirp and flutter of the birds relaxed him. The creatures moving about normally meant no demons or pursuers were breaking the calm. They were safe, for a moment.

Halting his pace, Peter watched Argia who seemed to be attempting to coax something from behind one of the large trees. Her silhouette was framed by a beam of moonlight poking between the trees.

"What's your girl doing now?" Peter slapped Kyle's chest.

"I gave up trying to figure her out when I fell in love with her."

"Smart man." Peter's jaw dropped a bit when he realized she was talking to a little girl. The kid appeared to be on the cusp of a teen. The child made frantic hand gestures at Argia. Then she ran off.

Peter jogged over to the girls. "What's up?" He spun around, checking the woods for a sign of anyone else.

Angel came up next to him. "The girl is homeless. She's here with her mother and wants us to go away."

"I get that, but did you talk her into taking us to her mother?

Maybe they can lead us out of here. We can't be far from the next Sanctuary." Peter rested his arm around her shoulders.

Before Angel could answer, the girl sprinted from between the trees. Her brown hair was short and dirty. Her pants and baggy shirt were wrinkled but clean. "You leave! There is a car. We think it works, but my momma can't drive it."

"Where?" Peter asked.

The girl stepped back, her eyes widened. "Th-there, straight through, a few miles, I think. At least it felt like we walked that far before we got to the water."

"Thanks." Peter held out his hand.

"Just go! We don't want company here. Too hard to stay safe." The girl thrust a flashlight into Angel's hand. "It will help."

"Uh." Angel started, but the girl ran off.

"Did you warn her?" Peter asked Argia.

"Yes, but she won't listen."

"Is she like us?"

Argia frowned at Peter. "No, she's like them. But I think she is a defector. It won't help them though."

"There's nothing we can do?"

Argia's eyes were watered. "No." Her head fell.

Peter took the flashlight Angel handed him. "Let's roll, this way. One step closer to answers."

CHAPTER 15

Peter cleared the branches out of the way and his jaw dropped. "What the hell?"

Angel lifted a dead branch off the hood of the jeep and gasped.

"It's our jeep. I thought it was totaled. It's even more beat up now, but hopefully it works. How'd it get here?" Peter tried the door and it opened.

"Yes! All our gear is in the trunk too," Kyle called from the back.

Peter released the air he'd held in his lungs. "Let's get outta here." He had a feeling something wasn't right with this set-up, but he didn't want to stand around and figure it out. He went under the dashboard, disconnected the pushrod to the ignition switch. Then opened the hood and jump started the motor.

Peter got in the driver's seat, said, "Ready?" then gunned the engine.

"God would be really smiling down on us if the tank was full," Kyle said, hitting the headrest behind Peter.

Peter glanced at the gas gauge. "Well, half a tank means He's watching but he wants us to sweat a little."

75

"I'll take it." Kyle laughed.

"So many coincidences, I don't know if they are good ones yet," Argia hummed, tapping her fingernail on the window.

"Maybe, there was a spy from the Decretum Venia that helped us? They've had some high-profile plants infiltrate the Extraho of Obscurum before."

Peter shook his head. "I don't know; I hope so. But I just don't get the feeling it was that kind of help."

Argia spoke up, "Lucien was careless this time. He's always been so."

Peter braced himself as he plowed the jeep over some rocky terrain and through some low hanging trees. "What do you mean about always?"

"He came to see me in the mental hospital once." Argia sighed and sat up, close behind Peter.

He felt her breath on his ear. "He tried to break my neck when they weren't watching. A sneaky one he is."

"He what?" Kyle bounced in his seat.

"Shh, I don't want Kyle to know, he is sensitive about those things."

"Was he trying to kill you this time?"

Argia tapped the curve of his seat in a rhythmic beat. "Maybe. I said he wanted to. Warned me, but last time he was quicker about it. If he hadn't gotten interrupted by a call from his brother, he would've finished me off. I'm sure of it."

"You don't think he was helping us, do you?"

Argia smacked her teeth. "No, he's a tease. Likes to play with his food."

"Yeah, I guess." Peter frowned and jerked the car way from a low hanging branch.

"You know they say his brother likes to eat his victims. Lucien just likes them young. He doesn't eat the flesh by choice I'm sure." Argia plopped back into her seat.

Peter thought about what she said. It wouldn't make sense for Lucien to let them go.

Angel rested her head on Peter's shoulder. He wrapped his free arm around her and held her as they broke through the trees. Peter maneuvered the jeep onto the road. "What do you think about our getaway?" he asked her.

"I think we need to be happy. Lucien wouldn't want us to escape; Gavin would kill him."

"Yeah, us doing so is pretty much the guy's death certificate."

Angel bit her lip. "Maybe not that bad. For some reason, Gavin really needs Lucien. He would hurt him but not kill him...at least, I don't think."

"Why?"

"It's the way the Order of the Dragon works. They need someone to pour their pain into. They do it by torture."

"Oh, you gonna pick now to remind me I didn't do my home-work?" Peter smiled. He was relaxed as the sun rose in the sky, and there was no one in sight.

"Well, if the shoe fits." She shrugged. "As I was saying, they work in pairs. Really threes. Gavin, his brother and Gavin's intended, which is likely some type of witch or psychic."

"So Lucien, the brother, can't have anyone?"

"Nope, he is to serve them when they marry. Until then, he doesn't have to serve Gavin's woman."

"What if Lucien died?"

"Then Gavin would not be able to lead. He has to meet all the conditions of the position. They have other ruling families who have the same structure in case they lose their leader."

"So, if he didn't intentionally help us – he's probably setting us up or planted something on the jeep."

"More than likely." Angel snuggled close and kissed him at the base of his neck.

"That I can deal with. I've got a plan."

"I know; you always have one." Angel laughed.

"They just don't always work out."

"Nope, they don't, but you are real good at the back-up planning."

"You would know; seems that's all I've been doing." Peter lowered the visor to block the sun. "I screwed up back there. That mistake could've ended everything."

"But it didn't, so don't dwell on a mistake that led to our freedom."

Peter watched a few cars come on to the two-lane road, and tensed for a moment. He pushed the gas and passed them. The cars fell behind. He figured that was a good indication that they were normal people taking a ride.

"How much further," Kyle asked. "A man's got to pee."

"Really? This is not the time."

"My bladder can't be controlled. Stop or get us there in five minutes."

Angel rummaged under her feet and came up with a plastic container that was curved with a top. "Here, and keep it back there with you." Angel tossed the bottle behind her.

Peter laughed. "Assume the position."

"You got to be jerking me! This sucks," Kyle cursed under his breath, yet a steady stream of liquid hitting the bottom of the bottle followed.

Peter laughed when Argia pinched her nose while observing Kyle as if she was inspecting an odd science project.

"Now answer the damned question: do you know how much further we have to go?"

"We'll be to a place I can park in about thirty minutes. Then we'll have to hoof it to the Sanctuary."

"Why are they so freakin' far apart?" Kyle asked.

"Well, we passed one, but it won't have what we need to figure out the location of the next Stronghold. Some of the Sanctuaries are just hiding places that are sacred and protected. Others have ancient scrolls or even angelic artifacts that will give us clues on how to destroy the Wall of Ash...and Gavin."

"Won't killing him be enough?" Kyle held out his hand and allowed Angel to squirt hand sanitizer into his palm.

"No. The demon in him actually opened the Wall of Ash, but its true owner is their king. Eventually, he will be able to release more demons from the realm to breach earth."

"Who's to say they aren't still here anyway?"

"They were killed in the BC, only loosely descended humans like Gavin and the Extraho of Obscurum are here. They are weak and childlike compared to what the supreme evil one would bring with him."

Kyle snorted. "Then kill Gavin and destroy the Wall of Ash it will be."

Angel pulled up her knees and rested a foot on the dashboard. "How will we stop them – permanently?"

"In all my dreams about the thousand year war, there is always good and evil. It's a balance. And basically, Earth is the demon's domain, we humans just happen to be taking up space here."

"So that means that one day our children will still be fighting the Order of Dragon and demons like Gavin carries in him?"

Peter let out a deep breath. "Yes, but they will never have to deal with the Wall of Ash."

Kyle kicked the seat. "Nope, that screw-up is all ours."

Peter maneuvered the jeep off the exit. The day was bright and cool. He rolled down the window and glanced at the gas tank.

They were out of gas, and Peter felt that time was hounding them, too.

He slowed the car and squeezed between a two other vehicles before stopping at a traffic light. The others had fallen into the quiet thoughtfulness that plagued them when they were too tired to voice their fears or strategize how to avoid the next bit of bullshit thrown at them.

Peter gripped the steering wheel and gritted his teeth. With all the dreams, the transformation through the *Book of Light,* and training from the Elders in the Decretum Venia, his original mistake still haunted him. It jeered at him in the moments of quiet, and reminded him that although they'd all suffered, he was the stupid one suckered into opening Pandora's Box, or the *Book of Light,* that actually gave Gavin the ammunition he needed to destroy them.

The hard fact was, in order to save Angel, he would've done it again. The selfish sucker that he was. He weaved in and out of traffic trying to figure on the best place to dump the jeep.

Peter didn't want to give Gavin another clue to what he planned.

At the intersection, Peter saw his opportunity. A sign that read: *Car Parts and Appliances.* He maneuvered into what appeared to be a side alley entrance. It was much larger than most alleys he'd been in, big enough to fit a large truck. The road was made of brick and the jeep bumped up and down.

"Where are we?" Angel asked.

"Someplace we can park in camouflage and come back if we need to."

Kyle asked, "How far will we have to walk?"

"We are hitching a ride a few miles, then walking another few."

"Can we grab some food?" Kyle asked.

"For that, we will have to dumpster dive. Can't be seen."

"Dude, dumpster dive? Piss in a plastic cup. We haven't been this hardcore in a year."

"The last place we stayed made us too comfortable. You've turned soft." Peter laughed. He drove between two large, beat-up trucks.

"You are fixing that assumption." Kyle snorted.

"Good. Let's get out. Girls, get the stuff. Kyle and I are going to push a car in behind the jeep."

"Damn," Kyle said. "It never stops."

CHAPTER 16

"C'mon." Peter led them between the cars and trucks in the lot. He searched for a back way that would put them on the street where they could blend in to the crush of people out on a weekday. It would be good cover for them for the next few miles.

"Give me some idea what direction we are going? I can put it on the cellphone Remmy hid in the trunk," Kyle said.

"No, we will get there. Just stay with me. If we get separated, meet up back here. Hide out or take the jeep and run."

"We will stay with you." Angel placed her hand on Peter's back.

He nodded. Angel didn't realize how her touch calmed his raging adrenaline. He adjusted the backpack on his shoulder and weaved in and out of the scattered vehicles.

The hairs on his neck rose at the first bark from a pit bull that skidded from between the cars to the right. "Run!" He grabbed Angel's hand and pulled her along with him. Behind them, three other dogs skidded from various places to chase them.

Kyle and Argia kept pace with them.

One dog caught up. Peter veered toward the fence just beyond a truck. It jumped. Peter sidestepped and kicked its nose.

"Go! To the fence." He released Angel's hand and pushed her forward.

Kyle hesitated.

"Leave!" The dogs were on them. Angel and Argia ran ahead.

Kyle followed.

Peter struggled to run and remove his backpack. His pace didn't slow. Neither did the dog closest to him.

"Who's got the pepper spray!" Peter yelled.

The girls were on the other side of the fence, Kyle was at the top. Peter hopped on the hood of a car, just yards from the fence. The dogs surrounded him. The barks grew angrier and more aggressive. Peter climbed on the roof. A branch from an over-hanging tree hit his head. He jumped and grabbed at one of the thick branches.

Kyle called, "I've got it. Come closer so I can throw it to you."

Peter yanked and jerked at the branch. Quickly, he removed the smaller branches, fashioning it into a wood club.

"On my way." Peter hurdled from the top of the car to the hood. He braced himself for a fight with the three growling dogs. Taking one glance at Kyle at the top of the fence waiting, he went for it.

Peter used all the super-human strength he had to beat down on the noses and poke at the eyes of the attacking dogs. He backed a few feet then ran and jumped over the disoriented dogs.

His leap gave him the distance he needed. Peter rounded the corner of a truck. Kyle tossed the pepper spray; he caught it with one hand. Then Peter dodged a fourth dog to catapult into its path. Peter hopped on the fence.

The fourth dog charged, and bit down on his calf. Peter tight-ened his grip on the fence. Then he twisted around to pepper spray the mastiff's eyes. The dog whimpered and the others caught up with it.

Peter didn't hesitate. He climbed the fence, and slapped hands with Kyle who was waiting for him at the top. Both jumped to the ground.

Angel hugged him, landing a kiss on his lips. Peter grasped her hand and took a moment to slow his breathing. "That sucked," he said against her lips. "But I made it." He shook his leg from the calf bite.

Angel smiled. "I knew you would."

Peter led them in a light jog that brought them to the main street of the busy city. He held Angel's hand in the crush of the crowd. It was morning and solemn-faced adults and kids were heading to work or school.

Peter observed those he'd squeezed by to make sure they weren't a threat. Angel didn't say anything about her discomfort with people brushing against her, but Peter knew it bothered her by the way she squeezed his hand.

To calm her, he wrapped his arm around her. "Relax," Peter whispered in her ear.

"I'm trying." Angel tightened her arm around his waist.

"When I was in the orphanage at Pastor Finn's, I loved coming outside. The moment I got a smell of that stank city air, I was hooked." He tickled Angel's side, trying to get her mind off of the noise and crush of the people.

She giggled. "Yeah, cities smell."

"The place where I grew up was on the edge of the business district. My father thought it was best to give me an access to the suburbs even though he wanted the convenience of working in the city."

"Did your mom stay with you?"

"Pretty much. She was able to work from home and took me to the school on our corner. Mom never let me walk alone though."

"She probably knew how dangerous it was."

"That's true; she did. That Caribbean-born woman was very protective."

"Do you still dream about her? Know what she looks like?"

"I remember everything about her. From her smell, to the long hair she wore at the top of her head in a messy bun. And the dreams…" Peter didn't want to talk about them. It seemed the only time he'd dreamed about her, she had warnings for him.

"What about them?"

"They don't come to me much anymore."

"Unfortunately, mine are not pleasant. So I try not to think about them."

"Someday, when this is all over, I want to be the only person you dream about."

Angel laughed. "I dream about you now."

"Really? What kind of dreams?" Peter raised an eyebrow.

Angel pinched his side. "You've been around Kyle's dirty minded self too long."

"True, he is a bad influence. You are worse though."

"Huh? No way. How am I worse?"

"All the compliments on how muscled I am. How my skin reminds you of delicious chocolate."

"I only said that once, and it was because you were tickling me to the point I had to go to the bathroom."

"Hey, you said it, I didn't."

"I said it under duress and to catch you off guard so I could squirm away."

"Naw, you want me."

"Well, maybe I do, but you don't need to always know about it."

"Yes, I do. I'm wounded here." He placed her hand over his heart.

"No, you are not. You remember all the girls I had to 'remind' at the last hideout that you were taken. It was ridiculous."

"They didn't have a chance."

Kyle tapped Peter's shoulder. "How much further? Argia's getting agitated."

Peter searched the street. They'd traveled a few miles, but they weren't close to where they needed to be. When Argia grew agitated, it meant demons were close.

"We have to hitch a ride." Peter walked over to the curb. "Let's hit the subway."

"On it." Kyle followed.

Peter crossed the street and proceeded down the stairs. They only had to wait a few minutes before the train came.

"When do we get off?" Kyle pulled Argia's small frame under his arm. The girl appeared spooked and whispered often under her breath to herself.

"Two stops." Peter was glad there was no one in their train car.

"Keep your head down though, don't want to be caught on camera," Kyle warned.

"Here it is. Let's get outta here." Peter held tightly to Angel's hand. He took the escalator stairs two by two and was happy Angel kept up.

On the main level, Peter searched for service elevators. He went to one end of the terminal and only saw the sign to the bathroom.

"What are you looking for?" Angel asked.

"Service elevator." Peter spun around and went in the opposite direction. He squeezed through a few pockets of people getting off the train on the top level.

The brand on his hand heated, almost as if it knew they were close to safety, or that there was a fight coming.

"How much further?" Angel asked.

"Depends what traps are waiting for us."

CHAPTER 17

"This is where we get on." Peter removed the yellow hazard warning tape blocking the entrance to the hallway. He crawled under the plastic barrier and searched the wall for a light.

"Here." Angel pointed and pushed the light switch that was in an odd position high up on the wall. The lights only worked in the depths of the hallway. Peter coughed from the dust and dirt that puffed from the floor with each step they took. He didn't stop until he stood in front of the service elevator he'd been looking for. The one he'd dreamt about at the end of a nightmare where he was running from something.

It was opposite a boarded-up employee bathroom. *Never Fear* was spray painted on the door. Several pieces of wood had been nailed on the entrance, with a signed that said, *Out of Service*. It was beat-up with dents and dust. No fingerprints or clues that anyone had touched the thing in years. The planks were criss-crossed from the top of the elevator to Peter's knees.

The lights flickered on and off. Then with a pop, they were thrust into darkness as the bulbs blew their last charge of power.

"Are you sure about this?" Kyle asked.

"Yeah, this is the place. I feel it." The brand on his hand came alive with tingles of flowing blood, turning it red and pulsing. Peter flexed his fingers. He kicked at the wood planks, and then wrenched at them to pull them free.

Angel placed her hand on his. "Don't take them off. If we are followed, they might not think we went in."

"Okay, can do that. " Peter pushed the elevator button. A whining sound came from the other side of the door. The tension pulley made groaning noises, but finally quieted. Peter tapped his foot.

"Cool it, dude, I'm going into coughing fits here," Kyle said.

Peter stopped tapping his foot and rocked back when the door creaked open. The elevator didn't appear any better inside. He was happy that at least the light at the top worked, even though it was dim. Peter motioned them inside. He glanced at Argia who appeared to relax a bit under Kyle's arm as he turned off the flashlight. The walls had peeling paint and were stained with yellowish and green spots that seemed to be mold.

They remained silent while Peter took a deep breath and pressed the button to B1. It was the lower level tunnel under the train they'd used to get there. Before heading here for their hideout, he'd researched the area around this sanctuary and realized the train station was built upon an intricate tunnel system created over a hundred years ago. The combination of his dreams and studying the books in the Decretum Venia's library confirmed the underground city. However, the internet searches didn't validate the hidden place, just the landmarks. The city had built its modern train station without realizing the tunnel system was there. He supposed it was used for trading and running liquor in the early days, but that wasn't evident in the web searches he'd done.

Peter never liked the process they had to follow to break into a

Sanctuary. Even so, it was necessary since some of these places were never to be opened.

"Is this it?" Kyle asked.

Peter shook his head. "Wish it was this simple." The elevator came to a stop on the bottom floor. "We have to find another elevator."

The door opened to a hall with pellets of light piercing from spots unknown.

"Uhum?" Kyle smacked the flashlight on his palm and it came on.

There was a faint dripping noise within the tunnel. This one had cedar blocks and spaces in the wall where pipes protruded. The ground was damp, and it had small holes in the corners where the wall met the floor. The cement was broken and cracked badly with chips on both the ground and ceiling. There were no light fixtures, but tiny punctures in the ceiling that flashed sporadically with glares of light.

"Are you sure this is a 'safe' place for us?" Kyle held Argia tight. She had her eyes closed and grasped his wrinkled shirt with her small, pale hands.

"Yeah, just follow me." Peter pushed past Kyle and grabbed the flashlight.

"Hey!"

"I'll give it back." Peter stepped over a rock. The elevator door behind them closed and the whine of the motor pulling it back in place echoed in the space.

Angel gasped.

Peter entangled his fingers with hers, and they stepped into the dark hall. He twisted around to take a final glance at the elevator and the glowing symbol above it. Before he could turn, the booming sound of rushing water filled the room.

"It's flooding!" Angel yelled.

Peter stepped back against the slosh of water at his feet. He traced the flashlight towards the ceiling and realized the water was pouring from the crease that connected the wall to the ceiling.

"Is that what I think it is?" Kyle snatched the flashlight out of Peter's hand. The light followed a large-toothed fish as it plopped into the water. "Piranhas?"

"Not easy. We have to make it to the end of this hall – alive."

"I say we get our asses back on that elevator!" Kyle hit Peter with the flashlight.

Peter kicked at the cold water filled with man-eating fish as it climbed up to his knees. He searched the hall again looking for a door, but there was none. But there was a faint blue hue at the end of the darkness.

"We run!" Peter tightened his grip on Angel's hand and pushed at high speed through the climbing waters.

"Wait!" Kyle called. "Science class memory-jogger here. If they aren't hungry, they won't attack. Take it slow."

"Do you think these things get much food down here?" Peter slowed.

Angel touched his arm. "He's right, we should go slow and easy."

"What else you remember, science boy?" Peter asked.

"Well, uh, they eat during the day." Kyle's voice sounded winded. "Um, and sleep at night. So, it's good that it's dark now."

"That's it?"

"No. One important thing, don't drop a bit of blood. That will draw them in like vampires."

"Thanks for the comparison." Peter reached back. "Now give me back the flashlight."

"I'm not sure I want to."

"Not funny."

"Yes, it is. And it's keeping me and the girls calm."

"No it isn't," Argia spoke up. "Give it to Peter. You play too much."

Peter grinned at that, and snatched the flashlight from Kyle. "Almost there." Peter pointed the light ahead, pushing through the water that was steadily climbing up his stomach. "Get on my back."

"Thanks." Angel climbed on his back.

"There are a lot in here now. I'm thinking over a hundred," Peter mentioned as one of the fish bumped against him.

"Don't talk numbers to me, dude. A few hundred of them could eat one of us in less than five minutes. Not making the 'calm' factor of us getting to this secret entrance possible."

"Do you have anything that could distract them?" Peter asked.

"Maybe. I grabbed a rock off the floor, and there's a knife and some beef jerky in my backpack."

Plop.

"Did you see that?" Peter tightened his hold on Angel's legs.

"Damn, that must be a king piranha." Kyle cleared his throat. "And he looked awake."

"The walls!" Kyle pointed to the left. "They are moving."

Peter slid Angel off his back. "Stay there and still."

"I'll try, but the water's up to my neck now," Angel said.

Peter sloshed to the wall. As it moved, a ridge widened at the top, creating a lip. Peter put the handle of the flashlight between his teeth, flexed his fingers and got closer to the wall. He nodded; the anxious bubble growing in his chest felt like it would burst. There were fissures in the wall, some wide enough for his foot and hands. With a hop, he wedged his fingers into one crack. Then he lifted himself with a grunt to slide the tip of his foot into another crack.

"It's getting closer," Kyle said.

Peter tilted his chin to shine the light at the water below. The king piranha was becoming agitated but was still a slight distance from the others. His heart sped up in his chest and he dropped his weight then sprang upward, barely catching the ledge of the top of the wall that was steadily closing in on the other. Breathing through his nose was getting difficult, and he slurped back the building saliva around the flashlight.

"Ow!" Kyle yelped. "Hurry."

Peter held himself upright, thankful for all those chin lifts he'd done in numerous bets against Remmy. He quickly made his way to the adjoining wall that had a blue glowing symbol on it.

"Peter! It's coming at us," Angel called.

He tried to drown out their cries and concentrate on placing his hand on the symbol. Balancing himself, he grunted as his foot slipped slightly. Peter reached, his teeth bared down on the flashlight. The splashing and yelling getting louder, he pushed himself a bit farther. Then slammed his palm against the blue light and winced when sharp pins stuck his palm to draw blood.

The sloshing water rolled through the alcove. The wall slid back; the crack at the bottom of the opposite wall opened, sucking in the water and the fish. Soon, the floor was damp, but empty of fish.

Peter jumped from the ledge just as it slammed back into its original position. He rushed over to Angel and hugged her close as he wiped the blood from her face. "You okay?"

Angel nodded. "They stopped attacking me when they bit me."

He kissed her. "Your blood. They knew you were a descendent of the Decretum Venia." Peter held her close as the entire wall slid upward, creating a doorway for them. "This is it."

CHAPTER 18

Peter's heart was still racing in his chest. The wall behind them moved back into place, and the entire hidden cave lit up. Glowing mineral rocks were everywhere within the entryway.

He couldn't help but spin with his eyes on the ceiling. The rocks were multi-colored, glowed or reflected reflections from the others and were in an intricate design of a legion of angels in flight.

"Whoa! Science project overload. These are extremely rare rocks." Kyle sighed with a goofy grin on his face.

Peter rubbed his hands on the wall as he walked further in. "No kidding, Sherlock."

"They are our protection. They smell of herbs and have an oily touch." Argia sniffed the air. "We are safe here." She ran her hands on the rough jeweled wall.

Angel jumped up and down. "Food? Think there is food in here?"

"Usually some of that dried stuff we just love to eat. How long can beef jerky survive?" Peter wondered what was at the split off of the two pathways leading in opposite directions from the main corridor ahead.

Kyle nodded at him. "We'll take this way. Meet you after we find a place to crash for a few hours."

Peter studied Argia; she was calm, tapping her chin.

She smiled at Peter. "We will find the answer here, I think."

"We have to." Peter grasped Angel's hand and walked down the dark corridor next to them. With each step, the jeweled walls came to life and lit their path.

"Clues to the location of the stronghold are in the scrolls." Peter intertwined his fingers with Angel's.

"Yes, that's where some of them were the last time we traveled to one. My only time ever going to a Stronghold was when my body changed."

"I know. This time won't be different. The stronghold has the most important secrets the Decretum Venia's angelic ancestors had to hide."

Angel sighed. "So beautiful."

"It is. Sometimes I wish we could just stay in these Sanctuaries. They have the scrolls of our forefathers and the protection against man and demons—everything we need to live a normal life."

Angel laughed. "I don't think I ever remember having a normal one. Living on the run with your parents, learning fighting arts without knowing why, and meeting a man who is more evil than the devil himself at my father's company party, was never normal."

"I get that. For me though, my parents kept the illusion until the very end. Then all hell broke loose when they picked me up from one of the few play date's they allowed me to go on with friends. Cars chasing us, Dad's drowning, and my mother being gunned down – blew up my fantasy life in my face."

"At least you had friends at the orphanage. That's something I rarely had." Angel stopped and leaned against the wall. Her palms lay flat on the decorated surface of flat colorful rocks. She moved her hands back and forth mimicking the making of angel wings in the snow. The rocks glowed up and lingered to create the illusion of illuminated angel wings.

Peter smiled at the sight of Angel with her eyes closed, and the glowing odd-shaped wings framing her on the wall.

"Yeah, I guess I did. And I'm sorry you had no one." He stepped closer and placed his hands on either side of her jaw. Then he leaned in and softly touched his lips to hers. Her eyes opened and brightened as she hugged his waist. Hungrily, she returned his kiss. Peter stood up, breaking the intensity.

"I had you, Peter. I am so glad I'd found you. Thinking back, the days on my own on the road, it made me stronger, and I needed to become stronger."

"I guess we all did." Peter nodded, feeling the kinship of the moment with her.

"I'm still a bit shook up from seeing Lucien." Angel shivered.

"I'm still angry I couldn't kill him right there when he touched you." Peter balled his fist and hit the wall above her head. Angel flinch but regained her stance.

"I could tolerate him as long as you were there." Angel ran her hand up his chest and wrapped her arms around his neck.

"We are still having a good time, right?"

"You're kidding."

"Maybe."

"I don't know Peter, I'm tired. Sometimes I am."

"Me too."

"But..."

Peter placed his finger on her full lips. "It doesn't matter. Everything will be worth it. We will earn our lives after this. We can do anything, be anything. This thing with Gavin, I will fix this."

CHAPTER 19

He tossed the dusty book in the air, then caught it and threw it to the ground. "We aren't getting the answers we need!" Peter sat on the long wood bench in front of the hundreds of warn, dusty books that filled the chamber. Floor to ceiling shelves carved from the rock of the walls held the glowing rocks within them, and they couldn't shine bright enough to burn off the thick dust collected on them.

Angel sat beside him. "There is a pattern to the way the books are arranged. You have to read them to find the time frame and the messages embedded in the text to figure out what section of books these are."

Peter smiled. "I guess me being the descendent of an angelic scribe seems a mistake since I've always had a deep hate of reading and books."

Angel's eyebrows rose. "Really?"

"Yeah. I read well. I was a speed reader. I always finished fast and passed my test with little study. I just didn't find pleasure in reading."

"What about writing? Do you like to write like your ancestor Luke 23?"

"No, I prefer typing and not for fun." Peter stood and selected another book, then put it back and stood on his bare toes to grab a rolled-up scroll.

"I believe we all are camouflage in a way. No one would believe I was a descendent of the most fierce warrior angel Michael 2nd. Especially, since I'm a five foot tall girl."

Peter placed the scroll on a nearby wood table. "No, the fiercest warrior angel was his twin brother Michael 1st."

"Yes, he was. He was the traitor who started it all."

"Right, it sucks." Peter shrugged. "But I know you are a bad ass that got my back and that's all that matters, right?" He winked at her.

Angel laughed. "It is." She flipped a few pages into the book she was reading, then frowned and absently picked up the scroll.

Peter helped her roll it out. "Found something?"

Angel nodded, her finger zigzagging down the scroll, then skipping over to the page she had opened in the book.

"What?" Peter asked, his eyes trailing the words and trying to decipher them upside down.

"It's not here. The location of the Sanctuary with the stronghold clues aren't in these." She pivoted around and waved her hand. "But there is something else we need to keep in mind."

"That is?"

"A potion. Only one ancestor could've made it, but finding his descendant is impossible."

"I found you; I can find the other."

Angel shook her head. "No. All the reading I've done here and studied since the beginning of my life...it just touches on how to destroy the Wall of Ash. The knowledge I gained by merging my memories with my ancestor Michael 2nd confirm that the maker of the substance never gave his DNA to a human carrier."

"So what makes you say that finding his descendent is impossible? You did figure out it was some sort of potion. Do you think he entrusted my ancestor with the secret to write down?"

"Negative. They didn't mention the angel who created it. I just have a feeling who it is from a memory. The passage I read stated, *'within the Ash there were the blood of angels, dissolved away by a thirst that was their own.'*"

"And that means?" Peter tapped his knuckles on the tabletop.

"I believe it means that whatever the demons take from the Angels captured in the Wall of Ash, it was used to destroy the thing from inside out."

"But we don't know what that is."

"Not yet, but you will when we get to the other Sanctuary."

"We still haven't nailed down the clue to where it is."

Angel smiled. She grabbed Peter's wrist, twisted it around, and pushed his branded palm in the air. Then she reached in her back pocket, pulled out a knife, and sliced the middle of the puckered red scar.

"Ouch!" Peter winced at the trickle of blood pooled into his palm.

Angel flipped his hand around and allowed a drop to fall on the seal of the scroll.

Peter frowned as he realized the seal matched the brand on his hand.

A simmer sounded from the wax and the mix of his blood. Then a tendril of smoke with a tip of blood pressed up from the wax. It had a thick gray, pin-like point that wove upward towards the tall ceiling. It whirled and twisted and formed an intricate map. It was suspended in the air.

"Yeah, I forgot I could do that." Peter flexed his hand, wiping the smeared blood on his jeans.

"I figured it out when I saw the seal. I knew there was more this scroll had to tell."

They stared at the floating gray map for a moment. Peter committed the image and landmarks to memory, blinking several times to make sure it stuck. "I've got it. You done?"

Angel nodded and sat back down on the bench.

Peter swiped his hand through the map and it vaporized into thin air. He sat on the bench next to Angel. "Ready to move on?"

Angel rested her forehead on Peter's shoulder. "Kinda yes and no."

Peter chuckled. "I feel the same way. But we should stay the night, and I have a feeling Remmy and Gil will be meeting us at the gas station nearby."

"So you told him where we were going before you told us?"

"Not exactly, but his angelic ancestor is a tracker, so he likely had a 'feeling' as to the general location of all the sanctuaries. He could do what I just did."

"Why didn't he show up here then?"

"As much as Remmy gets under my skin, he tries to protect the greater good of the Decretum Venia. It's given him something to fight for, I guess. At least it cured his obsession to beat up everyone around him."

"Oh, he was the bully at the orphanage you were at with Pastor Finn?" Angel stood and stretched.

"Tried to be. But I guess I was more of one than he was, since I usually cornered him and leveled his butt."

She smiled and gave him a quick kiss. "Yes, that is one of the things I like about you. Always willing to fight for the little guy, even though you act like you won't."

Peter gave her a sanguine smile. "I didn't use to. Hanna taught me a valuable lesson when she burned this mark into my hand. It just took me a long while to understand it."

"Glad you learned your lesson."

"Me too. Let's go hide out another night away from Kyle and Argia. I have a feeling they've been avoiding us for the same reason we've been avoiding them." He grasped Angel's hand and tossed a book on the floor.

"I don't know. They go a lot further in their amorous attentions than we do."

Peter halted his stride and pivoted to face her. "I will wait for you. Stop going to that dark place of doubt. Besides, I want all this...this hell to be over. So that when we are together, I can make it a beautiful beginning to life after—"

Angel placed her finger to his lips. "I want to do this before the fighting. So that no matter what, you know you were my first."

Peter bent and kissed her. Stilling himself, he pulled back. "You have no idea how much I want you. But we have no protection, and I don't want to risk this becoming something we aren't ready to deal with."

Angel nodded. "Okay."

"Now, to find someplace to sleep." Peter grasped her hand, gave her a smile, and entwined his fingers into hers. With each step, he willed his heart to stop beating so fast and his muscles to relax. Sleeping with Angel tonight without taking her up on her offer would be the hardest thing he'd done.

CHAPTER 20

Peter raked his fingers through his hair as the sun peeked through the clouds. The city street would take them straight to the meeting place with Remmy: a gas station he hoped was safe. Rosa had mentioned that people from the Decretum Venia worked at gas stops near sanctuaries in order to pass on information. Ever since Peter opened the second of the trilogy penned by his angelic ancestor Luke23, figuring out who was a safe informant had become easier. It was as if a larger force was working to connect the descendants of the Decretum Venia.

People on the street were scarce, so it was easy for Peter to spot the jeep with the redheaded guy leaning on it. He walked faster. Remmy's eyes followed their progress.

"Where's Gil?" Angel asked, keeping stride with Peter's long ones.

"Probably looking out."

"Better be looking out," Kyle stated. "Something seems off."

"I thought it was the walking and all the people that made you feel uncomfortable," Peter said.

Kyle snorted. "That's right. I just can't shake the fact that we got caught."

Argia giggled. "But this birdie flew, flew away."

Peter laughed. "Yeah, and took the rest of us with you."

Remmy walked up to Peter and the others.

Peter extended his hand, and they shook. Remmy pulled him into a quick hug, and patted him on the back. "Shit hit the fan."

Peter frowned. "What do you mean?"

"Another one of the sanctuaries was blown up. The one we were at wasn't exactly found, but the escapees were captured. Rosa sent me a message that our European headquarters is under attack. Big time attack."

"How is Gavin finding them?"

Remmy shrugged. "Rosa thinks they captured someone like her." He nodded at Argia. "Or he is stronger. They are seeing demons pop up and taunting them before their humans attack."

"A seeker? But those are hard to turn over to the darkness of the Extraho of Obscurum. Their angel guides help keep them centered."

"Well, whatever the case, the elders want everyone to retreat for a while. Especially, now that Gavin Steele and Lucien are seriously hunting us."

Peter paced in front of him. "I'm not backing down. I have to figure out how to destroy the Wall of Ash and get to the machine Gavin created."

Remmy grinned. "Gil and I knew you would say that. We've got your back."

"How?" Peter eyed him warily. His trust for Remmy was feeble, but at this point, it was all he had.

"Pastor Finn and Rosa said they have a rogue group still willing to fight. They'll wait 'til you get what you need. Meanwhile, some of us are sabotaging Steele Industry sites and building operations."

"Pastor Finn put you in charge of the kids fighting?"

"Yep, and it's about time they saw my worth. I'm going to make this happen for you. Pastor Finn is working on the European side of the establishment to get them to grow some balls and fight. Rosa is organizing the adults here, and I am making sure the rest of us fall in line."

"That's a bold, kick-ass move. I like that about you." Peter smiled.

"Feeling is mutual."

"Rosa told me to give you this pager; it will give you a code to where you can find her if you need her."

Peter turn the pager in his hand. "Likely I will."

"Expected, when you are ready to attack. Give her twenty-four hours to assemble everyone."

"Good." Peter touched fists with Remmy. "I trust you. How are you doing this without being detected?" Peter asked.

Remmy smirked. "They seem to want you the most. Apparently, they've got hundreds of kids in their dungeons across the globe. After you tell us the go-ahead, we are sending fighters to save those kids while you cause the Extraho of Obscurum to crumble with our final attack."

"You've got a lot of faith in my abilities, man." Peter raised an eyebrow.

"I know from experience how good you are at kicking ass and taking names." Remmy coughed. "Personal experience."

"Don't know if I want to gain your trust that way anymore. But thanks."

"Say the word if you need anything." Remmy nodded.

Peter put the pager in his pocket.

"There's another car on the corner of the building. Gil's been watching that side of the place." Remmy tilted his head in Argia's direction again. "We have another one like her."

"How'd you find a seeker?" Peter crossed his arms.

"Easy when you have someone like Rosa looking for them. This one was an escapee who conned his way out just before things got dicey. He gave us some good information on the inner workings and leadership."

"I will contact you with this when I'm ready to meet."

"Don't bother. Rosa has ways of finding you. She'll tell us all when it's time." Remmy turned and got in his jeep.

Peter and the others walked around the gas station convenience store where Gil stood wearing a lopsided afro and a big smile.

"Gil!" Peter jogged over to him. "Good to see you, man."

"You, too!"

"How's working with Remmy?"

"A real pain in my ass, but he gets the job done. And he's too arrogant to hold back on details, so it's working out. I chose to work with him instead of going with the Europe group that headed out." Gil dug a hand in his thick hair and studied Peter with serious brown eyes.

Peter smiled. Gil had hardened in the year since they'd escaped the children's home together.

"Kyle!" Gil opened up his arms. "Give me a hug." He grabbed Kyle's shirt.

"Back off." Kyle laughed and slapped Gil's hand away. Then grabbed him in a quick hug.

"Where's your girlfriend, Chloe?" Peter asked.

Gil shrugged. "We broke up. She went with Pastor Finn's crew to Europe."

"Sorry."

"No worries. It was best that way. She wasn't the same after we got her out of Gavin's underground cell." Gil pivoted and opened the passenger door to the car.

"I understand." Peter tossed his bag inside. "Thanks."

"No problem. See you at the meeting place. Got to catch my ride." Gil jogged towards Remmy's car.

"Yep." Peter caught the keys Gil tossed at him.

"And this time – let's finish off the bastard!" Gil pumped his fist.

CHAPTER 21

Lucien crawled to the door of his cell in the dungeon hidden deep within the recesses of Steele Manor. Through the agony in the effort of moving with his healing torn skin, he grinned. They'd gotten away. That was a kick in the ass his brother-demon deserved. He hoped Peter Saints would get the answers he needed.

There was a squeak at the door. Lucien lay down, giving up the fight to crawl closer. Mara, Gavin's fiancée came into view.

Lucien bit his tongue against the hate that rose in his chest. He'd known Mara wanted him instead of his brother. Lucien had never returned the feelings, although he played his cards well by flirting and leading her on. He never knew what would come of it; making her an ally instead of an enemy was always in his best interest.

"When will you learn, Lucien?" she tsked.

"Eventually." Lucien raised a hand to her, reaching for the water bottle tucked under her arm.

She put down the herb mixing bowl while moving her long skirt out of the way as she squatted beside him. "Lies." She handed him the water. "You like goading the beast. It will get you killed, but we both need you alive and well to serve us."

Lucien raised an eyebrow. "I don't mind serving you." He cleared his throat. "But Gavin? Well, he's a bastard with high maintenance tendencies."

Mara sighed and placed her hand on his cheek then leaned down and kissed him passionately. "I can't lie and say that you don't appear adorable here, broken and hurting. Yet, our duty to Gavin and his demon master can't be lax. You have to do better. He ordered me to have you ready for the preparation ceremony."

"Nice to know he cares." Lucien flinched when Mara rubbed healing salve on his back. He swore she added something magical to the pinch of soreness he felt.

"Is it heating up yet?" She rubbed deeper with her thumbs.

Lucien took a gulp from the water bottle she gave him.

"Not speaking to me won't help me heal you faster."

"I can take it." Lucien held back the venom in his voice, not wanting to show his irritation.

"It's about to get hot." She blew on his back and it seared him deep to the bone.

Lucien grunted. "It's nothing."

"I heard that when Gavin changes and touches you, it's the most painful feeling one could experience. Can you describe it to me?"

"Why? You could just piss him off and get him to give you some of the punishment that comes my way."

She slapped his back full of scabs and open sores. "Tell me!" she hissed.

It was a sign Lucien had pushed too far. Her demon mistress was coming out. Lucien didn't want that.

"It's as if I was being sliced open from the skin to the bone." He forced the dark memory into the hidden place in his mind with all the others. "Like a rattlesnake, there was a piercing in my soul. I was fighting for my last breath while drowning in a pit of fire that lit up my entire body."

"Ah! Beautiful."

"Yeah." Lucien coughed and pounded his fist on the ground. "Like being dipped into hell."

"Well..." Mara stood. "You will be ready to serve in a few short weeks. I must go and manage the preparation."

"What going on?"

"Jack's acting in your place. He's brought us some great success. He destroyed one of their hiding places. Jack claims it's because you set the wheels in motion."

"Success in..." Lucien winced and pushed himself up to balance on his knees.

"Capturing young ones from the Decretum Venia. We are able to start draining their blood for the preparation ceremony. There will be many in order to get the elite of our kind ready to use Gavin's machine to transcend to the enemy's gates for war. This time I will make sure they don't suffer death, as many of them have at your hands my love."

"I didn't kill them on purpose." Lucien allowed the lie to float from his lips as he gave her a seductive smile.

"I know. Your lack of control is what's so attractive about you. In this case, we can't afford to kill any of them. Gavin wants to keep their bodies in case we have to skin them for extra covering when passing through to the heavenly realm. It's a shame he prefers to feast on young woman for his powerful sustenance. I hate to waste all of that useful flesh. Well, back to work I go. We wouldn't want the demons that we invite in during the group meditation to be forced out of us before Gavin's machine trans-ports them to do battle."

"I see. You know I can be trusted. I could control it." Lucien's eyes skipped beyond her to the shadow that retreated from the cell door.

"I think not. These children are in the age group that calls to your rage. You get too heavy handed with them."

"But I..."

Mara's hand went up to stop him. "Your job will be to serve Gavin. The children have been left to me."

Lucien bent his head, showing his submission and hoping she would leave.

"Very well"—she blew him a kiss—"glad you are conscious now. I'll be back soon."

Just as Lucien relaxed and slouched down on his knees, someone cleared his throat.

Jack jiggled the keys and unlocked the cell door.

"Glad you could visit." Lucien adjusted himself, careful of his lower back. He crossed his legs and winced.

"You take too many risks!" Jack whispered.

"Someone has to or this won't be done."

"I want to see your brother fail so I can take his place, but he isn't quite human anymore." Jack paced in front of Lucien.

"I wondered when you would notice." Lucien closed his eyes at Jack's fury.

"Look at me!"

Lucien opened his eyes to Jack who was pointing down at him.

"I've sacrificed two daughters to this cause, thanks to your carelessness. I will not allow you to wastefully cause another of their deaths."

"I tried to save your daughter that Gavin incinerated. Can I get some credit for that?" Lucien calmly replied.

Jack's fists balled up. "What of my youngest? Tell me you didn't allow the guards to have access to her?"

Lucien raised an eyebrow. "Don't you trust them?"

"You sure you are on my side here? I told you the whereabouts of that Angel Ramirez girl. I allowed you to attend to her before Gavin and the others found out. What have you done for me?"

"I transferred an obscene amount of money your way. My trusted men of arms have been told to give you special access and treatment. You can now find the plans to the Transfero of Lux Lucis that Gavin designed." Lucien wiped a hand down his face. Little did Jack know Lucien had purposefully changed and ruined the plans and designs just so no other person in the blasted Order of Dragon could repeat this disaster? He'd also destroyed the blood and rare DNA collections used to create the ingredients that acted as authentication for the machine. No one would be able to uncover it again.

"That will suffice for now. But we have to make sure Gavin dies upon its use."

"I know, but it's dangerous to assume we can do this without all the players in place."

"What more do we need?" Jack looked over his shoulder to check that they were still alone.

"I don't know, but Peter Saints can find it."

"You put too must trust in a mere boy."

"I am sure of it. He's the only living person who has breached that Wall of Ash and survived. That is Balaal's realm. One Gavin stole and claimed as his own creation. There is no guarantee any of us will live through the ceremony."

"Fine." Jack tightened his hand on the keys. "You be a good servant for Gavin and heal quickly."

"Of course. He has to have a second, and I'm the only one for the job."

With a bow, Jack left the cell.

CHAPTER 22

Peter parked in an abandoned lot in a back alley at the edge of the city. Blood red and orange streaks of dust hung in the sky. The rising sun peeked above the building top, taunting him. The rest of them were asleep, lulled by the fact that Peter hadn't seemed fazed or edged off by any of the cars in the crush of traffic. He leaned back and saw a billboard for Steele Industries and their Grand Opening of a new physics-based lab that had something to do with dimensional portals or black holes. Peter didn't know. Didn't care. He just wanted the man gone.

Driving for the hours through traffic, always looking over his back was getting old. He'd be lying if he didn't admit he was ready for Gavin to meet his end. The man never gave up.

The city streets didn't do much to hide them. Peter deduced that the only reason they hadn't been hunted down again was that Gavin was focused on something else. Demons never came on their own. Gavin was definitely the one to send them.

He didn't know why or how, but the demon within Gavin – had *known* him. As far as Gavin the man, he was just a psychotic son of a bastard.

Peter rubbed his eyes and decided the time had come for him to seek more direction. He only had one ally close enough to help: Pastor Finn's brother—his youngest brother, one Pastor Finn only mentioned here and there. The man owned a gun shop in this area. They'd have to walk fast to get to the place before closing, but it was possible.

"Get up ya'll!" Peter banged on the dashboard.

Angel stirred beside him, and Kyle muffled a curse.

Argia sprang up and poked her head over the seat. "You ready? Uh, are we going?"

"Yeah, Pastor Finn's brother owns a gun shop here. It's a cover for people in the Decretum Venia."

Kyle's hoarse voice, heavy with sleep, boomed, "Can't we just go to the Stronghold!"

"It's still too far, and we need guns and a safe place to sleep for the night."

"And food, I could really eat a horse right now." Angel stretched.

Peter dug in his pocket and pulled out a wad of half-eaten beef jerky. "Go for it."

Angel crinkled her nose and took it. "Thanks." She bit daintily at it while getting her bag off the floor of the car.

Peter got out of the car. The flickering light on the side of the building that bordered the parking lot made him think some dark force was near.

"I thought they put guns in here?" Angel came to stand next to him and rummaged through the trunk.

"They did, but only two. It's not enough. Stun-guns are good, but we also need more herbs and oils for Argia to use. She is running low, and Christopher—Pastor Finn's brother, would have that at his shop."

"You've been there before?"

"Nope. But Pastor Finn wanted me to remember where to go if I needed help. The man rarely trusts anyone, so if he recommends them, they're legit."

"Is it on the route to the Stronghold?"

"Yep, directly in line." Peter grabbed the small handgun and the holster it was in and put it on. Releasing a long breath, he said, "Prepare for anything."

Argia nodded. "They...are...coming," she sang.

Peter turned from her, grabbed Angel's hand, and kept his eyes straight ahead while scanning for trouble.

"Did Argia say something's coming?" Angel squeezed his hand.

"Don't you feel it? A build up?"

"A bit, but it could be tension. The demons have been quiet. Contained, I think."

"They were, but I feel like they are awakening. Argia's getting more agitated. If they aren't moving on us, then they are seeking us out. Playing with us."

"Argia does provide a barrier for us." Angel pushed the button at the streetlight and the *Walk* sign came on.

Peter kept a quick pace as he crossed the street. They squeezed between two food trucks on the city block. The one named Badass Burger Wagon had a lady in front cleaning the windows and the other, Pimp Vegan Cantina, was vacant, with the exception of a black cat lying against it.

Not many people were around, except a few cops. He held his breath, put his head low, and slanted his eyes at the tallest cop who was staring him down. He swallowed the breath he'd been holding, until rapid steps raced behind him. Peter walked faster, pulling Angel with him.

"Run!" Peter looked behind him at Kyle.

The policemen started to jog. Peter picked up speed glad Angel was keeping pace beside him.

The cops yelled at them to stop. Peter gave Kyle the signal to split up.

"Meet you there, dude! You better make it," Kyle said, before cutting into an alley with Argia.

Peter scanned the streets for a place to hide. The sun was setting fast, and for that, he was thankful.

He and Angel turned the corner; a man was putting the trash out on the street. Peter and Angel ducked into a small restaurant. They passed customers, slipped between two servers, and through the kitchen. The employees moved about, not even noticing as they burst through a door in the back. Peter spied the sign that pointed up and read ROOF. He took the stairs two at a time. Angel was behind him.

He pushed the metal bar and opened the door. Air rushed in; the roof stood higher than many others on the street.

"Okay." Peter walked to the edge and peered over.

Angel stood catching her breath. "Are they coming?"

"Yeah, they are asking the guy about us."

"What now?"

Peter grinned. "Feel like jumping?"

"I don't know."

"Let's do it."

His forehead to hers, Peter whispered, "You can do this. Me first. You follow with everything you've got."

Rapid breathing, arms pumping, Peter backed from the edge of the roof, nodded to Angel, then gave her a quick deep kiss.

"Always." Angel clapped at him. "Now just do it."

Peter bent and took off into a powerful run. Pushing himself fast, he leaped over the edge. Moving his legs as he fought air, his feet hit the hard surface of the nearby roof. He rolled to break his fall.

Then rose to his feet.

Just as he pivoted, Angel's slight frame rolled at him. Gracefully she stood, flicked her hair back, and grinned at him. "That was fun!"

Peter nodded. "Yeah, it was." The rush he felt tickled his gut to his chest. He tugged her by the hand into his arms. "But this is a better rush." Peter leaned down and kissed her.

Several seconds later, Angel patted his chest. "Do you hear the sirens?"

"Yep, time to jet."

CHAPTER 23

Peter knocked on the glass door of the gun shop. The glass was beveled, and he couldn't see any light on the other side. A small peephole sat at eye level, and he closed one of his eyes to check if he see anything inside.

Angel hopped on the balls of her feet beside him. "Is anyone in there?"

"There's got to be, or we are screwed."

A light from a helicopter flashed through the sky. Peter grasped Angel's hand; they pressed themselves against the glass.

"Don't move." Peter flattened his hand on the window and closed his eyes while praying the helicopter would move on. It did.

Peter backed up, and knocked again.

"Stand back from the door," commanded a muffled deep voice from the other side.

Peter grabbed Angel's fingers and raised his hand to signal her to be still. She gave him a thumbs-up and stood behind him.

The door opened, and instead of some old man, Peter faced off with a dark-skinned guy around his age. The boy was a bit shorter than Peter's 6'3 height, but just as bulky. He had a long scar down the side of his cheek. And the guy's eyes were dark and cold.

"Where's Mr. Christo—"

The guy raised his hand. "I'm his assistant; he's out of town. Who are you?" His eyes trailed up and down Peter and then stepped back. "Oh, I know what you are. But there's someone behind you. I need both of your names before you get in here."

Peter sized up the guy, trying to figure out if he could be trusted. He couldn't read him, much like he couldn't read Argia when he'd met her. At first sight, she seemed like a normal kid – just like this guy.

"Peter." He figured only the first name would be needed if the guy was with the Decretum Venia.

The guy smirked. "And the person behind you?"

Peter inhaled a long breath. His palm didn't heat up, which was a good sign this man was worth taking a chance on to some degree.

The assistant stepped back and started to close the door. Peter stuck his foot inside. "Angel." He grabbed Angel's hand and led her in with him as the guy widened the door again.

Closing the door, Peter came face to face with their unwelcoming host.

The assistant to Christopher grinned. "My name is Micah. Welcome to a safe place, Peter Saints."

Peter relaxed his shoulders. "For how long? We have the police after us."

Micah's eyebrow raised. "I can't help you with the poh-poh, but the other things after you are not around. And that means the possibility of the dirty cops following you won't find you in here." Micah smirked. "For a little while."

"What does that mean?" Peter shrugged his backpack in place, just in case he and Angel had to head back out.

"It means that humans do evil on their own and don't necessarily need the influence of demons to tempt them. I should know."

"How long have you been working with Mr. Christopher Finnegan?"

"Not too long, but I'm a quick study with a lot of experience before he took me in. Once I escaped from the scum that kept me, well…" Micah stretched and stepped further into the store.

"Don't go there, man, I know the deal about Gavin Steele and the Order of the Dragon."

The floor was clean swept and the guns were in decorative cases spaced between paintings of various western heroes. Peter's gaze searched the place while Micah gathered his words.

"From what I heard, you didn't stay long enough for the full effect."

Angel stepped around Peter. "But I did." Her arms were crossed, and she rubbed at the hidden scars on her arms.

Peter placed a hand on her back, trying to give her strength to talk about her commonality with Micah.

"Uh, it's fine. I believe you." Micah stepped near the gun cases. The lights within the room brightened with each step.

Peter followed him; Angel walked double time to keep up.

"I have a place down under here for you to hide out until it's clear."

"I appreciate it, but two others are meeting us here in minutes, and I want them with us before we disappear." Peter also wanted Argia to check out Micah. Usually, he or Angel could tell when someone was on their side. A small vibe or calmness in the way they communicated—Peter didn't know exactly what it was—but from this guy, he got nothing. It was as though Micah was a void.

Micah turned and studied Peter a moment. "Suit yourself." He shrugged. "It's hard for me to open the door to the hideout when the door is opened. There's the risk the police could be with your friends when they get here."

"We'll deal with it. They are good at staying undetected."

Within moments of Peter's and Micah's stare-down, a banging came at the door.

Micah raised an eyebrow. "Sounds like your friends?"

Peter swallowed. "I'm sure it's them."

"I'm hoping so, for your sake." Micah moved toward the door.

Peter tugged at the guy's sleeve. "Check first."

Micah nodded.

Peter followed him, waiting to the side while he spied out of the peephole.

"It's a blond kid."

"That's him. Open up."

Micah unlatched the door and Kyle rushed into the room. Argia hopped in behind Kyle, her head down, and she fussed with her ever-ripping stocking.

Kyle turned slightly to take her hand, his smile wide. Peter went beside Argia to shut the door.

As Argia raised her head, Micah's gaze froze.

Argia stiffened and Peter had barely a moment to react before she fainted in his arms. Peter picked Argia up.

Micah snatched a gun from the back of his pants and pointed it square at Kyle. "Who are you and why is she with you?"

Kyle lurched forward. Peter grabbed his jacket and struggled to keep Argia's limp body secure over his shoulder. "Stop it, Kyle!" Peter yelled. "Gun! You'll get us killed."

Peter waited until Kyle relaxed and moved in front of him.

"Look...Micah, right? Do you know her?" Peter tilted his head towards Argia's blue tinged hair that fanned over his shoulder. The girl was so petite she fit in his arms like a doll.

Micah's eyes narrowed at Kyle. He glanced in Peter's direction before jerking his gun up to Kyle. "Yeah, I know her. What is she to him?"

"I'm freakin' standing right here, dude. Ask me your damn self!" Kyle snarled.

Peter placed a hand on Kyle's chest, praying his hotheaded friend stayed quiet. "Kyle and Argia are dating. She's a good friend to Angel, and me, too. We care about her."

Micah's eyes watered. "I love her and she loves me. How can she be with him?" He waved the gun at Kyle. "He doesn't understand her like I do." Micah pounded his chest. "Can't love her like I do."

Peter nodded. "But he does. Argia has a way of weaseling love out of the most stubborn people. I know this, though she wouldn't feel right if she woke up and you were pointing a gun at her best friends."

"I don't care." Micah faced Peter. "Give her to me. You all can go, but she stays with me."

"No." Kyle's response was deadly.

Peter put a staying hand up at Kyle. "Please, listen. We love her as much as you do. We have protected her for almost a year. Where have you been if you were doing such a great job?" Peter fought an anxious urge to charge the guy.

"Give. Her. To. Me!" Micah's desperation and longing for Argia burned from his eyes like a living fire.

"On one condition," Peter said, hoping Micah would give him an inch.

"None. She's mine. You go." Micah's gaze hardened on Kyle.

"Please, can you just put the gun away? I don't want her to get hurt by accident." Peter made his voice flat, so as not to anger Micah further.

"Lay her at my feet, then I'll put the gun away."

Peter glanced at Kyle who had a scowl on his face, with his fists balled.

"Kyle, you okay?" Peter hoped his friend could hold it together.

Kyle didn't move, except his jaw tightened.

Peter took that as a yes. Slowly, Peter walked over to Micah; his eyes didn't leave the butt of the gun. It shook, showing that Micah really didn't have it in him to be a cold blooded killer, but something about Argia made the guy protective.

"Put her there." Micah glanced at his feet.

Peter laid Argia on the floor.

Micah kneeled. Tears fell unchecked from his eyes.

Peter straightened trying to present a barrier between Micah and Kyle.

Micah caressed Argia's face. His wounded cry filled the stillness of the room. He slipped his arm around Argia's limp body and cradled it while he rocked.

Peter didn't know how to react to Micah's anguish and Kyle's anger, so he just watched the gun. It shook, but Micah kept it pointed at him since Peter had blocked his aim at Kyle.

Argia awoke with a startled cry. Without thinking she wrapped her arms around Micah.

Peter forced himself to keep still and let out the breath he'd been holding. Micah lowered the gun and tucked it back in his pants.

Micah and Argia embraced. Kyle roared and charged at them.

Peter pivoted swiftly and held Kyle back. "Keep it together! Give them a moment to work it out!"

"She's... No!" Kyle's head whipped back and forth.

Peter steadied him. Then all crap broke loose when Micah kissed Argia.

Peter could barely hold Kyle back. Angel grabbed Kyle's arms.

"Micah! She's dating Kyle," Peter yelled.

Micah pushed Argia away as though she'd burned him. Argia's gaze found Kyle's.

Kyle slumped in Peter's arms. "Why?" Kyle's voice broke.

Peter stared at Argia. He wanted her response as much as Kyle did. He'd thought she loved Kyle.

Argia folded her legs under her and rocked like she did when she got agitated. "I loved him before I met you, Kyle. I was trying to get to the Extraho of Obscurum any way I could to save Micah." Tears fell from her eyes and dripped from her chin as she rocked. "But I fell in love with you, Kyle. I didn't think I should, but I couldn't help myself. I was so lonely. Loving you gave me hope. I told Rosa that Micah was taken. She-she couldn't promise me he'd be alive. She advised me to go on with my life – with you, Kyle."

Kyle's fist rose and pressed against his eyes as he jerked from Peter.

Peter turn to work on Kyle.

"When can we leave here?" Kyle's voice came out hard and harsh.

"Wait." Peter touched Kyle's shoulder. He wanted Kyle to fight for Argia like he'd fought for Angel. Argia was strange, powerful, and whimsical, but she was good for Kyle.

Kyle shrugged away. "Get me out of here!"

Peter turned to Micah. "Is there a place I can go talk to him, with Angel, so you and Argia can figure this out?"

Micah's voice cracked, "Move the gun case on the back wall. There's a hidden hallway. Go down the stairs and to one of the rooms at the foot of the steps."

Peter nodded and grasped Angel's hand as they followed Kyle in silence.

CHAPTER 24

The back of the store was nicer than Peter expected. The hidden door opened to what could be considered a living room. There was carpet on the large rectangle of a space, with curved wooden doors on all sides.

Peter exhaled and crossed his arms. Angel sat in one of the overstuffed couches that lined the wallpapered walls. His gaze followed the diamond-shaped gold prints on the walls. There were statues scattered in decorative locations about the room and several bookshelves. Swiveling around, he made sure to keep an eye on a pacing Kyle.

"Sit down. We may as well stay the night here. We need information from him anyway."

Kyle grunted. "I want nothing from him."

"Kyle." Peter walked over to him.

Angel stood and Peter shook his head, hoping she'd give him the floor to speak to Kyle. She nodded and sat down. He smiled his thanks.

"I don't want to hear a damn thing you are saying. She ditched me. Like that." Kyle snapped his fingers. "And I loved her. I'd never allowed myself to love anyone else or trust anyone like I had Argia. But now, it's turned to something else."

"What? Disappointment? Don't hide hate within pain. Kyle, it's a fake and destructive cover."

"What do you know? You stayed weak in love for Angel, who flipped you off the moment you were gone, and cozied up to some other guy." Kyle snorted. "And you forgave that?" He threw up a hand.

Peter hit Kyle's shoulder. "Watch it!"

"What? You don't want me to tell you what I really thought when you turned away all those open invitations from the girls at the last sanctuary, just because you 'thought' Angel was waiting for you?"

Peter balled his fists. "You are asking for a fight? Let's not do this. It's not about me, but you. I can help you—"

"You can't help me do shit! You brought that crazy, spooked chick into our group. We were fine without her. Then you kept throwing her at me when she acted like she really wanted you. I don't think she can love anyone. Not with her messed up head and hearing things."

"Again, I tell you to stop blaming me and Argia for your mistakes. If you don't want to fight for her, to show her that you really love her, then that's on you. Your loss. It's a big one, too."

"Fight for *her*? Why?" Kyle shrugged and turned away as a tear fell from his eye. He swiped it away.

Peter grabbed his hand. "Because you never did! You made her fight for your love every damn day since the moment you met her." Peter flung Kyle's hand away. "She'd always wanted you, but Kyle the ego-maniac conceited blond gift to women, never gave her the time."

"You!"

Peter held up a hand. "No it's you, Kyle. She had one person in her life that loved her...just the way she was. I see it, you see it. That's what has got you pissed off. It was your missed opportunity to treat the woman you love like that guy in there did. Like she was perfect enough for *you*."

Kyle pushed his palms to his eyes. "I muffed up. God, it hurts so bad. So shitting bad."

Peter hugged his friend. He braced himself against Kyle's sobs. "Do you still love her?"

"Yes," Kyle murmured. "But will she still want me?" His broken question hung between them.

Peter didn't know. "You owe it to both of you to try. But give her time to figure things out with Micah. It's hard. I know it is, but you've got to do it if you want her. You need closure. If you think you love her enough to give her time to see the type of man you can be for her..."

Kyle nodded and pushed away from Peter.

"I've been there. And I was weak a time or two in the orphanage." Peter's gaze caught Angel at his admission that he'd never shared with her. "I'm not perfect. I made my mistakes, so forgiving Angel was easy. I wanted her to forgive me."

Angel got up from the couch. Her brows lifted, her eyes brimming with tears. Peter felt a jab, then hurt, in his heart at her confusion. He'd been a coward and never told her that while she was taken away from him, he'd waited just three months to try to find solace in another girl's arms. Then another, and another. He was too ashamed of his duality to let Kyle know what he'd done, to force his secret on Kyle's shoulders. He'd learned then that no one else would satisfy him and his body. He would just have to wait for Angel.

Kyle moved between Peter and Angel.

"You slipped up?" Kyle frowned. "And didn't tell me?"

Peter stared down at his feet. "I was ashamed. It made me feel like a user. I used them, to imagine that they were Angel. And I used them to hide my anger at the fact that I felt helpless to save her."

Kyle crossed his arms. "Wow. I'm going back in there with them. I don't care that she's talking to Micah; I want them both to know I'm present and here to be dealt with."

"As it should be."

Kyle frowned at Peter and mumbled, "Stupid." Then went back through the door.

Peter felt her staring at him. Finally, he was ready to face her. "I'm sorry." Peter blinked back tears. He bit his lip to stop from begging her to forgive him. Peter wanted to deal with the blow she dealt.

Tears ran unchecked from her eyes. "I know," she whispered. "But it doesn't hurt any less."

"What can I say?" Peter ran a hand through his hair. "Except that I was weak, I was angry, and lonely. It'd been so long since I'd been with someone physically, and it was the old way that I'd dealt with those feelings."

"I never did anything like that with—"

Peter held up a hand. "I don't care and don't want to know what you did with anyone else. I know what being held hostage by Gavin and his brother Lucien did to you. Don't ever feel like you not having sex with me will make me want that from someone else."

"But don't you...Why are we even doing this Peter? I can't be like those girls. Normal. Every time we get close, I have flashes of what they did to me. You don't deserve that."

"You can see that I can wait, that I'm worthy of your love, of your body."

Her face fell to her hands. "You shouldn't have to, Peter. When you had the chance, you didn't then." Angel shook her head. "My heart, my mind wants you so bad. This is destined to fail – we will fail, and it will destroy me."

Peter stepped closer and enveloped her in his arms. "Forgive me because you love me, not because you don't think I deserve you. I know what I want. Who I want. I have a strong mind, a mind that will control the needs of my body to have you."

Angel nodded. "I've forgiven you. But it still hurts knowing that another girl could give you one thing I can't. We can't last like this, even if we wanted. You have to know that."

"That's not the full definition of my love for you. Our bodies will figure it out when we allow ourselves to feel free of the Decretum Venia and the attacks from the Extraho of Obscurum. When we can just...be."

CHAPTER 25

Peter hated doing the right thing sometimes. But telling Kyle his shameful secret and being vulnerable was worth it if he could help Argia and Kyle reconcile. He didn't know what the secret had revealed about his and Angel's relationship, though. They loved each other, but it was a thin thread holding them together.

Angel had fallen asleep on the couch against the wall. It was obvious that given his admission of guilt, she wanted to distance herself from him. The lights in the room had dimmed since they were down for the night. Peter sat on a high-backed chair facing her. Just watching Angel sleep was enough for now.

After his admission to Angel, their conversation had been stilted, and he'd suggested she lay down and rest on something soft. It had been a while since they could just relax. She needed it; Peter wanted it, but he knew he wasn't getting it any time soon. He swung his gaze to the door. It had been over two hours since Kyle left.

The door's thick crease that held the one sliding door in the room moved silently aside. Argia's pale, petite form came though.

Her nose was red and her eyes were puffy. She walked towards Peter.

With a sigh Argia mumbled, "I'm sorry I never told you about my past, Peter."

He didn't know what to say. Peter never considered Argia the type to string along two guys at once.

"I've got one piece of advice for you."

Argia slumped down into a nearby chair. "Please tell me what to do." Her voice sounded hoarse and strained.

"Choose one, and tell the other as soon as possible."

She blinked slowly, and as her eyelids closed, more tears seeped from them. "It's hard. I love them both, but so differently."

"It's greedy, and damn cruel to hold onto them both."

"I would never do that."

Peter stood and walked over to her. "Then what are you doing? We've got to fight a lot of people to win this thing against Gavin and the powers behind him. Make a decision so we can deal with the bigger problem. I need Micah's help."

"Why? He's been through so much and barely escaped the Extraho of Obscurum with his life. I can't ask him to go back there for any reason."

"You're not asking, I am. But in order for him and Kyle to go to the Stronghold, both have to be able to play for our team. No screw-ups and be focused."

"I will do it, but I'm not ready now. I just want to disappear. Maybe...maybe, I need to let them both go. It would be for the best, right?"

Peter studied Argia, and he felt a fear—a caution tingling in his blood that what she was saying was a foreshadowing. That part of her would give herself up to death if she couldn't have the love of one of them. Peter didn't want that. Argia, although she'd had some strange behaviors, and refused to leave him alone since he met her, had become one of his friends.

"No. It's not for the best. If you don't choose and something happens to you, both of them would be ruined for anyone else. For themselves. Don't you get it?"

"I...I..." Argia started her agitated rocking, her eyes darting around the room as though she wanted to bolt.

Peter bent and grasped her by her upper arms to pull her into a hug. "Angel and I would be destroyed. We need you. You are our protector. No one can do what you do."

Argia relaxed a bit in his hug. "Micah can."

Peter released her and stepped back. "What?"

"Micah and I have the same abilities. We are like the girl, Hanna, who gave you this." Argia reached for Peter's hand and tilted it so the pale brand on his palm was visible. As she touched it, the scar rose up to meet her fingers.

Peter removed his hand from hers; the memory of Hanna's mark unsettled him. "Then we definitely need him. We must take him for his knowledge about Gavin's location and properties, and for his ability to blend in like you do."

Argia giggled; her face was wet, patched with red and her hair framed blue. To someone that didn't know her, she'd seem insane.

"Thinking?" Peter asked.

"I never blended in."

"No, you didn't. It's why Kyle fell in love with you. That guy wants a challenge." Peter smiled at her, and tried to lighten the mood.

"He does. It will always be so for us. He thinks me interesting, strange, and exciting. I feel that he keeps me centered, calm."

"And Micah?"

Argia bit her lip. "He was my first love. My first crush, my everything. Someone...somebody, like me. Around him, it was quiet. The voices didn't bother me as much."

"Did he do that for you?"

Argia tapped her nose. "Yes," she whispered.

"Do you need that more than you need Kyle's love?"

"No, but when I see him, I want him with the intensity that I want Kyle. Micah is safer for me I think. With Kyle, I love our differences, and there are many. But with Micah, I feel a peace and the fierce devotion of his love. It's contagious, and I guess always raged within me. I just tried so hard to put it aside as Rosa warned me to."

"That is a hard choice to make." Peter crossed his arms. "But you have to make it."

The door opened. Peter found Kyle standing there. Peter checked on Angel and walked over to Kyle.

"I need to talk to him." Peter put his hand on Kyle's shoulder. "You okay?"

Kyle nodded. Peter held back. Kyle's fisted hand showed he wasn't really okay. The guy would've had a wisecrack, stupid macho joke for him.

"I'll leave you."

Peter entered the gun shop and the door slid back in place. Micah was facing the wall with is head on it and his fists pounding on each side.

Peter waited.

Micah twisted around, his slanted eyes framed in a frown.

"I'm sorry things got screwed up earlier. But I'm glad you got to see Argia. She's been through a lot."

Micah bit his bottom lip, shrugged, and moved from the wall. "Well, so have I, but I didn't find someone to take away my pain... like she did."

"You're wrong there. Kyle didn't take away her pain. Argia

buried every bit of it deep inside and only protected us. She carelessly put her life in danger time and time again because she didn't value her life as much."

Micah smirked. "She could've fooled me. Seems like she values her life with him well enough."

Peter shook his head. "Not true. When I first met her, she told me she was searching for someone special that she'd known. That she was going to find him. I mistakenly told her to let the thought of saving that person go until we destroyed Gavin. If we buried the organization and the man, saving her friend would be reality."

"I can see your logic, I guess. But that didn't mean she had to attach to Kyle."

"That could be my fault, too. I pushed them together. Mostly, because I wanted to be alone with my girlfriend."

"Mighty generous of you. While Argia's 'friend' was captured, tortured, and then 'groomed' to be a psychic puppet for the Order of the Dragon, you 'hooked my girl up' with your best friend so you could screw your girlfriend."

"Man, you wanna crap on yourself, fine. But stop using me to do it for you. Those weren't my intentions. I just wanted Kyle to be a friend to her. She acted strange and scared the other people who were with us. Kyle was someone the others would follow. If he treated her like a friend, the rest of them would, too. It wasn't until we'd dealt with some pretty heavy stuff that their relationship changed. When someone almost dies in your presence, you don't waste a moment to find some joy where you can."

Micah released a long breath. "I get it. We were there before. Argia and I were on the run after my parents were murdered and hers were kidnapped. But that wasn't when I fell in love with her. Can your friend say the same?"

"I know you are dealing with the situation between the three of you now, but I have to ask you a favor."

"Bastard."

"Call me names, I don't take it personal. All I would like to know is: will you come with us?"

Micah snorted. "To the Extraho of Obscurum's headquarters? Or the guest house? Which hellhole of torture and dismemberment would you like me to follow you to?"

"Are you serious? Is the sarcasm for your benefit or mine? I don't have time to be nice about this or to figure out a better way to say things. We need you and Argia. Your abilities will help us destroy Gavin and the machine he is building—you can tip fate in our direction."

"I don't know if I can go that distance with you, even for the love of Argia. You have no idea the things I had to do to escape that place. Acts so vile and painful I wanted my life to end. Instead, I made myself believe Argia needed me to escape to save her. It kept me sane while I talked to demons when my body withstood tortures that would make you wonder at the fact I survived."

"You don't think you are the only person to feel agony and torture, do you?" He gave an abbreviated list of each of their journeys. "The list goes on, but I'm not giving up on destroying the bastard."

"I like your bravery, but if this blows up in our faces, I wouldn't survive. My cover would be known since I was Gavin's witch's favorite pet."

"What?"

"You heard me. Her pet. She knew I had psychic ability, but didn't know I could also talk to angels without either knowing. She performed spells, tortured my body to get me to reveal what the demons told me. Then she killed the weaker children in front of me as sacrifices. I escaped by selling my ability to her enemy: a man named Jack." He sighed. "What he charged me to get free..."

"Okay, I get it. I won't ask you to go the distance. There is more than one way to help us. There's a woman who mentors Argia; her name is Rosa. She is meeting us—"

"Rosa? You know where she is? I've been looking for her for over a year. Didn't she go underground, even to the Decretum Venia?"

"Yeah, she went into hiding, but this is what everyone's been waiting for: a way to end this."

Micah laughed bitterly. "Don't you get it? This will never end."

"It will."

"No, it won't. The boogeyman never goes away," Micah whispered and placed his index finger to his lips.

"Maybe not, but he can be put in his place."

CHAPTER 26

He'd done it. Peter knew without a doubt that Micah would
come with them. At least as far as their first stop at Rosa's.
After that, it would depend on Argia.

Peter adjusted the pillow under his neck and tried to get
comfortable on the chaise lounge. His feet hung over the side. It
was the only thing left to sleep on since Kyle lay on the couch next
to him; Argia slept on the loveseat across the room at some strange
angle. Her hips were curved over the armrest, and her face hung
over the side while her butt was pushed up. Peter had always
wondered what kind of dreams she had that made her sleep in the
weirdest angles.

After most everyone was asleep, Micah passed through their
room and went into one of the doors. Peter faked snoring to give
the guy the break he needed, and allowed him to believe all
was calm.

"You sleep?" Kyle asked, groggily.

Peter rolled to his side and faced the couch. Kyle sat up and
tossed his pillow to the floor.

"Yeah, I slept some."

"I'm ready to leave here."

Peter sat up and pushed his pillow down with his palm. "About that."

Kyle's eyes narrowed.

"Micah's coming with us."

Kyle shot up, grabbed Peter's shirt and growled low, "The hell he is."

Peter didn't budge. "He has to. We need him. You have to eat your trashin' until Argia decides, and we part ways. The guy is powerful; Argia is more powerful with him."

Kyle pushed Peter's chest, releasing his shirt.

"Listen to me. I went through this with Angel. It was hard, but necessary."

"Necessary? For who? We were doing fine without the dude. Argia was powerful enough to lock Gavin into the hellish Wall of Ash. She and Rosa did that alone. Why does this Micah guy have to get involved?"

Peter wondered if he should tell Kyle everything, then decided against it. "Kyle, just one day at a time. Taking him to the Stronghold will give us answers on how to use his power with Argia. I don't know if he's even been 'activated' like the rest of us who fought against Gavin that day."

Kyle cursed. "I will never be 'activated' since I'm not a pure blood. Maybe, Micah isn't a pure blood either."

Peter sat up and faced Kyle. "You know when we opened the last scroll with Angel that every pureblood had a type of death before they became 'aware' of their connection to their angelic ancestors. But that doesn't mean they were in warrior roles, or had the ability to form the angelic weapons needed to kill Gavin and the demons that are able to cross over to our realm."

"You're right, some of the kids at the bug-out compound said they just became aware of their ability to form weapons by looking at you and some of the others that manifested them during the battle. Otherwise, they wouldn't have known they could do that, even with their new awareness."

"Well, the consciousness is more acute when in battle, or around others like you. Otherwise, it only comes out during a demon attack. It's possible Micah has been safe here, that his DNA was never ignited to expose his full abilities."

"You are killing me with this. I haven't even had a chance to talk to Argia. Every time she looked at Micah or me she started to cry. We both stood there like statues while she sobbed."

"I'm sorry."

"No more than I am. This sucks...and watching her fall apart is making me die inside. I wanted to lay with her tonight. It's been a while since we could be comfortable, and the way she walked stiffly over to that couch, I knew it wasn't going to happen."

"She'll come to you when she is ready."

"I hope so."

"We should leave tonight. Micah told me there is an exit further underground that goes through the city for miles."

"Then we'll do it."

"Thanks Kyle, for staying with us."

"Where else would I go? I may not be a full blood with abilities like you and the others, but common sense and a bad attitude goes a long way."

Peter lifted an eyebrow. "Besides, you love us, bro."

Kyle snorted, "Sometimes," and turned to face the couch.

"Oh, I see I've been dismissed."

"Yep, now go back to sleep while we can."

Peter knew he couldn't, but lying down for a moment was just as good. He'd need all his strength to hold them together. Whether Kyle had their abilities or not, Peter knew in his chest, in his being, that Kyle was right where he was supposed to be.

With them.

CHAPTER 27

The cleared area in the middle of the dense forest led to a private beach entrance. It was one of Gavin's family's largest estates. It also coexisted with one of the Steele Industries labs, and Extraho of Obscurum's main conference location. Gavin stood in front of the group of followers that he considered his most trusted. He enjoyed the location; it was why he'd decided a while ago to have the production of the Transfero of Lux Lucis built there. The machine was his personal masterpiece. It would give him the power to transcend to the Heavenly realm, a dimension his demon master and his king couldn't breach. Balaal was strong and well positioned as demons went, but Gavin wanted to lead them all. Pleasing the demon's current master would be preliminary to destroying it. As Balaal and he were fused, he would get eternal life and ultimate power.

Gavin flexed his fingers, itching at the hunger of holding so much control in his palm. His pale hand was littered with blood blistered spots at his hands, it was the only sign that his hand had been sliced. He extended his fingers and watched with the edge of his lip hike up over elongated teeth as his nails grew. Then the burn of the talons, exposing themselves through the nail shaft, itched him. Releasing the demonic body he'd trapped inside had become addictive. Its power was unspeakable.

He had to fight its lure though. Each time he tapped into the power of Balaal, he felt the beast becoming more confident in taking over. That couldn't happen. Gavin's temporary incarceration in Balaal's level of hell was unimaginably addictive and torturous. Even as he experienced his own type of hell that he found to be unique for every person, Gavin had freed himself but kept his hunger for it.

Jack walked up next to Gavin. "It seems to be growing."

Gavin observed the tornado of gray with slivers of black within its cords of smoke and ash. Although, many tornados moved, and were loud with no control, his Wall of Ash was steady. It was a quiet, breathing, an evil force of its own. The instrument of destruction was a living portal to the entryway to unimaginable evil and carnage.

"It is." Gavin waved his hand, and small snake-like creatures, mouths crowded with teeth, slithered in and out of the mass, snapping their teeth. His movements pushed the creatures back within the wall's depths.

"Can you control it?" Lucien asked. "We need it to back off to get to the Transfero of Lux Lucis and finish the work to complete it."

"Of course, I can. It's my creation." Gavin lifted his palm toward the Wall of Ash. "You sure you wouldn't want to take a peek inside?"

Lucien crossed his arms. "No. I'm not trying to go to hell any earlier than my appointed time."

Gavin grinned. "You don't know what you are missing."

Jack stepped up next to Gavin. "You speak as though you've been there."

"I have. Balaal accustomed me to the place briefly. I only got to enjoy the first level."

Gavin frowned a moment; he moved his hand sharply, willing the massive portal to move back just enough to reveal the machine. He lifted his other hand and pushed both hands out. The Wall of Ash separated briefly and expelled the Transfero of Lux Lucis before reconnecting.

"Wait! I didn't see anything," Lucian said.

"You don't 'see' hell; it is an experience," Gavin added.

Jack's eyelids lifted. "Tell me, what was your experience?"

"It happened within a blink of an eye with the lure of rotting flesh. Then beauty, a young girl took my hand. It was soft, yet I was blinded by her light. I felt as though she touched me, but I couldn't touch her back. That brief interlude was followed by hooks that tore my skin and yanked me down onto a hot but firm floor. Then, the fun began."

Jack frowned. "Uhm, that's enough." He placed a finger in his collar to loosen his tie. "Doesn't sound difficult. We all have experienced cuts and torture."

Gavin couldn't help himself; he smiled. "Then you wouldn't mind having a small taste." He slashed his talon fingers down Jack's neck. Immediately, the man started convulsing. "Now, the rest of you, call in the work crews." Gavin turned his back to Jack who was on the ground, foaming at the mouth.

Lucien stepped closer. "What do you need for it to be ready?"

Gavin considered his brother. Lucien's loyalty had been impeccable in the last few weeks. "The sacrifices you've brought me to be offered up should be sufficient. Mara was happy that thirty of the fifty children you gathered had psychic ability."

Lucien smiled and rubbed his hands together. "I handled them personally, brother."

Gavin narrowed his eyes. "They are supposed to be chaste and full of life. I expect that you contained your cravings and left this group of offerings alone."

"I assure you, Gavin, that as soon as I went with the crews to pick up the captives, I had the women handle them with strict threats on their lives if they fondled any of the merchandise."

"Good. In that case, the men working on the Transfero of Lux Lucis will have to be possessed by their demon master. Make sure Mara and her recruits get to work. I will need about fifty of our best scientists, physicists, and engineers working on this to be finished in time for the blood moon."

Gavin willed his fidgeting to subside. Ever since he returned from the near-death experience that held him in the first level of hell for over six months, he'd been like a junky for pain. Pinching and tearing at his skin nightly with his sharp demon master's talons was never enough to fight the call to return to hell. It was a place no one in their right mind would choose to visit but those who had seemed to have an unhealthy desire to return. Gavin would fight that desire because in his current state, if he returned, Balaal would wrestle control back from him. Now, he rather enjoyed holding Balaal captive within the in-between of the dimensions that trapped the beast between hell and earth.

His brother was quiet. That wasn't always a good condition. Lucien observed those walking around the Transfero of Lux Lucis that appeared in the shape of a huge beehive with rounded edges and a slightly pointed top.

"Brother, how does the machine work? Do you even know if it does? We are risking many in this beta-test effort."

Gavin bit down on his tongue to restrain himself from attacking his brother for his idiocy. "It works. I don't need to beta test it because this machine was built before. The captive human who visited the heavens created it. When Peter Saints opened the sacred scrolls, I started dreaming of the designs stolen from the man by my master Balaal. I used those messages to further enhance the machine's abilities."

"Why didn't Balaal remember the plans?"

"The time was erased and the secrets of their war were hidden from them. I needed that boy to release the secrets. Once he did, the plans were plain as if they sat in front of me."

"I trust your instincts, brother."

Gavin snorted. "About time you did. Now send someone to take Jack to his room. He'll wake in a few days. Enough time for me torture some information from his wife."

CHAPTER 28

Peter stood in front of Micah's van while the others packed
their things into the back. Micah was staring at him; he felt
it. The boy's mistrust and frustrations flowed off him like waves. It
was as strong as Kyle's, and Peter found being around them and
Argia difficult. They didn't speak, not even Argia—and for her,
that was completely out of character. Usually, they couldn't stop
her random singing, dancing, or urgent whispers to an unknown
audience.

"You're going with us, right?" Peter studied Micah, who hadn't
packed his stuff in the van yet.

"I'm still debating if I should. I'm supposed to keep this place
open as a safe spot for others like you." Micah slid his hands into
his jean pockets.

"Have you had anyone here since you were left in charge?"

"A few kids who'd escaped the Extraho of Obscurum. It seems
the group had a huge push to kidnap kids and upped their pick-
ings from runaways to kids with special abilities to just any kid
they found alone."

"Really?" Peter wondered at that. "How would they find the ones who were different?"

"Many of them end up in mental wards, or with doctors feeding them huge handfuls of colorful drugs to keep the voices away." Micah shrugged.

"How would they get those kids?"

Micah snorted. "They own stock in many of the pharmaceutical companies, doctors are on their payroll, and police are in their pockets. There's no one and nothing those guys can't get."

Peter nodded. "Did you know Argia was in a home for the mentally ill?"

Micah raised an eyebrow. "I'm not surprised." He shrugged. "She escaped?"

"Not only did she escape, but she stabbed one of the masterminds in the Extraho of Obscurum, Lucien."

Micah took a step back, almost stumbling. "Lucien? Gavin Steele's brother and the stepstool to Gavin's witch bride?" He shivered.

Peter nodded and swallowed the sour taste that threatened to spill from him at the thought of Lucien and Gavin. "We had a run-in with Lucien before we got here. He specifically took Argia from us. She got away and saved us. If we had been captured..." Peter shook his head not wanting to ponder the grim possibilities.

"Aren't you the one who started this? I heard about you, Peter Saints, and I don't know if Argia or I should continue with you on this path. We have the most to lose if we are found out. You all will die. Go to heaven, live happy. But Argia and I can have a different end game. We could be leading ourselves to an earthbound torture and a spirit realm prison."

"I'm sorry. I didn't know."

"Or didn't care."

"I care. I've made mistakes, but at least I'm not trying to hide them. I'm going to fix them."

"Is that possible?" Micah laughed bitterly and stepped toward Peter, pointing his finger in Peter's chest. "How exactly did you fix them? By opening those sacred scrolls?" He lifted an eyebrow. "By giving the Order of the Dragon knowledge to bring Armegeddon to Earth and the heavens?"

"It's not..." Peter tried to answer, but Micah's stare held him.

"You don't know what you've done. I do, I was bound while their witch and their leader's brother schemed over me as they drained my blood, over and over again. Every step you think you are taking to save us all will lead everyone to their deaths."

Peter stepped up to Micah, chest to chest. "I've seen the outcome of this story. We won this war before, and we will win it again. Just trust me."

Micah sighed and backed down. "I'm not here for you. The only reason I am standing here contemplating helping you is because of my love for Argia. She alone is why I am about to risk my life and my freedom, following you. But get this, if she gets hurt, if she dies, I will turn on you and everything you stand for."

"You won't need to. I'm giving you my word we will see this through, and I"—Peter pounded his chest—"will continue to protect her and my friends as I've done this far."

Micah smirked. "So...you...say." And with that, he pivoted around and went around the van.

Peter slumped back on the hood and held his head against the building headache. Micah would be trouble, but Peter felt it in his chest, in his heart, that Micah was the secret weapon they needed.

Angel came up next to Peter and gave him a kiss. "Is he coming?" She placed her hands in his back pocket and laid her head on his chest.

"Yeah, I got him to do it." Peter smiled. Angel could always tell when he was agitated.

"I think Argia sold him on it." She tilted her chin up. "Can Micah or Kyle sit up front with you? Argia wants me between her and one of them."

"Are you serious? She's going to avoid both her ex-lovers the entire trip?"

"I think so."

Peter raked his fingers through his thick, curly hair. "She needs to start making things less tense or it's not going to help us when we are in danger."

Angel sighed. "Do you want to break it to her?"

"I'll do something better." Peter gave Angel a quick kiss and went to the back of the van where Micah had just closed the back hatch. He walked behind Argia who was crouching under the van.

Micah gave him a nod. "You got the keys, right?"

"Yeah." Peter tossed them up and caught them. "You mind sitting up front with me?"

Micah searched around as if he was looking for Argia. "I was going to try to sit next to—"

Peter put up his hand. "She's not ready for that, and neither is Kyle. I want to get to know you. Angel is going to sit between them. Or, Argia will have to sit up front with me."

"Then she should. There's no reason why you should be at ease when the rest of us feel like we've been tossed over. At least, I won't have to worry about her and Kyle making eyes at each other until she and I can talk more."

"Look, what are you trying to prove? She is in love with both of you."

Micah grumbled. "No. The only way I will get in this car is if she is sitting with you and not him. I don't care who she loves; I care who she *is in love* with."

"This time." Peter tapped Argia on the head.

She smiled up at him, apparently relieved.

"Don't say nothing. Just get in." Peter was ready to go.

It was going to be a long ride.

Peter got into the driver's seat and cut on some music. He hoped Argia would take that as a sign that he didn't want to talk. No such luck.

He pulled off just as she opened her mouth. Giving her a scowl, Peter pressed the gas and drove out of the tunnel where the van was parked. Not even two minutes passed before Argia started humming.

"You are so good to me, Peter. The first time I saw you, I knew you would be my savior. Even when I...ah..." Argia hopped in her seat.

"Stop. You gotta stop. I get that you aren't used to dealing with having two guys fight over you, but I don't want to be called your savior. It's a bad position to be in. I should know, I was in the same situation with my girl, and it hurts. They are hurting. Don't make it a game."

Argia's hand touched Peter's shoulder, and while he stopped at the light, he caught a glimpse of a shimmer of tears in her eyes.

"It's not like that for me, Peter. I just want to die. Micah and I met in school. It was when I was at a safe place in my life. He knew my parents and protected me even though he didn't know I had a crush on him for the longest time." Her head dropped.

"Let time work it out." Peter gripped the steering wheel, glad to be in the city where there were lots of people, and he could pretty much hide in plain sight.

"Time didn't work out things with Micah. I failed him. My plan was to sneak into the Extraho of Obscurum's dungeons where I figured they'd be keeping him. But...I met Lucien and the demons surrounding him. I was frightened and ran."

Peter snorted. "Anyone would've. The guy made me uncomfortable, and I looked him eye to eye. There's an edge of darkness and sadness he carries. It makes him unpredictable."

"Yes, in some ways. He made it clear he'd kill me before he took me to the headquarters. Lucien held me and whispered all the ways he planned to torture me before my soul slipped away." Argia sighed. "I was too afraid to go with him. Afraid that I would die and never save Micah."

"I get that, but why Kyle if your heart was focused on Micah?" Peter asked the question for selfish reasons.

"Loneliness, I guess. Both Micah and Kyle allowed me to lose my fears in their love. The nightmares, the sadness—it all stopped when I was around Micah and...Kyle."

Peter frowned. "You sure it wasn't me that calmed you? Kyle's only a half-blood of the Decretum Venia."

Argia gave a sanguine laugh. "You attract the demons. I spend a lot of time diverting them. But I realized that when I was around Kyle, they acted as though he was invisible. It's strange really. I also couldn't read him. It's like his aura is masked by some invisible force."

Peter bit his lip and leaned back in this seat. Maybe Argia's observation was a clue.

Kyle could be more than he seemed.

CHAPTER 29

Lucien didn't have much time. Getting to the recuperation room where Jack was had to happen immediately. The main hall of the mansion was filled with people eating and drinking. The main course of human flesh with a side of virgin blood was scheduled to be served within the hour. It was the perfect time for him to escape to the lower dungeons where Jack was being held. Those rituals always turned his stomach, he was glad to be able to escape it.

He hoped the witch, Mara, wasn't below. Likely, she would be preparing the sacrifice for dinner instead and left one of her ladies in training to guard him. Lucien walked quickly but made sure he took the time to smile or wink a hello to those who knew him. He had to keep up the act. Make it believable if his plan was going to work.

The stairwell had a few cats scattered on it, sleeping comfortably in the corners. They barely glanced up at him as they were used to people coming and going here. Especially him since his lab and experiment room was on the lower level. A girl at the bottom of the steps was dressed in a white dress. It flowed to her ankles in a transparent wave as she turned in his direction.

Her face beamed. The brown wavy tresses were pulled up and curls framed her lack of a chin.

"Lucien." She sounded breathless.

Lucien catalogued the names of the girls who surrounded Mara and remembered her name. "Daisy." He bent slightly and kissed the corner of her red lips. "Congratulations on your promotion. I heard it was recent."

"Th-thank you." She sighed with a hungered desire that many of Mara's servants did since they knew he could never marry. However, he could have children with any of the servant witches he wanted in order to increase the bloodline of the dragon. They saw power and opportunity in seducing him.

Lucien touched her arm and slid his hand downward, using the flirtatious effect he had to get her to tell him where Jack was. "Can I ask you something, beautiful?" He slid closer to her. "I need your help."

"Mine?" She blinked her large green eyes.

Lucien wanted to take her misplaced innocence and torture her in it until she choked on it.

"Yes, yours. My friend was brought down here ill. He made me promise to help him to the dinner tonight. It's not often we have a living sacrifice that has the second sight and is considered a girl at the peak of her beauty."

Daisy nodded vigorously. "It will be my first time to partake. My mistress told me my sister was one of the best sacrifices they've had yet."

Lucien swallowed the taste of vomit in his throat. This girl wasn't sweet or innocent like she portrayed; she'd turned her sister over to Mara to gain her place as the witch's servant.

He laughed, then leaned in to kiss her. Daisy nipped at his lips and pushed against him. Lucien slowly released her; the disgust was hidden in his chest.

"Mara is possessive of me now, you know," Lucien whispered.

Daisy stepped backwards and peeked around as though she was afraid Mara was present. Her hand nervously went to her neck. She narrowed her gaze at him.

"You are worth it I heard." She licked her lips. "Your friend is on the below ground infirmary. Sasha is watching over him, though I suspect she's sleeping on the job. All that weight she carries around with her is dragging her down. My code is 45839 for the infirmary."

Lucien raised an eyebrow. "Thank you." He bent and kissed the curve of her neck. "We will meet again. I will repay you for this deed," he whispered. "Don't tell a soul we met, and I will visit your room at dawn after the festivities are over."

Daisy caressed his cheek. "I'll be waiting."

Luck was with him, and Lucien didn't take it for granted. He went through the dimmed room to the far door and pressed in the girl's code. The stairwell to the dungeons was reached on the outside of the home and other hidden locations throughout the house; however, not as many led straight to the clinic below. Lucien had his own code; he just didn't want to use his in case his brother or the guards decided to check to see who was going and coming.

The lights flickered. It was dim but efficient. Lucien cautiously opened the door and saw the other girl sitting in a chair on the opposite side of the dingy hall, asleep. Her lush brown hair framed her heart-shaped face and dimpled chin. Although she was heavier than most of the girls Mara employed, she had a beauty about her as did the others.

Lucien quietly closed the door behind him. He turned from her and sauntered down the hall. Many of the doctors were upstairs with the others. Though the infirmary was available, not many people stayed long. Usually, the doctor tended to them, and Lucien's family offered a room in the back wing of the mansion that overlooked the gargoyle garden. Unfortunately for Jack, Gavin hadn't made that offer.

The odor in the infirmary was difficult to breathe, for most people not used to the taste or smell of blood. However, Lucien had loving family to thank for his addiction and acceptance of the smell of blood mixed with rotting flesh. It was another of those things he hated about himself, but had given up the futile act of seeking a savior from it.

Moans emanated from a few of the rooms. Lucien peered in some of the closed doors through the two-sided peepholes in each. None of them were Jack. The more he walked, the more he relaxed he became. The nurses must've bailed, since not many were around.

Finally, he heard sobbing that sounded suspiciously like Jack. He had his doubts about the man crying. He'd known Jack all his life and the guy loved being tortured. The guy was made of iron will and could kill an adversary with his bare hands. The man seemed inhuman the way he withstood any punishment the Ancients doled out on him.

Lucien took a chance and opened the door. He heard the sobbing and mumbling, but didn't see Jack on the bed. The walls were stained and yellow with no pictures or windows. No dressers or closets for anyone to hide.

His gaze dropped to the floor. He halted. Jack was under the bed, trembling and sobbing like a broken man. Nothing like Lucien had ever witnessed, even when the vilest of their Ancient priests in ceremony administered torturous cuts and devices on Jack to open him up for possessions.

"Jack?" Lucien called, hoping it would help the man pull himself together.

Jack's hand reached for him. The nails were bloody and bitten almost to the middle of the nail bed. "Lucien," he breathed in a hoarse hiccup. "What are we going to do?"

"Kill him and send Balaal back."

Lucien bent to help Jack from under the bed.

"I don't know if we can. What...he did to me." Jack trembled.

Lucien sat Jack on the bed, pushed the man backward, and covered him with the comforter. "Tell me. What was it like?" Lucien was curious, knowing that when he'd finished the deed with his brother, it was where Lucien would end up one day.

Jack's hand slid down his face. "Like nothing I ever want to experience again."

Lucien sauntered to the chair in the corner and slid it in front of Jack then sat down. "You don't have a choice. That's our future, unless we get a miracle. We signed up for it, remember?"

"I don't know anything other than that. We're born to this. I have been so stupid to want that power."

"Is it power?" Lucien asked, studying Jack.

"It's a lie. We have no power in it. No joy. It's a deception. All of it."

"I'll need to make sure you will be able to go through with our plans." Lucien cautiously leaned forward and placed his hand on Jack's shoulder.

"Now more than ever, we have to do this. I need to get well, get the flashes of what I suffered in that realm of hell to release me from their crippling effects. My daughters...I wouldn't wish that dark twisted place on them." Jack's voice cracked, and more tears fell from his eyes.

"When will you be ready? We don't have long before Peter Saints shows up. The final ceremony will need him. My brother confided in me that the missing link hasn't been revealed to him yet. Peter holds the key to that."

"What's missing?"

"Two human portals. Apparently I had one in my possession. A girl named Argia, a rare find. The other girl like her, Hanna, escaped with her father. She was killed in a car accident." Lucien didn't reveal that he'd made that car accident happen. Even then, he had an unnatural desire for his brother's mad intention to build the machine to fail. He'd deliberately blocked most of his brother's possible successes. Maybe out of jealousy, but if he was deeply transparent with himself, he'd been compelled to do so from some unknown force of power. Something deeper than revenge. An atonement of sorts.

"Then how was she found out? How did he know about her?"

Lucien shrugged. "After he bonded with Balaal, his knowledge of the demonic workings and manipulations became apparent to him, I guess."

"We will do it, but you have to promise me you'll find a way to free my daughters from the fate upon me."

Lucien chuckled. "Unless they are accepting applications with our enemies from the Decretum Venia, their fate is what you made it."

Jack's stricken expression aged the man.

"Chin up, man, at least you can make their time here on Earth as safe and pleasant as possible. Isn't that better than what they are suffering now?"

Jack sniffed. "I suppose."

"Well, I look at it like this: if I'm going to burn in hell, I'm going to fight my way there on my terms. No more accepting my fate."

Jack nodded and lay down, pulling his knees up to his chest.

Lucien hoped, for all of their sakes, he and Jack could follow through. At this moment, he had his doubts.

CHAPTER 30

Peter hoped Rosa could fix this disaster. Getting to her was important now more than ever. Argia had grown stronger after meeting the woman.

Peter tried to ignore the tapping of Argia's knee against the door. The girl never seemed to be completely still except when she was sleep. He wondered if she was always that way, or had she become like that after she was found by them.

"Peter?"

He groaned under his breath; the girl had just stopped rambling about every store they passed on their way out of the city.

"Peter? You hear me?"

He rolled his eyes, and bit down on the mint he'd held in his mouth. "Yeah. If you wanted to talk so much, you could be in the back, talking to your harem of men fighting over you."

Argia peeked behind him. "Your girlfriend is doing a good job of keeping them entertained. They are playing a card game."

"Great."

"Can I tell you a secret?" Argia whispered.

"Sure, why not, you shared everything else." He tapped his finger on the wheel as he waited for the traffic light.

"Micah...he was my first, everything."

Peter coughed, then choked on the pieces of the mint before swallowing them. "Why are you tellin' me this? Not my business." He shook his head and put his hand to his forehead. "You just put really uncomfortable images of you in my head."

She shrugged. "Sorry, I have that effect on people." Argia touched Peter's arm.

Peter jumped. "Don't touch."

"Okay. Well, I am telling you because, I—Angel and I are friends, but I don't want her to think of me as an 'easy' girl."

Peter held in his laugh. "She wouldn't think that."

"Yes, she would. You know, since she told me that you and she hadn't—"

"Stop right there!" Peter cleared his throat. "Not your damn business."

"Well, I didn't mean to upset you. I'm just talking through my dilemma here."

Peter inhaled and then released the air through his teeth, "Talk. No judgment – okay?"

Argia hopped in her seat and moved closer. The girl had no understanding of personal space, but Peter was used to it.

"Micah and I had been acquaintances for over a year. I wanted more and I think he did, too. We were like two kindred spirits forbidden to be together because it would endanger us both."

Peter bit back a sarcastic comment about her sounding like she was retelling some fairytale or Shakespeare play. "I get that."

"That's why when we were on the run I felt I should, you know, do it. I lost hope that I could actually be with someone forever, so I wanted a piece of him for that moment in time."

"And Kyle?"

"Well, you know with Kyle, he played the cat and mouse. He pretended to hate me, call me names, and act like I scared him..."

"Uhum, Argia, that wasn't play acting."

Argia laughed. "It was. I know it was. He was just scared of what we could have together. Kyle was lonely for so long and so was I."

"O-kay." Peter allowed her the fantasy, but he distinctly remembered Kyle demanding they ditch the *crazy chick* more times than he could count.

"Micah got caught." Argia hiccupped, her brief brush off laugh turned to a whimper. "He did it to save me."

"I believe that."

"I promised to find Rosa; he knew her, you know."

"He mentioned it."

"I didn't find her before I met you. So many bad things happened to me."

"I know the feeling. Did you get far?"

Argia reached in her pocket and handed Peter a piece of gum. "You'll probably need this fresh one."

Peter eyed it, noticing some dirt on the wrapper, then watched her quickly unwrap it and press it to his lips. He opened his mouth.

"I got pretty far. It was hard remembering everything Micah taught me. I stayed pretty hidden until I tried to get money when I heard how you could get food when you donated blood for DNA samples."

"What?" Peter had been somewhat ignoring her, but caught the DNA sampling part.

"That's when things went bad. I didn't realize the Extraho of Obscurum was using that as a way to find descendants of the Decretum Venia. I went for the food and ended up fighting the police to get out, stabbing a doctor, and being put into a mental institution. It's a blur."

"Dahum."

"That's how I felt. It worked out, though. I escaped. On that day I talked to the angels, I figured out when I was angry the demons didn't bother me as much."

"Were you still looking for Rosa?"

"Yes, but I'd lost the paper with her address. I did sort of remember it. Then when I was feeling pretty low, I asked the angels to kill me."

"You..." Peter couldn't believe it.

"Then, I saw you and Kyle. The air around you crackled. I felt it was a sign."

Peter laughed. "A bad sign."

"No, you saved my life that day. If it wasn't for you, I wouldn't have found Rosa, and Micah wouldn't be sitting here with us."

"Did you tell Micah that?"

"No, I couldn't. I felt like I'd betrayed him by taking so long, and well, then there is Kyle and I."

"Why didn't you tell Kyle about Micah?"

"Peter, nothing good happened to me after Micah except Kyle. There were bad men and boys out there who hurt me. I got away sometimes, and other times..."

"I'm sorry." He patted her arm.

"It's okay now, I don't dwell on it. Being with Kyle helped me erase the way I felt about love and showing it after Micah. I needed that to recover. I don't regret it."

"You shouldn't regret love or being loved, Argia."

"I know. I just regret hurting them both. I won't choose you know. I can't be with either of them. I understand my position now. We have to take both of them. Micah is very powerful, and if I need more power to fight Gavin, he can do it."

"What are you talking about, Argia?"

"If we go back to the Wall of Ash, the only way to destroy it is we have to go inside."

Peter skin crawled. He'd been there and he never wanted to go back. "There's got to be another way."

"There isn't. I thought about it, and remember everything we studied in those ancient books. The dreams and the transformations that happened when we released our angelic DNA all confirm that someone has the formula to destroy the Wall of Ash. However, a person with my ability can go through the wall without being noticed. A person demons can't help but want to speak to—someone like me."

CHAPTER 31

The night had fallen. Their gas tanks were empty. Peter watched the gauge and felt a tingling up his neck at the thought of stopping at a station in one of the small towns off the highway. He could risk it.

Argia whispered, "There were no scrolls to tell us where to go at Micah's Sanctuary." She stretched and adjusted so her knees were up under her, and her seatbelt rested at an odd angle.

"I know. There is another one that is better hidden. Those are usually the ones that have the historical records."

"Will we be able to talk to Rosa before we get there?"

Peter checked the gas again and frowned. "I believe she is in an abandoned doomsday prep site that the rogue members of the Decretum Venia built."

"I thought we trusted each other more now."

"That trust is fragile. Pastor Finn and Rosa don't stay at the recorded Sanctuaries anymore. It's too dangerous after our enemies destroyed some of the locations."

"When we find her, she will tell us what to look for. I hope it's easy this time."

Peter pulled off the two-lane highway; several of the lights were dim or busted, but he took the exit anyway. It was the only one he'd seen in a while that had a gas sign.

He peeked in the rearview mirror and found Angel sleeping with her head rested on Kyle's shoulder. Kyle was staring out the window, quieter than he'd ever been. Micah's eyes were trained on Argia.

"If we can't get to Rosa safely, we'll have to go straight to the next Sanctuary. Otherwise, the stronghold we need to find won't be revealed."

"How do you know where they all are—by memory?"

"Dreams." Peter shrugged and slowed the car as he rounded the curved road off the highway and onto a one-lane road. "And sometimes, I uncover them when we are in a Sanctuary. After that, my memory kicks in."

"Rosa told me that she knows where many of the Sanctuaries are because she reads the ancient scrolls and teaches them. She doesn't share the locations unless she has to."

"Then someone else that had access to the scrolls must've given them to Gavin Steele."

"It could be anyone. They have an office in Europe that manages the orphanages and makes sure they are staffed with a trusted member. Many of those places have been hidden in the sanctuaries known by the Elders. I remember them sending some guy named Dr. Phillips to the Sanctuary Kyle and I were in. That guy killed our caretaker trying to find out about me. He was playing double sides."

"It is possible. I know his name." Argia frowned and started pinching her arm. "He checked on me at the hospital just before Lucien and I first met." She shivered.

"That can't be good. Do you think he's like you? The man could be playing both sides."

Argia shook her head. "If he was willing to sacrifice my life to keep his secret."

Peter snorted. "Mine, too. And if he killed Mr. Boswell, our caretaker, then it's doubtful the bastard was playing on anyone's side."

Argia started humming. "So maybe we should just let Rosa contact the people who can help us."

Peter nodded. "It's the only way to roll it at this point." He went silent and blocked out Argia's chatting as he drove on the dark road towards the lit up gas station that seemed extremely packed with people to be so far off the road.

"Dude, don't stop there." Kyle leaned up to warn Peter.

"No choice, we are out of gas."

"I may not be psychic, but this doesn't look right. We go here, we'll be easy targets."

Peter watched the bikers hanging out at the station. There was a bar on the back side, and many of the people had drinks in their hand. Music played in the distance and there was laughter.

"They're just partying."

Argia climbed on her knees and released her seatbelt.

"What are you doing? Sit down." Peter pushed Argia back in her seat. "Kyle, you go in and pay for the gas."

"Oh, I get it. Send in the 'token white boy' who fits in with the bikers." Kyle grunted.

"You got it, bro," Peter said.

"Stop the damn car. You better not forget this favor I'm doing for you." Kyle sank back into the seat.

Peter chose the pump furthest from the bikers.

Kyle got out the car and came around to Peter's window. "Open the back so I can get the gas can." Kyle turned his head to study the group.

Peter smirked. "And the gun."

"Hell, and the knife, too. Be ready, those son of butts are looking over here."

"I am." Argia slid a small gun from under the seat. Then she shrugged. "I found it at Micah's."

Peter snatched it from her. "Give me that."

Kyle winked at Peter. "Thanks for looking out. I'm going in. If I don't come back in ten minutes, just leave me. I can hide in some of these woods around here."

"Not happening. We've got explosives in the back. I'll blow this mofo up before I leave you here."

"Thanks, good to know I'm needed." Kyle peered over Peter to stare at Argia. "Right?"

"Yes, needed. You are needed." Argia smiled back at Kyle, bounced on the seat and clapped.

Peter flinched when Micah leaned on the seat, his elbow close to Peter's neck. Micah cleared his throat. "Am I needed?"

Peter responded in spite of Argia's sanguine smile. "Essential."

"By who?"

"Me, I need you, Micah." Argia reached out and touched Micah's hand.

Peter got out of the car to give them a moment. He folded his arms and watched Kyle's exchange with the cashier.

A hand slid onto his bent arm, and a head rested on him.

"This won't be a bad stop."

Peter entwined his fingers with hers. "No, I don't think so."

Peter had his doubts, though; several of the bikers were watching them. Their expressions changed to a fake distraction. He had a feeling it wouldn't be the last time he'd see them.

Kyle rushed over to them and nodded.

"Where outta here." Peter smacked the top of the van and opened the door. "Argia, it's your turn to sit in the back."

"But I..."

"No. You will deal with it. I need to talk to Angel."

Argia nodded and slowly opened the door. She made a big deal of the snail's pace she moved each leg off the seat. Then she twisted around. "My gun, please?"

"No way in hell." Peter lifted his eyebrow at her.

"Fine. I got another one in my pocket anyway." Argia slammed the door behind her.

Peter turned and enveloped Angel into his arms for a quick kiss, his eyes never leaving the one biker, tall, bleached blond and gray eyed, who wasn't smiling back at him.

CHAPTER 32

Peter knew it was too good to be true. The gas station was far
behind them, but the revving of motorcycles wasn't too far
away that he didn't hear them in the distance. Angel held his
hand, and he kept his eyes on the road.

"Why are you squeezing my hand?" Angel squeezed his back.

Peter sighed. "There are motorcycles behind us."

She laughed. "We are on the highway."

"I know, but I've heard them for miles. There was this one guy
at the bar staring at me. He was smiling, but it didn't reach his
eyes. I haven't been able to shake the bad feeling."

"Well, you were out of place. It was a 'white' motorcycle bar. So
you and Micah would stick out. I can pass for 'white' until I open
my mouth and my accent gives me away." She laughed.

"You're Hispanic and Argia is Asian; you think that bothered
them, too?" Peter smiled at her.

"Maybe, but they were really staring at you. Micah stayed in
the car, so no one really got a good look at him."

"As long as they don't make a move on us, we should be alright
until we have to ditch them to get to the next Sanctuary."

"A break would be nice." She squeezed his hand again.

"Thanks for sitting between the guys in the back."

"I knew you wanted to make sure Micah didn't leave, so I didn't mind."

"So, how were they takin' it?"

"Not good. I understand how Micah feels. Betrayal isn't a good taste. I also, know how Argia got into her situation. It made me regret what I put you through when you found me again."

"Can we forget about it?" Peter hoped so. He'd forgiven her for seeking comfort with another when he wasn't around. "I hope you can."

"It's complicated, Peter." Angel released his hand and leaned toward her door.

"Forgiveness isn't complicated. You either can or won't." Peter tightened his fists on the wheel. This was ticking him off. He never wanted her to know his mistake and how it made forgiving her easier.

"I forgive you, Peter, but you have to know that our situation isn't the best for you – or even me. I don't know when I will be able to overcome my issues. It's not fair for me to expect you to wait. Even though I'd thought you had before when we were apart. I don't think the sexual part of our relationship is the only problem. It's other parts of me that I can't seem to reveal that I think I should if we were to make what we have last."

Peter's heart pounded in his chest. He wanted to hit something. "You thought I wouldn't try to forget? Find someone to help me with the isolation and anger when you were moved to another facility? I had to go through hell and high-water to find out where you were."

"I'm sure you did." She snorted.

"I did. It started out that way at first. I flirted with girls who were in the computer room of the facility. Kyle worked on getting the guys to give us information, that's how Gil got involved and ran with us."

"Okay, but you?"

"I didn't volunteer to go after the girls; they were already seeking me out when they heard you'd left. It was easy enough."

"Easy to do what? Get information or into their pants?"

"Angel? Are you really going to ask me to give you details on my crap-storm of a mistake? Don't do this to us. To yourself or me." Peter felt her gaze on him. His skin heated from it.

"Did you not ask me in detail, several different ways, what happened with me and—"

"Don't say his name. Just stop." Peter mumbled a curse. "Let's talk about this later."

"No, let's stop right now. This relationship is a disaster. I can't be honest with you about the details of that time I was with Lucien and Gavin. If I don't cross that line and unlock nightmares I try to pretend aren't there, I can't share them with you. We can't work them out. We won't, because to face those fears, I have to relive them. I won't; I just won't, not even for you, Peter. What are we holding onto? If we survive this battle, you and I won't have a common enemy anymore."

"What the hell does that mean? That's a good thing. We want to have a normal life. So we can see where this goes. Keep your secrets; hide them until you are ready to share. I will be ready."

"No! I will never do that, Peter. I am able to fight Gavin with you because inside me, there is so much hate for him—for his brother—for the Extraho of Obscurum that I want them to die! I even hate myself and what I had to become to survive there. I want them to go to hell and never return. I can never forgive them for taking everything I have. My love for you sometimes feels as though it's the only good thing in me left. Then I feel unworthy, since I can't forgive myself for the horrible things I did."

"We can build on that love and destroy our hate when we destroy them. We have every reason to hate them. To want justice for what they did for us. We can't find it in the legal system, in this 'system' of law we have. So we will do it ourselves. You did what you had to in order to survive. It wasn't your true nature."

Angel's foot pounded the dashboard. "You are not listening to me," she sobbed. "I can never love you the way you want. Never give you everything you deserve. We should just do this and let it go. I can't even love myself anymore. I'm so cold inside sometimes."

"No. There is no freakin' way I am letting you go. Ever. You can push, you can scream and fight, but we will work this out. I won't allow you to let me go. When you can't fight for us, I will. Now isn't the time though. Let's deal with the big bad-ass monster in the room. After that, we rebuild us."

"Hey!" Kyle yelled. "Someone's pulling up on us fast."

"I knew it! Guys, get weapons out. We got to make it to that bridge."

Kyle tossed a bag onto the front seat. "On it. Your guns."

Peter held out his hand. Angel handed him a gun.

Angel rolled down her window. Then took off her seatbelt.

Peter put the gun in the cup holder. "Micah, you got anything that will blind them?"

"Yeah, smoke bomb. I'm dropping it now."

"There's eight of them! How'd they sneak up on us so fast?"

"I saw them a way back. I got distracted," Peter said.

The smoke bomb hit the pavement behind them. A blast sounded. Peter pushed the gas pedal.

"Hold on, going up!" The mountain curved upward sharply. Normally, Peter would have preferred to take the road in daylight, but the cover of night would help. He just hoped no one was coming down.

He pushed the car as fast as he could. No guard rails were around to guide them. The shrubbery that bordered the outer edge of the elevated mountain road was short and ragged as the light from the headlights hit.

Peter constantly shifted in his seat to steady himself from the jerking; his hand went out to brace Angel; she shoved him off. "I'm okay."

Grinding his teeth, he squeezed the wheel and sped forward.

"Car ahead!" Kyle called.

Peter didn't wait for the other car. "I'm takin' it. Get guns ready in case they're with the guys on the motorcycles."

"Just so you know," Micah responded, "those bastards are still behind us."

"Damn!" Peter sped up. His headlights bumped a flash of light over the one car road and the front of the car on the other side. He pounded the accelerator. Then he jerked the wheel before hitting the front bumper of the other car that was trying to take the one-lane spot before him.

Peter peeked at the back lights of the car they were leaving behind. "Can you toss another smoke screen for us?"

"On it!" Micah tossed the bomb out the window with a back hand flick of his wrist.

"Good throw." Peter had to give him credit. He smiled at the fading light of any of their followers as the blast behind them emitted smoke and fire on the dark and winding road.

"Football," Micah commented.

Peter didn't slow down; they had several miles to go, to the breaking point on the mountain, to drift back down and find the bridge.

They had to make it there in one piece. He needed time to work on Angel, to get her to see that this battle couldn't be won if he didn't have her love waiting for him on the other side.

CHAPTER 33

T he road widened as they descended the opposite side of the mountain. Peter slowly expelled the breath he'd been hold-ing. The bridge wouldn't be far. The moon was yellow and full. Rocks from the pebbled road flew from the tires to hit up against the bottom of the van.

The knocking was soothing but not enough to calm the raging beat of his heart. He was glad they wouldn't need gas. The journey, though, wasn't getting easier.

"I've been checking the phone Pastor Finn encrypted for us. The news has us as missing kids, but dangerous."

"No kidding," Peter snorted.

"That's not all. On the black web, we each have a million dollar prize on our heads—except Peter, you, dude, got a cool ten million, and it keeps growing."

"Thanks."

"Anytime you need me to tell you how special you are, let me know."

"Peter?" Argia asked and rested her head next to his. "Are we close yet?"

"Close enough."

"They have our scent, you know. The demons are hunting us by larger numbers than before."

"I don't doubt it. Gavin's awake and Lucien probably told him he'd caught us."

"No. Lucien wouldn't do that," Micah stated. "He'd be punished if he failed to capture you. I never met Gavin, but the rest of those creatures that call themselves humans are like rabid dogs on a bone."

"How d'you know?" Peter adjusted in his seat as he pushed the speed of the van.

"I spent a lot of time with Lucien. More than I wanted to."

"Sorry," Peter added.

"Sorry doesn't take it away. Lucien was charged with preparing me for sacrifice. He tried to kill me though."

"You escaped?" Argia asked. "I knew you could, Micah."

"I didn't do it alone. I had a lot of help. Some important people in that organization don't want Gavin to succeed. Because of that, I was able to get information from the demons surrounding them. The demons that thought I was working for them. I know the Decretum Venia had undercover operators there. They were possibly like Argia and I."

Peter glanced at Micah's stone-faced gaze in the mirror. "You played their game?"

"Yeah, and won. I used one of their own to help me escape. Unfortunately, someone else died in my place. But the girl was one of their psychics, nothing as powerful as me or Argia."

Kyle's accusing voice deepened, "So you thought it was alright for someone to die in your place?"

"No. She was going to die anyway. Either in one of their cere-monies or during their psychic exercises where she had to contact demons. Most average psychics can't survive the experience of speaking with demons without a demon wanting to jump inside."

Peter frowned. "So a demon can't get inside you or Argia?"

"Not just us, but anyone in the Decretum Venia. It's not easy for them to get inside anyone. They have to breach the barrier that separates them from our reality. And they have to convince their human host to leave the body. Some people don't realize the signs. Drugs can be used to allow this; meditation also leaves a person vulnerable. Hypnotism is another tool. Some people though are stupid; they invite the scum in."

"Well, then, maybe just ignoring them will be all we need to do," Kyle added.

Peter shook his head. "No way."

"You can't ignore something that can throw things at you, that can scratch, burn or use objects to kill you. And although they can't possess you, they can eat you and drag your body into their hell...until someone decides to save you."

"That I believe is true," Peter said.

"They can also drive you insane and seduce you to do things that you are weak in. Like if you like to drink, they get you to drink more and more until you are drugged to the point they can slip in."

Peter lifted an eyebrow. "Not surprising there."

"That's why I never touched the stuff. I knew what I was risking to do it." Micah turned toward Kyle. "But those who sell the poison may as well be demons themselves."

"Now wait one damn minute; you don't know me, so why are you looking at me like that?"

"I know what you've done. You don't think I researched you? The early crime reports and records on you said you were a drug dealer."

"A dealer gives to those people who want it. Trust me, those evil spawns' offspring I went to school with wanted it. They were kids of people in the Extraho of Obscurum."

"And you preyed on them. Those kids still had a chance. They could have escaped. You were just feeding their own poison."

"You don't know a thing about me. What I went through or what I did there!" Kyle yelled.

Argia placed a placating hand on both of the guys.

"Micah, give Kyle a break," Peter said. "We've all done things we weren't proud of. I changed, Kyle also. And the way I see you, I think you changed. We have the power to be what we want to be now. Not what our circumstances tried to make us."

Micah clapped. "Good speech. I hope you are right." Then he sank back to his seat to turn towards the window.

Peter fell into silence. He was glad the others did, too. The traffic was thickening up on the road. He'd hope the bikers hadn't spread the word on them or the possible direction they were heading.

"The bridge ahead...see it?" Peter pointed. Aqua blue seawater surrounded the base.

"Never seen anything like this before. The water is so clear and blue." Micah's usually gruff voice had a lightness to it.

Peter smiled. "It goes on for miles."

"I wish we could stop for a swim on one of the beaches," Argia said, hopefully.

"Oh, we are going for a swim." Peter caught something moving fast towards them in the rearview mirror. "Brace up! Trucks." The tractor barreled between a few scattered cars.

He gunned the engine and swerved around the few vehicles in front of him. Argia's hand was pinching the top of the seat behind him.

"In front! Something's stopping traffic on the bridge," Angel yelled.

"Doesn't matter as long as we get on it." Peter swerved between the cars. The van slammed against a jeep then a compact car that veered onto the opposite side of the road. Peter dodged another vehicle and fishtailed the van into the left lane to pass a blue car that was keeping pace with him on the right.

"Don't kill us," Micah said. "There's a break up there."

Kyle hit the seat. "Guns! They are pulling out guns ahead."

"I see it, breaking through, on the bridge – now!" Peter hit the accelerator and barreled between two cars before getting on the bridge.

Angel fell into Peter's shoulder. "The bridge is going up."

"Damn! Hold on, we got to make it to the other side." Peter gunned the engine, and Angel braced her foot against the dashboard.

Kyle pointed a gun ahead. Micah held onto Argia.

The van hit the air. Peter's eyes never left the ascending edge ahead. The van bounced down on the opposite side of the bridge. A gunshot rang in the air. Kyle was slammed back; the gun fell out the window. The vehicle jerked and swerved, a tire blew, but Peter kept pounding through the line of cars.

"Roll the windows down!" Peter yelled, then jerked the wheel.

Argia screamed. The van broke through the guard rail and crashed into the blue sea. A whirlpool formed; Peter held his breath.

CHAPTER 34

Peter's window was down. Water rushed in, and he grabbed Angel's hand to yank her out. Micah and Kyle were struggling with Argia.

Argia's skirt was caught in the seatbelt. Peter hit the closed back window, then swam to the opposite side where Kyle's window was open, and gave him the knife Peter kept on his belt.

Kyle nodded a thank you and sliced through Argia's seatbelt. Micah pulled her with him into the front seat. Then through Peter's window while Kyle tried to squeeze out of his, then Kyle gave up to follow them through Peter's window.

Peter waved at them to follow. Angel was struggling to hold her breath. Peter tucked her under him, put his hand around her mouth, and swam as hard as he could to the rock he'd dreamed about under the bridge.

He was thankful Argia's scream caused the whirlpool; it was what he needed to jar open the sanctuary doorway.

Peter smiled. There were statues embedded in a large seamount in the ocean. The one he was looking for would be the entry. He remembered from his dream that there were places to grab air. He frowned and focused on the open mouth of the warrior with a sword drawn in the rock littered with algae.

Angel's body went limp as he fished into the open mouth of the statue for the tube. Frantically, he pressed his hand inside, Kyle joined him. Relief rushed over him when Kyle yanked out a tube with a metal tip at the end. Peter flicked the metal off, and air blasted out of it. He slid it between Angel's lips. Weakly she grasped it and took a breath. Bubbles came out of the sides of her mouth. She nodded a thank you at him.

He held her close under his arm and searched for the entrance. The underwater mountain had a smaller statue—one of a child, tiny compared to the large warrior. Peter left the others, taking turns breathing in the tube, and swam close to the smaller statue. It was completely covered in green algae with the exception of its right hand that was up as though the child was waving at someone.

Peter placed his hand on the statue's hand and within seconds, tiny needles pricked his fingers and palm. The brand heated as blood flowed from it. The needles retracted, and the entire statue sank within the rock. A blast of air pushed out, creating a pocket of constant air where the statue had retreated. Peter waved to the others and forced his way through the air pressure to a tunnel within the mountain. Once he fell into the tunnel, he sucked in air that tasted stagnant but good, considering he'd felt near passing out before entering the cave.

There were steps and noise from the others behind him. Angel held on to Kyle, whose eyes were shooting daggers at Micah while he carried a coughing Argia.

"We need to go deeper. There'll be another door." Peter led them down into the cave. Every spot in the tunnel was dry. It held an ancient smell. He ran his hand on the rock.

"This place is unbelievable." Micah's shocked voice echoed through the cave.

He'd come up beside Peter who was focused on the small light at the end of the downward spiraling tunnel.

"How'd you know about this spot?"

Peter slowed. "Many ways. It started with dreams. Then Pastor Finn, my guardian, showed me the first one. I had some hallucinations, or what seemed like it, that showed me a map of all these Sanctuaries."

"I wish I'd known of these. Maybe things for Argia and me would've been different."

"Maybe, if hiding from your destiny and letting other people take the fall for the evil in the world is what you want. I thought I wanted that, until I found Angel."

"I understand the motivation of loving someone. Would you do this if it meant losing her?"

Peter pondered it then stopped to follow Micah, who'd gone to the nearby cave wall to trace the symbols on it.

"I would do it now because I love this broken, mixed up, mad world we live in. I'm a part of it and finally see how real it is. I appreciate my bullshit I had to fight through to get to where I'm standing now. It's bigger than the love I feel for Angel. It now includes the love I allow myself to feel for me. I deserve a chance to change this. I'm taking it." He slapped Micah on the back. "There's more to show you. The good stuff is inside this. It will tell us where the big answer is."

"There's more?"

"Yeah, what we call a Stronghold. Ancient artifacts are hidden inside. We can only find them if we go to the right Sanctuary."

"I protected a sanctuary. We had scrolls, not many, but it was a safe place from enemies."

"The Sanctuary is where warriors planned battles. This kind is usually uninhabited by anyone. The secrets inside are much too valuable."

"And you found them?"

Peter continued to descend down the sloping cave; he wiggled his eyebrows. "You do know what the Decretum Venia members are, right?"

Micah shrugged. "Yeah. Some have different kinds of abilities or none at all."

Peter nodded. "But we are an engineered and genetically modified race of a human and angel hybrid. It's as if angels dissected the best part of themselves and gave it to us."

"Doesn't seem like it."

"It was a secret virtually unknown by many except the Elders, until some stupid guy opened the first book of secrets, which revealed it."

"Who the hell would mess with something so sacred?" Micah's eyebrow went up as though he was mocking Peter.

"Me. Isn't it obvious?"

"Yep."

"The Sanctuary will tell us the location of the Stronghold, and that is when things will get interesting."

"What will happen when you reveal the last secret?"

Peter shrugged. "I don't know. I try not to dwell on it too much. If I did, I wouldn't go there."

"Why? We don't have to do this. It may give Gavin the upper hand in the end."

"I won't believe that. Our angelic ancestors, with their human supporters, defeated the king of evil himself. Gavin isn't that strong or powerful."

Micah appeared to shiver slightly. "He wants to be. If there were ever humans I considered as evil as a demon, it would be Gavin Steele and his brother."

"No argument from me on that score. But both of them are still human. They can die, they can be stopped, their demons are immortal until we find a way to destroy them. We have to destroy it all."

"I'm with you on it. At first, because I didn't want to leave Argia. Now, I don't know how that's going to work out; I want to help you with this."

"Thanks, man. If it's any consolation, I had a similar issue with Angel. We still haven't worked through it, but if she'd chosen the other guy, it would've hurt like hell. I would still be here doing this though. I would have to find a way to move on."

"I'm not there, yet." Micah glanced behind them. "Neither is he."

Peter came to a stop at the bottom of the cave near a small boulder with carved symbols in it. He turned his palm up; the blood gathered caused it to appear red and swollen. Suddenly it formed into a symbol of three intertwined circles with words within them.

Micah gasped.

Peter ignored it and slammed his palm on the exact same symbol on the rock barrier. The pricks of the needles came fast; the symbols lit up with a glow from within, and Micah stumbled back jarring Peter's arm.

The boulder sank into the ground, and the cavern opened.

CHAPTER 35

Peter got a thrill when he witnessed someone entering the most secret and ornate Sanctuaries of the Decretum Venia. Very few in the Decretum Venia even knew where they were.

"I-I had only imagined a place like this in my dreams." Micah's eyes widened. His hand reached out to touch the gold-plated wall inside the rock and jewel covered door to the cavern they'd travel through.

"Many of us had visions of this place if our ancestor had been in them during the time of the thousand year war." Peter leaned against the wall as the others made their way closer.

"I'm going to find a room to put her in," Kyle said gruffly as he adjusted Argia in his arms

Micah grimaced and nodded a terse concession to Kyle.

"I'll tell you where we are," Kyle added, his voice broken.

Angel followed Kyle and gave Peter a pensive gaze before she turned away.

"Seems like ya'll came to an agreement about things." Peter crossed his arms.

"In a way. But it's not finished yet. She won't decide."

"Argia is...complicated."

Micah laughed. "You got me there."

"C'mon, let's check out the place. There's usually lots of rooms and clues in these Sanctuaries. We need to find a hint to a hidden place where the warriors created their strategies and war plans. It's also the place that holds the books I made the fatal mistake of opening."

"Ah, Strongholds you called them."

"Yeah." Peter glanced over the inlaid gold wall. There were some strange imprinted symbols. Every part of the wall and ceiling was covered in the gold overlay that had messages written under warring angels. It was hard to tell which were demons and which were not. Peter stepped back and noticed that if he were a closer distance to the mural some of the angels changed to demons.

"Can you read these?" Micah's hand traced some of them.

"Not all of them; it's as though the ones I 'need' to know appear to me and their meaning is...revealed. It's a strange way to explain it, but it's as if the symbol lights up, pushes itself off the wall, and twists around into something I can identify with."

"Amazing. I am having the same experience. It's blowing my mind."

"Been there, and it still makes me feel disoriented when it happens."

Micah sighed. "Those guys after us—you know they were planted, right?"

Peter frowned. "What do you mean? The gas station was a set-up?"

"We have been hunted for a while."

"I know, but this is different. Those guys there, it was like they were waiting for us."

"How would they know to do that?" A few doors had wood and

jeweled fronts. The jewels were usually fashioned as a piece of art that had clouds, terrain, or animals on them. He didn't feel as though the scrolls were in those rooms, so he passed them by.

"I had a guy on the inside of the Extraho of Obscurum who helped me escape. He told me that I had to keep his cover. Until..."

Peter frowned. "Until when?"

"Until I was no longer useful." Micah slapped his hand on the wall. "He thinks I'm working for him and the Extraho of Obscurum, but I'm not. I didn't want to leave the store I was at because I didn't want him to get a tip-off that I was still alive."

Peter wiped his hand down his face. "We can't get caught now. Usually, these Sanctuaries have a passageway exit that is different than the one you come in. When we get out of here, they won't find you. Also, hopefully, those who were after us will think we died in the crash."

"Maybe, but what if the police get involved? They'll fish the van from the sea."

"But they won't find us, no matter how much they search. Hopefully, they'll suspect we were swept out by the current."

"We hope." Micah shrugged.

"Now, I need your help with the scrolls. We don't have too much time. Finding clues to what destroyed the Wall of Ash, and the angel who did it is important. Then I will be able to find a lead to the Stronghold."

"Sounds doable." Micah stepped away from the wall.

Peter started walking and then turned left at the fork in the hallway. The corridor was dimmer than the other, but Peter felt a pull for him to proceed.

He studied some of the shapes and symbols on this wall, and they were guiding the way. There were no doors in this corridor, and Micah fell silent behind Peter as though he was following along.

"It's down here." Peter pointed at the end of the hall. The rock had a glow that brightened the path. There seemed to be a closed partition—no door, just a wall with a repeated symbol. Peter knew the symbol; he'd studied it on his hand every day since Hanna died.

"Wait, there's no door." Micah stopped.

Peter grinned. "There is always a door." He rubbed his hand on the beveled surface of broken stones and drawings. A thin layer of smoke slithered out from the brand on his palm. It heated; he was used to the burning, even though he didn't like it. He removed his hand to reveal the symbols on it were slashes of light.

"What the..." Micah stumbled back.

"Don't leave...just watch." Peter needed Micah to see this. To understand that even though Gavin was powerful, they all held their own power, and together it could beat Gavin and his demon. Peter needed Micah to tap into his deeper strength; they all would need it when they got to the stronghold.

Peter turned his palm upward. The circular brand lifted, throbbed, and the blood seemed to glow and burn. A pin of smoke formed from the middle of his palm, it weaved its way upward from his skin.

Micah's jaw dropped.

"This is how I found the first clue to the Stronghold. It was through this brand that a girl named Hanna gave me. She was like you, like Argia." The point of smoke lifted and made a symbol of a curved moon, the symbol for the Angel Gabriel. Peter knew it from the times he was sent to the void history that wasn't supposed to be repeated, only accessed through the treasures uncovered in the strongholds.

As suddenly as his palm heated, it went cold and the smoky symbol disappeared.

"What did that mean?" Micah's hoarse question echoed in the cavern.

"It means that is the clue. Let's find the symbol on the wall." Peter searched the crowded overlapping symbols. The ceiling was at least twenty feet tall.

Micah frowned. "It could be anywhere."

"True, but at least the symbols are glowing." Peter squinted at the crush of symbols from as high as he could see. Zigzagging his searching downward, he smiled as his vision collided with the one symbol that wasn't illuminated. A half-moon sign, just above his reach.

"You find it?" Micah asked.

"There; it's high, but I can stretch to get it." Peter reached, then bounced on his toes.

"Or you can let me lift you."

Peter nodded. "Good bet."

Micah bent, and Peter climbed on Micah's back then braced himself as Micah stood so Peter could sit on his shoulders.

"Higher." Peter reared his hand back a bit and then smacked it on the symbol.

Crack.

Slivers of cracks in the rock formed on the sides of the wall. Peter jumped off Micah's shoulders. "Now, your knowledge begins."

CHAPTER 36

Peter stood in awe of the room that was revealed. Gold and silver was everywhere, with statues of Angel warriors in each corner of the wall. Books trimmed in gold, brass, and silver were embedded in their own crevices. The design was indescribably a piece of art within itself.

Micah slowly turned around. "Unbelievable."

"I know. We need to find any hints to the final stronghold. Maybe, something that talks about a place of planning and protection, or somewhere that all the warrior angels met to win the war."

"Just want to point out that there are a lot of books here. It will take years."

"Nah, there is a system and order to the way they are cataloged. Rosa taught us how to figure out the pattern. Well, Argia and Angel know better than me, but I remember enough to find the clues."

"Well…" Micah shrugged. "May as well start at the bottom." He walked around a large wooden table with tips of gold on each side. The benches and table were tall enough to fit a person eight feet tall.

"How long have you known about the Sanctuaries?" Peter grabbed one of the books and jumped back when a small scroll fell out behind it.

"Since I was a kid. My parents taught me all they knew about the Decretum Venia. They were well connected in the organization. I met Argia when my parents were told to provide a safe house for them."

Peter laid the book on the table and bent his knee while watching Micah's awestruck face as he traced the jeweled case of a book he was holding. "So, how many were you in before the one where we found you?"

Micah tensed his shoulders. "None."

"Let me get this straight; you knew about these but never went to one? How did you find the one you were in? We were expecting an Elder to be there." An uneasy feeling about Micah being at their Sanctuary and the original Elder not being present teased a warning of discomfort in Peter's gut.

"I was smuggled out of the Extraho of Obscurum's dungeon by someone working both sides. I told you, my stay there was chaotic and complicated."

Peter teased his chin with his thumb. "Who?"

Micah hesitated. "I don't feel comfortable telling you."

"I don't care. I risked a lot bringing you here. I need to know exactly how you got out of the Order of the Dragon, who helped you, and figure out why."

"There was a man named Cadman who worked for a high official in the Extraho of Obscurum. He was Lucien's right hand man. He smuggled me out then gave me to another man who took me to the Sanctuary where you found me."

"What did the Cadman guy look like?" Peter wanted to know. There was a guy that smuggled him out of the dungeon in one of

Gavin Steele's homes after he'd helped Angel and Kyle escape. He vaguely remembered the guy's profile and stature.

"He wore a hat low down on his face." Micah stared ahead; he seemed to be reliving a moment.

"How big was he? Was he muscular? A beard?" Peter wanted to know.

"The guy was about my height. Real thick, like body-builder big, but he was graceful. He had a neat, dark, and trimmed beard that covered most of his cheeks. The mustache was thicker. He was pale like he'd never seen the sun. But I remember what he smelled like the most." Micah cleared his throat.

"Like what?" Peter swallowed. The guy Micah described reminded him of the man who practically dragged him out of the Steele mansion when Peter had first ripped the demon free of Gavin Steele.

"Cigars, with mint."

Peter gulped in air and then cleared his throat, hitting his chest. "I know him."

Micah's eyebrows lifted. "How could you? The guy was stealth. He was Lucien Steele's shadow at that place."

Peter felt sick at that knowledge, but then a flood of warmth covered him at the knowledge that the Decretum Venia had well placed spies in the Extraho of Obscurum.

"Anyway, the guy he sent me with gave him something I think was real important. They didn't speak, just nodded and exchanged a bag and some encased box that had a dagger in it."

Peter frowned. "A dagger?"

"Yeah, I thought that was strange, but I didn't care. I wanted to be free of that place."

"The guy who took you after that—what did he look like?"

"White old guy, buzz-cut with some balding in the back. Cold eyes, but I felt safe with him, like he'd kill anything or anyone who tested him."

Peter chuckled. "That sounds like my caretaker. Pastor Finn."

Micah frowned. "Finnegan? That was his name, same as Mr. Christopher who owns the gun shop I worked at."

"Damn, that old man is more of a mystery than I knew." Peter sucked his teeth and smiled thinking of all the trouble he gave Pastor Finn growing up.

"He was a good man. What about Christopher, the Elder you were working with?"

"Mean, and knew his weapons. That old man could put some dude from an old west movie to shame. He was scary with guns and knife throwing."

Peter frowned. "Sorry, man, that you went through that."

Micah shrugged. "So am I, but surviving is sweeter because of what I went through."

There was a noise in the archway. Argia and Angel cautiously stepped inside.

Angel spoke up first, "You guys started playing with the books before we could get here? So stingy." She giggled as she tiptoed inside.

"You should let us help you; we'd get done faster." Argia went over to a book near Micah while giving him a side-glance.

Peter smiled. "Argia, you might want to watch where you are go—"

Argia bumped into Micah who was staring at her. She swallowed and lifted her eyes to his. "Thank you, Micah, for helping Kyle save me."

"I will always save you, Argia." Micah's voice was gruff.

Peter put down his book and stood behind Argia. "Then let's get to work."

"Oh, Peter, you are a pest," Argia hummed, then bounced away to snatch a book off the shelf. She climbed onto the large bench. She rested the book in her lap and ignored them.

Peter raised an eyebrow at Micah. "Back to work." Knowing, Micah's explanation of Pastor Finn and the guy, Cadman, who were working together to free kids and overthrow Gavin Steele, Peter's chest expanded with a new energy and hope.

"The Stronghold."

CHAPTER 37

S tretching, Peter followed Angel into one of the main rooms of the Sanctuary. It had large pillows, exotic patterned rugs on the wall and floors. A bed protruded from the wall; it was made of rock and covered in thick blankets and pillows. The colors in the room were vibrant burgundy, emerald green, and gold.

Peter sighed, wiped a hand down his face, and wondered what to say to Angel. She hadn't spoken to him for hours as they searched through the books they could easily reach in the hidden library.

"Where are you sleeping?" Her voice came out hesitantly, low and broken.

"Depends on what you want, Angel. I'm trying real hard here. I've made my mistakes, but I am trying to hold onto you. To us."

Her eyes watered. "I know Peter, but why? It's too hard to work through. Some other girl—"

Peter placed a finger on her lips and stepped closer. "Who doesn't know me. Who can't fathom all I've been through to get to the other side of this nightmare. Love is about overcoming the struggle and staying together through it...after it."

Angel shook her head. "You don't understand. I watched my parents stay together when they were both bitter, angry, and scared at what would happen to me. It festered, even though they were fighting to save me."

"We are not them. If we make it through this, we can make it through anything."

Angel wiped the tears with the back of her hand. "We are becoming them. I don't blame you in this, Peter. These are my feelings. I want the comfort you are offering, but I can't depend on it. If things go bad with Gavin and the Extraho of Obscurum again, I will die to protect you and the others."

"I don't want that. I can fight my own battles."

"You're not supposed to. Your angelic ancestor was a scribe: a recorder of our angelic sponsor's history. My ancestor was a warrior. Michael 2nd was sent to save his traitor brother from following of the king of demons himself. Where my ancestor failed, I won't. I made a promise to him and myself when you took me to that Stronghold where I died."

"We are not them. They were just our DNA donors. We get to decide this new fate. The new ending."

"I know, but Peter, I just feel…" Angel rubbed her arms and fidgeted with her t-shirt. "I have a feeling that one of us isn't going to make it out. It's like, if we go to the Stronghold, we are putting wood on the fire, and there will be a fight to the death that we have every chance of dying in while trying to overcome them. Gavin wants his victory."

"He won't get it. I'm not a scribe. I'm not writing anything like Luke 2nd did. I am living this, fighting this. At the end of it, I want you. My prize, my ride or die girl. We have to let it go. Stop rehashing this wound. or it won't heal."

"I thought talking things out was how we resolve them? Saying it a million times until we figure out an answer, maybe…" Angel's eyes searched Peters. Her hand shook as she raised it to his cheek. "Then let's do it, Peter. Help me overcome my fear of intimacy. Don't stop until I have a beautiful moment with you that I can hold onto."

Peter grasped her hand, kissed it, then leaned in to kiss her. He slid his arms around her and deepened his kiss. Angel sighed into it, slowly relaxing.

Her body molded to his and shivered. Peter's cloudy mind fought the urge to take it further. Grudgingly, he pulled away from her shaking body and felt the dampness of the tears flowing from her eyes.

"Not this time, Angel. We'll do it when I know you are ready. It will happen the right way, not with you offering yourself up to me like a sacrifice."

She sobbed. "Peter, I am a failure at this. Can't you see?"

Peter jerked her back into a hug and slid his hands in her hair. "No you're not. Just let me initiate it when I know you are ready. Trust me to know, okay?"

Angel nodded.

"Let me hold you tonight. We'll sleep in the bed and this time, with only our underclothes. Can you do that? I promise to just talk. Tell me everything about what scares you. About what you did. What you endured. Cry on me, hit me, scratch me. Make me the vessel you pour out your hurt on until there's nothing left between us."

Angel relaxed and sniffed, wiping a tear that fell on her cheek with the back of her hand. "Yes, I can do that."

Peter slid his hand down to her jeans. "I'll help you with these. I won't touch you, but I will help you out of them."

"Okay." Angel's shaky reply came out in small breaths as she placed her hand on Peter's covered chest to brace herself.

He slowly unbuckled her jeans, trying not to jar her or rush in any way. At an exceedingly slow pace he unzipped then slid her jeans down her slightly muscled legs. He smiled at her striped boy shorts she wore for underwear.

Angel released a breath. "C-can I help you?"

Peter smiled at her bravery. "Always, babe."

She smiled. Her trembling hands grasped the bottom of his shirt.

Peter fought to remain completely still as she came a step closer. Angel was initiating intimate touch, and Peter was shaken by it. She didn't realize how much this proved to him that if he waited, he could help dampen the memory of Gavin's torture and show her how much love could change her.

He lifted his arms and waited until she finished tugging off his shirt.

Then he stood, still not touching her. "Are you good?"

Angel smiled at him. "Yes, I feel like I'm tingling all over. I keep seeing images of things that happened to me, but I am fighting through them because I love you."

"I love you, too."

She took a deep breath. "I'm ready to finish." With shaking hands she started at his belt.

Peter smiled because he had regular shorts under his pants. He hated wearing typical underwear. At least these wouldn't freak her out.

When she pushed past his hips, her hands stopped shaking, and she relaxed. Peter helped her finish by kicking off his shoes and pulling his feet out of his jeans.

He relaxed and watched and waited for the tenseness in her shoulders to disappear. It did.

"We've slept together; it's not like it isn't cold in here, which would make the skin to skin more comfortable."

"I know. Hopefully my nightmares and confessions won't separate us."

"We'll work it out like we have been."

"I'm trying, Peter, but..."

He kissed her, and slowly her lips relaxed on his. Peter waited until her hand moved from his chest to around his waist. Then he scooped her up. "My princess Angel, will you marry me?"

Angel laughed and smacked his chest with her hand. "Not yet, my warrior king."

"Ah, a challenge." Peter kissed her cheek and then laid her on the bed. He slid in next to her, never ending contact with her body as his hands moved from cradling her to snuggling her into a spooned embrace.

"You like a challenge," she replied with lightness to her voice.

"I love you, and you challenge me to be a better me."

Angel took a deep breath; her body trembled as Peter slid his hand under her t-shirt.

"I'm just touching your stomach; that's all I'll do tonight. Promise."

"I trust you."

"Let's go to a different place than we talked about before. Take me to another place in your dreams we would travel to after this is over."

Angel's trembling hand rested on top of Peter's. "To Ireland? My parents talked about going there, and we even watched videos on planning the trip."

"Sounds good. I could go, drink beer since you don't have to be twenty-one to drink there."

"You like beer?"

"Yeah, Remmy smuggled some cans of it with a pizza into the dugout while everyone was asleep. Kyle, Gil, Remmy, and I drank it all."

"Yuck, I never liked the taste of liquor. I'd tried my parent's wine."

"I used to drink beer when I snuck out of the orphanage Pastor Finn ran. It was my escape from the guilt and anger. I'd only have one or two, but it relaxed me."

"Do you think Pastor Finn drank it?"

Peter chuckled. "Oh yeah, he had a stash in the cellar. That's why he didn't want me down there."

"Was he a real pastor?"

"Nah, we named him that. It stuck, and he even kept the title when he met with other people in the Decretum Venia. He was a retired cop with a lot of anger and control issues before he was handed us kids to take care of."

"Rosa spilled his story to you so honestly?"

"Rosa's honest, and a little bent, like Argia."

"What do you think of the Argia and Micah situation?"

Peter pondered the question. "I think Argia is undecided. She's got a deep history with Micah. He sacrificed himself so she could escape. Kyle, even though he's my best friend, was a total prick to her for months when they first met."

"He was, but isn't that just the way Kyle is?"

"I guess, but she really had taken a lot of teasing and mean talk from him. With Micah, the guy seems to think she is perfect. Kyle had to figure that out."

"It was easy for me to choose you over anyone else. That wasn't my problem. Now, tell me about..."

Angel was silent for a while. Peter traced circles on her belly; her hand continued to rest on his.

"I was ashamed. Argia seems as though she isn't really here or in our reality, most of the time."

"True, it is like she is always somewhere else. But she is still watchful and protective of us."

"I know. Maybe, I will talk to her, too."

Peter kissed the top of her head. "I just want you to release your fears tonight with me. Let me listen, comfort you."

"Peter, I hope I'm worth it," She buried her nose in his neck "When they threw me in the car, and you were running down the steps to save me, the bad things began."

Peter held her close while she recounted her terror from the moment she was kidnapped from him. Peter let her tears soak his chest while his own slid down to pool in her hair. It was difficult for him to not squeeze her tight to him to the point of suffocating her. She trembled as she spoke and stiffened as the tale grew darker than Peter's worst nightmare.

He didn't let her go, and with each word, he fell deeper and deeper in love with her.

CHAPTER 38

They held hands and walked down the cavernous hallways
of the Sanctuary to the library. Angel's hidden terror had
been replayed for him every night until finally, she was done
telling it. And when she had, each time she cried less. He would
end the night telling her how strong she was, how he loved her,
then talking about their victories.

They arrived at the library. Days had passed. Peter was getting
frustrated with their progress in finding the stronghold. He knew
the clue was here; they just couldn't seem to unlock it.

"I'm glad we found the dried nuts and fruits, and the fresh
water filtered to the wash closet." Angel squeezed Peter's hand.

Peter lifted her hand and kissed it. "I am sick and tired of it
though. We got to figure out the answer."

The others were already there, spread in three corners of the
room, and silent. Peter observed each of them and realized that
none of them were paying attention to what they were reading.
The tension was thick.

"Anybody find something?" Peter asked. Both Argia and Kyle's
heads were bent over books.

"We are getting close, Peter, I know it." Argia moved her regard from Peter to Kyle then darted to Micah, who was still staring at his book.

"Sure." Peter smacked his teeth. "Awright, let's cut this now. Kyle and Micah, Argia's not going to choose. I thought we made a truce when we came here. This has been going on for days, and we are running out of time here. So, I suggest we work in shifts. Your drama is slowing progress."

Micah faced Peter. "No. There's nothing else to do here but read the books."

Argia hopped up and down. "There's artifacts with utensils, jewels, and tools we can uncover."

"I vote we work together." Kyle stepped up behind Argia. "We are working through this situation."

"I get that, but staring at books while throwing fight signs at each other when Argia's not looking isn't working. There is a pattern to these things, and if we don't find a clue soon, we are screwed."

Argia cleared her throat. "I found clues."

"Why didn't you tell us?" Peter frowned at her.

"Well, I guess I was a little bit"—Argia hummed—"distracted."

Peter sighed. "We are all friends here."

"Speak for yourself, ex-friend." Kyle crossed his arms over his chest.

Peter narrowed his gaze at Kyle. "Oh, it's like that now?"

"Damn right. You can't be his friend and mine." Kyle dropped his book on the table and crossed his arms.

"We have to be friends in this situation. Acting like this is screwing up our progress."

"We had a truce. I'm respecting that," Kyle said.

Micah put down his book and turned toward Peter. "Me, too."

"Then what's the damn problem?" Peter frowned.

Angel went next to Argia and held her hand. "They can't stand being around her without wanting her." Angel peeked at both Kyle and Micah. "And wanting to fight each other over her."

"Doesn't matter, I'm not going anywhere until we have answers and get out of here," Kyle said.

"Me neither," Argia added.

Micah leaned against the wall. "Not giving up or leaving now."

"Fine!" Peter dragged his fingers through his hair and shook them in frustration. "Argia, tell me your clues."

"The clue is; the location of the stronghold is not in any of these books."

Peter wanted to shake her. "What the hell is that supposed to mean?"

"Hold up, don't talk to her like that." Micah stepped toward Peter.

Peter took a deep breath. "Sorry, Argia. What do you mean by that? How are you sure?"

"I read rather fast. I guess I'm a speed reader, and, well, I capture the picture of the pages in my head."

"And?" Peter put his fisted hands on his hips.

"They have a pattern. I didn't notice it at first. When you stare at the pages, they form shapes."

Kyle opened his book. "You're right. I thought I was seeing things."

"Each of these books has jewels that are in different shapes on the front." Micah traced his book's gold cover with jeweled design on it. "The design that shows a 3D impression inside my pages' matches." Micah walked over to Argia. "Her book."

Peter lifted an eyebrow. It was obvious that Micah was quiet but had been watching Argia enough to discern the emblem on the book she'd been studying.

"How do we know the order?" Peter took the book from Argia.

It was heavy, the covers made of hallowed silver, the jewels framed within fitted divots. His brand on his hand warmed. Itching, which meant it wanted him to do something. He placed his hand on the emblem. The jewels warmed under his palm then pricked his brand. It was quicker than the other times, and in the top right corner of the book, a number appeared.

"Do you see that number?" Peter asked them.

Argia moved in closer. "I don't see a number, but it's some type of symbol."

Peter swallowed. "I see a number two there."

Micah stood behind Argia and touched it. "This isn't a number that we can understand."

"I am tellin' you, there is a number two."

Angel touched Peter's arm. "Don't you think you are the only one who is supposed to see it? Your ancestor Luke 2 was the one who hid the history he documented."

Peter nodded then circled around the room and counted all the books on the wall. "There are hundreds of these books."

"Then get ready to shed blood for your answers," Micah stated.

"There's always blood to pay. Bring me the books, Kyle and Micah."

"I will put them out on the table," Angel volunteered.

Argia removed the book from Peter's hand. "I will remember the symbols and the numbers you reveal. I promise."

"I trust you to do what's right, Argia." Peter gave Micah and Kyle a piercing stare. "Even if others don't."

CHAPTER 39

Peter stared at the wall, then down at his sore hand. He felt a bit dizzy from the blood he gave up to get the numbers revealed on those books so they could place them in the correct order on the wall. Each book locked into its own indented niche in the rock.

"The puzzle is finished. Now what?" Micah asked.

Peter didn't have an answer. Each time he uncovered the location of a stronghold, there was a different scenario. So he stared at each book, each number, and each symbol. Then he lifted his sore hand and noticed the brand had sunk back within his skin. "Can ya'll leave me alone?" He'd usually found the stronghold locations when he was alone. Maybe that was it.

"Peter." Angel touched his arm. "You don't look well. I think you gave up too much blood too fast. We can do it in the morning."

He couldn't explain it, but something in him at that moment wanted them all gone. Maybe being a bit dizzy would help in uncovering the answers. He fought against his desire to yell at them to leave. Even Angel's hand on his arm irritated him.

Pulling in a deep calming breath, he flexed his branded hand. "Please, leave, and close the door."

Peter didn't know if she nodded in acknowledgement; he never let his eyes leave the wall of books facing him. The heavy creaking and grinding of rock behind him alerted him to their departure. He was relieved.

"Luke 23." Peter tried to compel his angelic ancestor to speak. "Tell me what to do. Should I do this? If I have a chance of winning this thing, let me know what to do."

Peter felt nothing. Heard nothing. Saw nothing, even though he stared at that wall and each book until head hurt.

He released the breath he'd been holding.

"Typical, you never answer when I ask you to save my ass."

Peter walked backwards, not blinking or thinking until his back hit the wall. Through the blur in his vision, the jeweled fronts of the books lit up—not the complete emblems, but parts, here or there. It formed a symbol of a circle and within the circle, only one book's emblem was fully lit.

Peter's palm burned; he lifted it, daring himself not to blink, and faced it toward him, and the symbol on the book and his palm were identical.

Peter rushed forward. He pushed the large bench next to the wall. Then climbed on it. Jumping up several times, he was finally able to wedge the book out of its alcove. His palm was burning now. Literally on fire. On removing the book, the emblems on the books all lit up, flashing colors within the jewels flooded the walls, and in an instant stopped. It reminding him of club lights as the room came to life.

The breath he'd been holding escaped his mouth in a succession of coughs. He blinked at the map on the walls of the library that weren't filled with books. It was beautiful. Almost 3D in appearance.

"Unbelievable." He hopped from the bench to the table and sat on it, then laid down with his hands behind his head, committing every turn, curve, and warning to memory, until everything went dark.

CHAPTER 40

Peter was awakened by rough shaking. The lights from the jeweled books were gone, and the book he held was back in place. He didn't remember putting it up on the wall. He moved his head back and forth to oust the fogginess. Then closed his eyes tightly again.

"Wake up, you nut!" Kyle yelled at him.

Peter peeked through his eyelids just as Kyle was pulling his hand back to land a big slap to his face. He grabbed Kyle's wrist. "You are one sick pleasure-seeking bastard."

Kyle smiled. "You know me too well. I wanted to land that slap, too. Would take the edge off me."

"You don't get to use me as your punching bag because you can't beat up Micah and look like a dumb-ass to Argia."

"She knows I'm a meathead and loves me."

Peter lifted his eyebrow. "How do you know?"

Kyle smiled. "She kissed me."

Peter slid off the table, stretched his arms above his head, and flexed his hands. "When?"

"This morning when I asked her to walk with me to check on you."

"Where was she sleeping?"

"With Angel. Before you crashed here, she slept here. Alone."

"Micah didn't try to stay with her before? He knows how to decipher these books as well as she does."

"He tried, and she begged him to leave. He even told her he would sleep outside the door to make sure she was okay. I wanted to choke him when I heard him trying to convince her to let him."

"You were just mad that you didn't consider offering that first."

"Maybe, but I'm not that kind of guy, you know."

Peter chuckled. "No, you never were the type to be a gentlemen or to put Argia in a place where you felt you had to protect her at all costs."

"Who the hell's side are you on?" He pushed Peter's chest. "I do those things."

"Sometimes, like an afterthought, or like you are figuring it out as you go." Peter placed a hand on Kyle's shoulder. "I know that's not the place you came from. I understand your story and having to put yourself first. Getting used to caring about someone keeps you guessing."

"Maybe, but it's exciting, too. Well, being with Argia is like trying to hold a frog in your hand. Just when I think I got her figured out, she always surprises me by jumping off in another direction. Most of the time, it was good surprises." He winked at Peter. "Real good."

"Stop. I'm getting uncomfortable images in my mind with you winking at me."

"Sorry you're not getting none. I am feeling your pain since the dude arrived." Kyle scratched the top of his head. "By the way, how are things with you and Angel?"

"Man, it's getting better I think." Peter crossed his arms.

"How?"

"I don't want to talk about it."

"Not working with me." Kyle pointed at Peter. "I spilled, you told me I suck; you get to spill to make me feel like I'm not the only one trying to figure out the female psyche."

Peter frowned at Kyle's logic. "She can't get over what happened to her when she was captured. She'd opened up to me these last few days. I didn't notice until we were at the Sanctuary with Micah that Angel's been repressing memories. I wracked my brain trying to get her to relax so we could..."

"Take things to the next physical level?" Kyle wiggled his eyebrows.

"Your mind is always in the gutter, man."

"Don't act like yours don't go there." Kyle put his hands in his jeans pocket. "Now finish."

"I don't just want to have sex with her. I want Angel to be my wife one day. When I'm over this and finish college and can take care of her. But sex is important to me. I couldn't live with her for the rest of my life and not be with her in that way. It's hard now, it would be hell then."

"So what are you going to do?"

"I am being patient with her. Trying to get her used to the intimacy and to telling me everything that she's been hiding." Peter rubbed his hand down his face. "She even offered herself to me a few times, and I wouldn't go through with it."

"Why the heck not? I would've given her what she wanted." Kyle smiled.

Peter shook his head. "Her mouth was saying it, but the fear in her eyes stopped me cold. I never want her to look at me like that. And she was trembling as soon as she did it. I felt like I'd be raping her. I don't want to do it that bad. I want her to want to."

"I don't know what to tell you to do. I suck at being sensitive. I just hope we all make it with our relationships intact after this."

Peter shrugged. "To be honest, I don't know how things will end with Angel and me. I'm hopeful. It's just that sometimes, she acts like she is fine. Then some situation makes her regress to the day we found her tied to that table in Gavin's basement."

"Remember you told me to take this life one day at a time?"

"Yeah, and what about it? The advice sounds good, but it feels like a crap shoot."

"I know, but it's doable. If you just focus on the small wins."

"Right." Peter smacked his teeth. "Great way to screw someone's day by waking them and throwing garbage in their face."

"Well, I aim to please." Kyle tapped Peter with his fist. "So did you figure out where we have to go? This hideout diet is killing me."

"I know where it is. We should pack and get out of here."

"Do you know how?"

"Yep, it will be easy. There's a shaft that puts us on a main highway. After that, we'll have to figure out how to get mobile."

"Great, every time I try to leave my life of crime behind, you lead me astray. I'll get us a ride."

"I know, man." Peter elbowed Kyle. "You have a talent."

"You don't know the half of them."

"Got more?" Peter walked out the door of the study. He turned around and placed his hand to a protruding rock on the wall that framed the entrance. Then he pivoted around to catch up with Kyle who was still walking. "What other talents you got?"

"Chemistry whiz. I can make a poison that will put everyone to sleep at the Steele mansion while we break in."

Peter frowned. "What about getting the captives out?"

"Not a problem, I'll give the rescue crew an antidote to make the captives inhale. I dabbled a bit with the stuff before I went on the run."

Peter rubbed his neck. "Why would you do that?"

"Uh, I told you the type of school I went to."

"Yeah, but you make it sound like you had a plan to put all them to sleep."

"No, I had a stash of the chemicals to make that gas if they tried to take me to the cellar in that school and do to me what they did to the other dealers who disappeared."

"Oh, couldn't you just use a Taser? Pocket knife?"

"No, they had metal detectors and police security at the school. All of them, I think, were working for the evil side."

"So you went home and played alchemist to create a sleeping gas for your escape. A bit overboard. But whatever floats."

"Eh, well, I liked mixing stuff. I made use of several of my concoctions while on the run. No gun, no blood, no mess. And my attackers probably lived through it."

"You talk like you aren't sure."

"I didn't hang around to find out. I dropped my powders or stuck them with the stuff, and when they hit the ground, I ran."

"Kyle, you scare me."

Kyle winked. "I know."

CHAPTER 41

Gavin paced the conference room on his estate grounds. The key members of the Extraho of Obscurum watched him in frightened silence. All of them had seen the bite of his true nature and the demon Balaal's power.

They were uneasy; he liked them that way. But his brother was his most irritating problem. Although Lucien had excelled in most areas of Gavin's demands, the taste of fear Gavin observed from his brother was altered. Now, Lucien's gaze was obedient with a hidden layer of defiance.

"We are meeting today to finalize some loose ends that have held us in limbo regarding the use of the Transfero of Lux Lucis. Now, like never before, we have to make sure every piece of this puzzle is in place."

Lucien leaned back in his chair. Gavin studied his brother, from his slightly curled blond hair to his dark blue eyes. Nothing seemed out of place as Lucien stared back at him unwavering.

"Gavin, why the urgency?"

Gavin narrowed his gaze, fighting off the growing power of his imprisoned demonic master. Leaning forward, he wrapped his fingers around the edges of the table to brace himself against the inner ripping of his soul. Balaal was angry and aware of his effects on Gavin, but Gavin's will in this wouldn't falter. He would be the one to storm the gates of the heavenly realm with the bodies of the humans favored by the creator there.

"Gavin?" Mara started to stand.

Gavin lifted his hand to stay her. His fingertips elongated a bit as his exertion weakened. "The longer we delay, the weaker my demon head gets. There is a measure of strength required by my combined soul and it. The psychics we've gathered aren't strong enough. We need one younger, more pliable of a sacrifice."

"I will get that for you, brother. There are some special cases at the various hospitals and drug rehabilitation programs our organization owns around town. We've been especially fruitful in the suburbs lately...since we've been bribing the physicians there to prescribe more opiates to their patients. Both young and old." Lucien tapped his pen on the table.

"That will help. There is one important fact that we've overlooked." His gaze skipped from Lucien to Jack.

Jack squirmed in his chair, his hand nervously rubbed on the back of his neck.

"Jack?"

"Y-yes, sir." Jack visibly forced his hand from his neck back to the table.

Gavin smiled, the acrid taste of Jack's heightened fear filled the air. It was a gift from holding the demon Balaal captive within him, the power to enjoy someone's fear in a palatable way.

"I want you to take over the search for Peter Saints. My demons warned me there is another seal he can open. If he does, there is a high probability that we could be deterred from my goal."

Lucien cleared his throat. "Gavin. I'm fully capable of carrying out the task. The kid is not normal. My men..."

Gavin allowed the change to overcome him. The sweet, torturous knives which sliced the inside of his soul, his body, almost brought him to his knees with its sadistically painful ease. Gavin slivered his tongue against his lips like a snake in pleasure. The tearing of the skin from his face, the burning of the healing of his skin as his and his demon master's bodies fused into one.

Gavin grinned; he was the one in control.

He turned to Lucien. "You, brother, I am trying to figure out if I can still trust." Gavin sniffed the air. "I smell a defiant spirit within you now. It is a strong, sour taste on my tongue. Something I will deal with later."

Lucien went silent.

Jack stood, and on apparently shaking legs, walked around the table to stand in front of Gavin. Never lifting his eyes, he fell to his knees and kissed Gavin's clawed red toe. "Whatever you need me to do, I will make happen, master."

Gavin's lips stretched over his crowded mouth of teeth. "Kill him! He must die before he releases the last seal. Bring-me-his head!"

CHAPTER 42

The others couldn't keep pace with Peter, so he slowed a bit. The images from the sanctuary that mapped out the stronghold and its location drummed in his mind. Mountains— tons of them—clustered together behind the trees that lined the base and surrounded the main highway they trailed.

"We need wheels?" Kyle asked.

"Would be nice." Peter resolved. Not a single car had passed them for hours. His feet hurt, and Angel was avoiding him again.

"There's a car up there just sitting. Maybe I can get it moving."

"Yeah, right. It's on the side of the road for a reason."

"Most of the time, people don't know how to fix their cars. If it's a woman or teenager, they usually just leave it."

"Fine, let's check it out." Peter signaled to the others not to follow, and they ran the quarter mile to the vehicle on the shoulder of the road.

Peter walked around the car. It was rusted in spots. The passenger door was bent. The tires looked good, not new, but in decent shape.

Kyle opened the door. "Old accident. The person who left it

213

figured no one would want to mess with it." He popped the hood. "Believable I guess, but I bet the piece of junk doesn't run." Kyle rummaged around with his hand under the passenger seat while Peter watched him from the partially rolled down window.

"Jackpot!" Kyle pulled out a screwdriver then slid across the seat to unlock the driver's door by pulling the handle.

"Okay, what are you going to do with those?"

"I'll figure it out."

Peter glanced to the backseat and realized it was damaged badly. The sharp springs in the seat protruded in the middle, making it a hard ride for anyone who sat in the middle. That meant they only had four seats for five people.

"You got this?" Peter asked.

Kyle smiled; for a moment Peter felt like everything would be right with them. Micah came up behind him.

"Is the car able to start?" Micah asked.

Kyle's irritation was obvious, his eyes skidding up and behind Peter to land on Micah. He mumbled, "Open the hood."

Peter leaned on the driver's door. He wanted them to deal with each other. He pointed to the driver's seat. "Get in, see if you can start the car."

Widening the door, Peter pointed to the screwdriver. "You can use that to start it. Have you done it before?"

"Yeah, not a problem." Micah ducked under the steering column. There were several clicks, but the engine didn't start.

"Kyle, we can't turn it over." Peter called to Kyle who seemed distracted under the hood.

"Starter probably," Kyle said.

"Can you fix it?" Peter asked.

"Maybe, I'm going to tap it with the hammer."

Peter turned to Micah. "When I give you the signal, try and start it."

Kyle got under the car and tapped then signaled to Micah.

"Nothing," Peter said. "Try it again."

They tried it four times. Finally it started.

"Yes!" Micah pumped his fist.

The girls jumped up and down at the side of the car.

"Squeeze in, someone will have to sit on a lap."

Micah got out of the front seat. "Argia can sit on mine."

Kyle slammed the hood. "Hell if she will."

"Okay, back off. Both of you. Angel?" Peter hoped she could help.

"She can sit on my lap." Angel opened the back door, and slid in the middle.

Peter frowned at Kyle, then Micah. "Really? I got to do this with y'all? Kyle, up front with me."

Peter got into the driver's seat, ignoring Kyle's burning eyes on the side of his head.

They drove in silence for about an hour. Smoke started coming from under the hood, seeping into the car. Peter rolled down his window, coughing and holding his forearm over his nose.

He gripped the steering wheel and rocked back and forth willing the car to keep going until they got off the highway exit. He maneuvered into a spot at a gas station in the middle of various rest stop amenities and buildings.

"We'll have to switch cars here." Peter searched the truck stop. There was a car dealership and garage on the side.

"I'll find us something." Kyle snatched the screwdriver from Peter. "Meet me at the rear of this place in about thirty."

Micah got out of the car as Peter opened the door.

"Look, I know Kyle is ticked, but I'm not backing down. We'll get to that place you are taking us. I'll go all the way if that's where Argia is going. But I'm not leaving without her."

"I hear you, Micah, but can you stop pushing Kyle's buttons? We are trying to stay alive here, and I need all of y'all to do that."

"Got it. But I lost touch with her two years ago when we got separated. You've got to understand why I can't back down on this."

"I understand, but a lot happened in the two years since then. The year and a half she's been with us has been a stormfest for all of us. You weren't here, but Kyle, my best friend, was. I'm not picking sides in this. I like you as a person, but we don't have the history Kyle and I do."

Micah stared at Peter as though considering what was said. "Empty words about taking sides. You just contradicted your ability to be fair." Micah squared his shoulders. "I'm going with the girls to get some food."

Peter nodded. "Meet us in the back; I'm going to help Kyle." There was nothing left to be said.

CHAPTER 43

L
ucien was nervous. Jack could mess up the plan. He paced
in front of the car he'd parked in their secret meeting place
in the cover of the woods off the main road. His men had reported
a sighting of Peter Saints and the other kids with him. There was
no way Lucien could risk them getting caught.

Jack's car pulled up next to Lucien's. Lucien moved his features
into the usual casual and comfortable expression he put forth. *Best
to act the fool than to play the hand.*

Lucien opened Jack's door. "Glad you could make it."

Jack appeared visibly shaken. "Barely got out of there without
that witch on my tail. This is getting more dangerous."

"We've always thrived on danger, right Jack?" Lucien leaned
against the car.

"What's the plan? I promised your brother I would send my
men after that kid. Gavin is on to you. He is the one who personally gave me their location. Apparently they were spotted by
several people—or things—in your brother's personal employ."

Lucien stifled the shiver that traveled up his spine. "My

brother controls demons. They persuade and manipulate people. It must be how he can track them."

"Whatever his methods, how do we know he isn't tracking you? Me?" Jack asked. His eyebrows rose as his lip quivered slightly.

"He can't. I have a man working with me that gave me a covering chant. When you are with me, you are invisible to his demons."

Jack crossed his arms and teased his chin with his finger. "Are you sure the man can be trusted?"

Lucien grinned. "Definitely." He wasn't giving up his contact with the enemy. Cadman served him well. He trusted the man with his life. Besides, Cadman had powerful allies. The Decretum Venia had someone who wanted the same thing he did. The man had miraculously survived an attack by his brother, and seemed angrier for it. Just the type of ally he needed.

"I don't know. My name is going down with yours in this. My demon master has gone silent in my head. I don't even know if he still has the strength to do this."

Lucien narrowed his eyes and frowned at Jack. "If you want me to ensure your wife, concubines, and your remaining children live after the ceremony, you will follow through on your part of this plan."

Jack sighed. "Damned if I do, and damned if I don't."

"Being damned for killing the abomination that is my brother, and gaining the rightful power of your demon, is what you threatened me with when we first went into this bloody deal together."

"I know, but now, after what I know Gavin is capable of, I fear that my time in the realm of hell will be worse than I had imagined. We'd been fed lies by our ancestors and the demons that raped them."

"You got what you wanted, Jack. Power. Here and now, you are the third most powerful and rich man the Extraho of Obscurum has to offer. Second only to my brother and me."

"Yes, well, I am starting to feel it's not worth it."

"Not a decision we can make this late in this game. Now. Are you going to let the kids go or what?"

"I have to make it appear like we will take them."

"Fine. Let your men do their best, and I will provide the kids a diversion. We can't let Gavin stop what they started. I don't believe he knows what his demon wants of him. To get that Transfero of Lux Lucis to work, those kids have to finish uncovering the secrets," Lucien lied. It would likely be the last chance they all had to stop his power-hungry hybrid demon of a brother from ending the world as they knew it.

"I hope your diversion is good, because my men have orders to kill and decapitate, bringing each captive's head to your brother."

Lucien smirked, euphoria flooding his blood. One thing he knew how to do was kill or be killed. Jack just didn't realize all his men were about to be sacrificed.

"I will cover it." With that, Lucien pivoted away from Jack and got into his car.

CHAPTER 44

Peter trailed Kyle, searching out cars that they could use to keep moving. They weren't far from the Stronghold, and Peter pondered on how close the secret hideouts of the Decretum Venia were compared to their enemies. Either they'd been watching or spying on the enemy, or The Extraho of Obscurum was spying on them.

"Over here; this one is even open." Kyle waved at Peter.

Sirens went off around them. It was hard to tell if they were police or ambulance.

Noise of people running and yelling drew Peter's attention. Tingling on the back of his neck alerted him that something was off. "Kyle! Hurry up and get the car started." Peter ran towards Kyle and jumped over the hood, sliding off the car in front of him.

Peter opened the passenger door, but stood behind it while his gaze frantically searched for the others.

Men, dressed in various outfits, stood above the surrounding customers. They were huge, muscle-bound men who fought their way through the crunch of people while pointing at Peter.

Peter's fingers tightened on the window. "Weapon. I need a weapon."

The car started. "Got one. A damn car will run them over."

Peter slid into the passenger seat and closed the door. "They see us. We have to get the others."

Kyle maneuvered out of the parking space. The men halted in place, aimed, and shot at the car.

"Hold on! Dodging bullets here." Kyle laughed. "My kind of diversion."

Peter braced himself as Kyle swerved the car to and fro. Several bullets connected; most missed.

Pointing, Peter yelled, "Over there! They are surrounded."

Micah was fighting off men approaching them with a metal pipe. Angel swung a gas hose at them and then squeezed it, soaking them men with gas.

"I'm on it. Honking the horn at them to get their attention."

"There's gas everywhere, they've got six or seven guys surrounding them."

"Add the two cars behind me now."

One by one, each of the guys surrounding Micah and the girls heads jerked to the side before blood gushed out from their necks and chest.

"What the hell happened? Someone's shooting them." Kyle sped up, almost hitting a few of the scattering people rushing to their cars.

"Someone's killing them." Peter pounded the dashboard. "Hurry up!"

"Risking bad guys behind us catching our asses now!" Kyle skidded and fishtailed beside Micah and the girls.

Peter opened his door. "Get in!"

Micah, Angel, and Argia scrambled into the backseat with

barely enough time to close the door before Kyle hit the accelerator.

"More cars close behind us." Kyle pushed the car; shots were fired.

Pellets of fire sprang up behind the car. One bullet pierced the back window and went out the front as Kyle dodged their pursuers' shots.

Boom!

The gas station exploded as if someone had pointed a bomb at it. Smoke and fire enveloped the road and one of the cars pursuing them.

"Still got one riding us," Peter called. "Too far for him to shoot."

"Hitting the highway, should get us some distance," Kyle said.

"I've still got my gun," Micah said.

"How did you hold on to it all this time?" Peter asked.

"I have my methods, I strap them to me. After all the dirt I've been through, no way am I going anywhere without a gun on reserve." Micah leaned up next to Peter. "Want me to use it? It'll give us some space."

Peter held on as Kyle pushed the car to over ninety miles an hour while he zigzagged through cars, vans, and trucks.

"Yeah, we can't have them follow us." He spied a car through the rearview mirror.

"Lucky I'm a good shot. Slow down a bit so I can blow one of their tires," Micah requested.

Argia climbed over Micah's lap to change places. Kyle jerked the car, causing Argia to slam into Micah's chest.

"Dumb move, Kyle, eyes on the road. I'm trying to live here." Peter braced himself.

Micah cut a hard glare at Kyle and rolled down the window.

"On my signal, slam the brakes," Micah said.

Peter twisted to follow the timing. "Wait until we get clear of most of the cars."

"Not doing that. We need them to block us."

Peter pointed. "Got that, okay, the car ahead has their signal on, they want to change lanes away from us."

"Do it now, dude!" Kyle yelled.

Micah shot, missed, then shot two more times, finally landing one on the wheel of the gaining car.

"Go!" Peter called.

Kyle accelerated and they slid between the two cars ahead just before the one attempted its lane change.

The pursuers car slammed into the one changing lanes and several cars crashed in behind them.

Peter's heart pounded in his chest. "That was close."

"Is it me, or did it seem like we had a little help?" Angel asked.

"Don't care where it came from; all I know is we needed it." Peter relaxed back in his seat. "Almost there."

Kyle drove in silence, never stopping from pounding the accelerator at top speed.

All Peter could think about was how this Stronghold would unleash evil and answers; he prayed it would save them.

CHAPTER 45

"Kyle, you can slow down now. We don't need to get stopped by the cops." Peter bent to see the light from the yellow moon. No one was on this side road. He was glad about that. He didn't care that they'd driven until it was dark. Peter was just glad the car had a full tank and only had to be filled once since they left the scene of the near catastrophe. Getting caught would've meant death, and that couldn't happen on Gavin Steele's terms. If Peter was going to die, he would do it trying to repair the mess he'd made.

"I want to hurry up and get us to this damn place so I can switch places with you and go in the backseat."

"You had the chance to do that when we stopped to siphon gas out of the car on the side of the road."

"Negative, butt wipe in the back didn't get out to use the bathroom like everyone else."

Peter peeped behind him to Argia, asleep, her head rested on Micah's chest while his body was adjusted to accommodate her in his sleep. Angel's head was resting on Argia's shoulder.

Watching Angel felt like a punch in Peter's heart. Even though the nights they spent in the sanctuary made them closer, Angel was still pondering over what they shared. She'd become more quiet about her doubts, but her body didn't lie. Her muscles were still rigid against him, even when she slept. He'd stayed awake hours, it seemed, just watching and waiting for a sign she could relax, but those moments were so brief, he started thinking he was imagining it.

"Don't give up, Kyle. Your girl is still conflicted." Peter offered Kyle hope with the possibility that his heart would listen. Reality was apparent, it felt like his was breaking all over again like it did when she'd been taken from him. He refused to wallow in that dark place; if this didn't work out with Angel, he doubted he could ever fall in love again. At least Argia had been able to love someone despite what she'd endured. Her strength and hunger for any bit of affection made her fight her way into a friendship with them and a relationship with Kyle. He felt bad for his friend.

"Easy for you to say; Angel came back to you."

"We aren't done with our issues yet. Didn't you notice she is distancing from me now, even after all we shared with each other at the last Sanctuary?"

Kyle shrugged. "I didn't pay much attention to it. I was watching after Argia since I thought bringing her with us was bad luck."

"I'm glad you saw she wasn't."

"I guess. I just... I could punch something." Kyle turned his head and scowled at Micah. "Or someone."

"Keep it together, man. She hasn't chosen yet."

Kyle shook his head. "I might have to choose for her. I can't take this aching wound crap. I want to get the knife in my heart in with one jab, then be over it. This is a killer and the misery I'm feeling won't let me think straight."

"Been there. You'll survive, even if she doesn't stay with you."

"Have you loved anyone else besides Angel?"

"I thought so. But it wasn't real. She was shallow. Angel and I connected on a deeper level."

"Well, I never did allow myself to fall in love. My parents' relationship was abusive, and I didn't want anyone to have the power to hurt me or make me beg for their love."

"But—"

"No buts, I didn't want to fall in love with Argia. I fought it. I fought her. I treated her like dirt in the beginning because some part of me wanted to just take care of her. I regret it now. The guy back there—he didn't do that to her."

"It doesn't matter, she knows you well enough to understand where you were coming from."

"That doesn't make it right, does it? It's not going to make her think about me the way she does Micah. The guy risked his life to save her from the get-go. I put her through hell and made her beg me to kiss her." Kyle wiped a hand down his face. "I'm shit, and I feel like it. I shouldn't even be with you."

Peter touched Kyle's shoulder. "You belong here. Every one of us came together for a reason. Something in our makeup brought us together. You belong here."

"It's not easy when I see what you and the others can do, but I can do none of it. I can't make weapons appear out of the air."

"You have other skills that saved us all. Stop beating yourself before you find out if you won her over."

Kyle glanced back at Micah. "Then why does my heart feel like I've already lost?"

Peter said nothing. He'd felt that frustration with Angel sporadically through their relationship. But he couldn't let her go. No one else made him feel worthy of her love. Angel wasn't pushing Peter away because of what he did to her. She was pushing him away because of what she thought she was doing to him.

That made him keep his mouth shut, because as much as he wanted to believe Kyle was the better man for Argia, the obvious truth was, Kyle wasn't.

CHAPTER 46

The stronghold.

Peter felt tingling all over. It was close. Real close. They'd parked the car on the edge of the side road. Kyle made sure to hide it under the cover of trees.

Peter stood in front of the border surrounding the overgrown driveway. What was once a gravel road to a secluded piece of land was overgrown by grass, weeds, and thick trees intertwined with thorny wild roses and wildflowers. The moon was bright and seemed to bounce through the clouds, casting a glow on the forest of branches.

"Now what?" Kyle asked.

"Thinking about it," Peter's mind seemed blocked, and he didn't remember the part of his dream that guided him through unlocking the stronghold.

"You know these things always have some vicious surprise waiting for us," Kyle whispered.

"Yep, I know." Peter released the breath he'd been holding.

"What is he talking about exactly?" Micah asked.

"The fact that a stronghold was a highly protected location for warrior angels of the Decretum Venia. They set traps to keep humans that were working for the demons out of these places. Even though the location is protected from demon invasion, they sent their humans to kill the angels during the thousand year war."

"Traps to kill us?" Micah folded his arms looking at the copse of intertwined trees. "This place doesn't seem to have much going for it. I don't see anything that makes it appear to be a fortress of war." Micah leaned in, moving some of the branches out of the way. "No way can we get through there to see anything."

"Isn't that the set-up? Look around for a small opening." Peter stepped back and searched the huge mass connecting the thorny trees.

"Who'd plant acres of honey locust and thorn trees with rose bushes?" Micah asked. "Whoever it was wanted to keep us out."

Peter answered, "That's their plan, but with these places, if you know what you are doing, you can unlock them." Peter pivoted; he grasped Angel's hand. "Walk with me?"

"Okay." Angel tightened her fingers around Peter's. "Are we really going to do this?"

"Have to. We made it this far and it's obvious now that Gavin doesn't want me to open it. The bastard must be scared of something we'll find out."

"I don't know; he's been playing with us and manipulating this from the beginning. Do you want to trust that?"

"I have to. We've got no other option."

"There are always options, Peter, we just don't want to take the less obvious ones."

Peter ran his gaze upward, following one of the thorn trees, seeking differences between it and others. Although they were different heights, they all appeared the same. Then he considered the bushes at the base of the trees that ran the tangled mass of several yards in front of them.

"Do you see a pattern?"

"To the trees?"

"No, the roses. They seem to be spread an exact distance from each other."

"Yes, they are. That's strange, they are the exact same width and height also." Angel stepped in front of one and studied it. "They even have the same number of flowers on each branch. How is that possible?"

Peter released a sigh. "I have no idea." He brought her hand to his lips and kissed it.

They walked a bit farther. Argia was alone and singing loudly while spinning around with her hands spread wide.

"Why is she doing that?" Peter frowned.

Angel smiled. "I bet she found something."

"Let's see." Peter released Angel's hand and jogged toward Argia. Even though they had some sunlight, the fog cast a dim hue on the land. Peter stood in front of Argia. With a jerk, she stopped spinning, the last note barely out of her lips. "Here is the entrance."

"How do you know?" Peter asked.

Micah and Kyle came up from the other side.

"One rose is pink, not red."

"We are going to need something to cut through this," Micah offered. "I'll check the trunk."

"Yeah, do that." Kyle put his hands in his pockets.

Peter narrowed his gaze at him, and Kyle responded with a shrug.

"I'll pick the rose." Peter hoped that was all he needed to do to release the trap of trees. He stepped forward, and placed his fingers on the rose, allowing a sticky thorn to pierce his skin.

Angel gasped and stepped back from him. "All the roses fell off."

Peter found thousands of rose petals on the ground. "That doesn't help. The barrier is still here, and this pink one didn't fall."

Argia squeezed the same thorn as Peter had. The rose bushes sank into the ground as though they were being pulled under by some unseen force. The thorn-riddled trees remained. They were crowded together in the dim light of day, giving no indication that there was possibly an opening between them.

Micah returned with a tire rod, and an axe. "Looks like the guy who owned the car was some type of mechanic or fireman."

Kyle grabbed Argia's hand and wiped the blood from her fingers.

Peter's breath caught in his lungs when welts formed on Kyle's hand. They thickened turning red to travel up his arms like veins.

"Ahhh!" Kyle doubled over, dropped to the ground, and started convulsing. Argia fell on her knees beside him.

Peter knelt. "I'll hold him."

Kyle's body shook, bent backwards almost to a bow. His eyes rolled around in his head.

"Put something in his mouth so he won't swallow his tongue." Argia's voice was strong and sure.

Micah handed her a flat piece of plastic tag off the axe he was holding.

Peter fought against Kyle's bucking to hold him down. Argia wiggled to straddle Kyle's waist. She placed the plastic piece into his mouth. Micah and Angel stood by in tense silence.

With a few more jerks, Kyle lay still.

A deep grumble came from Micah who stumbled with his mouth open. Argia reared backwards like she was burned. Thick tracks from Kyle's veins in his hands were bright red, crisscrossing on his body like a vine. They pulsed, thickened, then sank back within his skin as if never present.

"What was that?" Peter asked, his gaze passing between Argia and Micah.

Argia shook her head. "I don't know. I, uh, but he…"

"He's different." Micah's stare met Argia's eyes and a silent agreement seemed to pass between them.

"Tell me." Peter's voice was gruff, his fist balled as Kyle mumbled through trembling lips.

"We don't know; I think I can get the answers if I research it," Micah answered.

Peter snorted, disgusted that Micah seemed like he was holding something back. "Argia, I want an answer."

"I don't know either, Peter." She visibly swallowed and even scooted off of Kyle. "I can't say right now." Argia twisted her hands together and rubbed them up and down her arms.

Peter nailed her wandering eyes with his. "What did you do to him?" He leaned in towards her. "What did you do!"

Micah stepped closer. "Watch it, man. He's fine."

Kyle rocked his head back and forth. Then he sat up holding his stomach, and placed a shaking hand to his head. "What the farts happened? Damn, I feel like I'm on fire." He was sweating, his hair plastered to his head. "I'm a…okay." He stumbled while standing, and then staggered a few steps before throwing up.

CHAPTER 47

Peter waited with his hands on his neck while Micah axed through one of the trees. Their trunks were littered with long, ragged thorns, which were in patterns that allowed them to create a virtual fence around the massive forest that seemed to be cloaked by dark trees and brush. It basically went on for miles with a 'keep out' sign posted on the path leading there. The tree limbs were twisted and dark with specks of silver that flashed like metal whenever the moon peeked out from the clouds. Peter frowned and let the dull thud of the pounding axe fade in his mind.

What the hell had happened to Kyle? Peter turned his gaze toward Kyle. He had his arm draped around Argia's shoulder. She was rubbing her hand on his back. Something had changed. Peter could swear Kyle appeared larger, bulkier than his formerly slender physique. It was possible that his eyes could be playing tricks on him, but he doubted it.

Peter walked up behind Angel who was using a tire rod to break some of the branches so Micah could wiggle between them to chop at one of the trees.

"It's about to fall." Micah stopped swiping the axe. "Watch out. The thorns are pre-historic sized."

The tree tilted forward; the crackling sound of splintered wood challenged the sound of crickets that played in the night. Peter put an arm in front of Angel to protect her from the splinters.

Micah slipped and fell forward. "Ahhh!"

Peter reached for him, but Micah had been stabbed by one of the large thorns about six inches in width and several inches in length. His shoulder was bleeding. Peter yanked him back hard with both hands on Micah's shirt; the thorn extracted and fell off the trunk.

"You alright?" Peter helped Micah regain his footing by steadying him at the shoulders.

"I think so. Hurts bad. But I can deal with it." Micah's hand pressed against the bleeding spot on his upper chest.

Crack.

Pop.

"Watch out!" Peter twisted his body around to bow over Angel's.

Tree after tree toppled forward. One by one, several fell to the ground piling on each other to form a pathway. The fallen trunks flickered from the metal pieces littered within them. Those metal shards lit up with a bright orange hue that seemed to spurt fire. The lines of fire laced orange lines through the trees, and with a pop, the trail of fallen trees combusted to ashes.

Peter stood up, pulling Angel into a tight hug to his chest.

Kyle staggered over with Argia supporting him under his arms.

Micah stepped back, shaking his head with one hand on his bloody shirt, and the other on his forehead. "What the hell are we doing?" He wiped his hand down his face.

"Breaking into a stronghold. This one wants blood proof from all of us, I guess." Peter slid his hand down Angel's back and held her hand.

"I don't know, Peter." Angel laced her fingers in his. "This is a bad omen."

Peter had a tingling in the back of his neck and the hairs rose on his arms. They didn't have a choice. It had to be done.

"I don't think this is a good thing." Micah rubbed his shoulder.

"No kidding, Sherlock." Kyle's ragged response was sharp and deep. "What other choice do we have?"

"He's right," Peter added.

Kyle stood up straight. "I'm with Peter on this. The answer we need is in this place."

"He's right, Micah." Argia's soft voice pitched higher with authority. "I've been with them since I left you, and the things we've been able to do together after experiencing the knowledge in the Strongholds has allowed us to freeze Gavin and his demon inside the Wall of Ash."

"You haven't seen the thing." Peter walked over to Micah and placed a hand on his shoulder. "The Wall of Ash will make it difficult to get to the machine Gavin is building. He summoned the portal around the device he is using to follow the steps of Jakaan, the human that ascended to the heavens. We are his Trojan horse."

Micah shook his head. "He's crazy. How can anyone do that?"

"Gavin will figure out how."

"I didn't sign up for this. The guy who helped me out didn't say I'd be paying with our lives," Micah growled.

"Who helped you?" Kyle asked. His arm tightened on Argia's shoulder as he limped closer.

"An important man."

"Pastor Finn." Peter's heart pounded in his chest. "I know there is more to his involvement with Lucien's right hand man. We will have backup if we see this through. From the inside out I'm sure of it." Peter scratched his head.

"Fine." Micah studied Argia. "We may have done something that could hurt or expose us. Maybe there is a way we can fix it."

Peter frowned at the exchange between Micah and Argia. "Is there something going on we need to know about?"

"Nothing." Micah shrugged and started walking down the path of ashes, the remaining tall thorn trees lining his way.

Peter squeezed Angel's hand, tugging against her planted stand until she gave in and followed. Something had happened between Argia, Kyle, and Micah. It was a déjà vu flash in time to the moment Hanna traced her blood on Peter's palm. From that moment on, Peter hadn't been the same. It was if Hanna's Seer's blood activated a deeply held secret in his own DNA that gave him an awareness of secrets he was never supposed to have known.

Did Gavin's demons, or Lucien, manipulate Argia to do the same? Peter wondered as Argia and Kyle followed him. The fact that Lucien allowed Argia to escape, and since then, they'd met Micah, who also escaped, seemed off. Lucien shouldn't be that careless—or was it another set-up by Gavin to get them to open the last scroll revealing the ending to the Thousand Year War that the Creator of All erased from human history?

They walked the path in silence, the putrid odor of smoke from the simmering trees alongside their path filling Peter's nose.

Behind them, there was a thunder of branches breaking. He turned around and the standing trees moved, grew their branches then shifted to recover the path.

There was no turning back.

CHAPTER 48

The land beyond the trees that circled the clearing was rock-covered and dry. A huge abandoned mansion appeared ahead. It seemed to be encased in metal as if someone built the structure then poured metal on it from above. It was in the distance and Peter wondered what was waiting for them.

The mansion had indentations of where elaborately designed windows would be. Several doors were indented at the base of metal-encased stairs with spiked handle rails that made it impossible for someone to hold them for balance.

Several statues framed the corners of the mansion. Huge muscled warriors with swords in several positions of rest. Some had shields, and others were covered in strange armor.

"I can help Kyle," Peter offered and went to place an arm under Kyle's.

Kyle narrowed his eyes at Peter. "Argia's got me."

Peter smirked. "I bet." He slowed his pace to follow the group. Angel was talking to Micah, walking a bit ahead of him and pointing at bats soaring above.

Argia and Kyle stumbled in front of him. Peter snatched Kyle's arm and braced him against his side.

"Argia, I've got him." Peter waited while a waterfall of expressions flash on her face.

Argia bit her lip and slid from under Kyle. "Thank you." Then, she rushed ahead, walking behind Micah.

"You suck," Kyle grumbled.

"You're stupid. She couldn't help you stay steady for long."

"She's stronger than she looks, and it got me close to her." Kyle slumped a bit against Peter.

"Seems you were weaker than you let on." Peter adjusted Kyle and took more of his weight. "You should've had me or Micah help."

"I don't want his or yours. I just wanted hers. I don't know how much longer I'll have her...you know." Kyle's voice softened.

Peter hated to admit it to Kyle, but he felt the same. Argia was fighting it, but Micah was fighting the hardest.

"Going silent on me? No words of encouragement or advice?" Kyle squeezed his arm around Peter's neck.

"I got nothing except to say, let's just live through this. One thing at a time right?" At least that was Peter's hope.

"See, I knew you had something to say."

"I try."

"How much further?"

"Far." Peter adjusted Kyle weight again. "How are you feeling?"

"Like crap-shit. My head is beaten, my veins feel like they are on fire, my joints ache and I am seeing double."

"We'll help you." Peter hoped.

"Like how? I don't feel like I can make it out of this place with you. I just keep feeling worse and worse each minute. I'm fighting this, but I really just want to go somewhere and sleep forever."

"You don't feel stronger?" Peter wanted to know if he'd changed like they did.

Kyle laughed. "If you consider a strong urge to pee and throw up a force of strength."

"Not at all." Peter studied Kyle and noticed that although the red veined marks had dissipated, his hand still had the marks.

"Wait, got to scratch." Kyle adjusted himself and removed his arm from Peter's.

Peter frowned; the marks on Kyle's hand and wrist were symbolic. It wasn't just a mask of vein-like scars; it was a symbol. A marking he'd seen when he was at the last Sanctuary.

Peter snatched Kyle's wrist, twisting it up so he could see it close-up.

"Watch it! Are you trying to knock me down?"

"This, on your hand." Peter pointed and moved so Kyle could place a steadying hand on his shoulder. "I knew it. I've seen this symbol before."

"Doesn't look like a symbol to me." Kyle concentrated on it, then his head reared back in shock. "It moved."

Peter saw it. "It's raising up, like the brand on my hand."

"What the..."

"Was your hand cut when you held Argia's bloody hand?"

"Not at first, then I scratched it in the thorns on the rose bush." Kyle swallowed and his eyes met Peter's.

"Hanna. Argia is like Hanna, the girl who gave me my brand. Her blood mixed with mine on my hand. Then she drew a symbol on me." Peter remembered it like it was yesterday.

"Argia didn't draw on me."

"Maybe she didn't have to. All of us are different. With each book I open, we get more powerful in our understanding of what our angelic ancestor knew. It seems like a fogged dream that we act on without realizing it."

"I don't get it."

"Argia probably didn't have to mark you to 'activate' your engineered angelic DNA. It's like yours was different than ours. Yours was hidden in two layers. Micah and Argia must have known they revealed some secret in you that neither was aware of. That's why they both seemed guilty after that happened." Peter dragged a hand through his hair. "I hope we didn't unleash something we weren't supposed to."

"Trust me, the way I'm feeling, like a bird under the wheel of a truck, nothing is unleashed in me."

Peter smiled. "I hope not."

"C'mon, let's catch up to the others." Kyle reached around Peter's shoulder.

They'd just started walking at a fast pace when Angel screamed.

"Go to her! I'll use the rest of my energy to catch up. Send that bastard Micah back here to get me."

Peter nodded and steadied Kyle before running towards Angel. Micah and Argia were a distance from her and were stumbling backwards.

Peter didn't stop, but picked up full speed to push past them.

"Peter no!" Argia called.

Peter didn't stop; his heart was racing.

Then he staggered to a stop. Scorpions all different colors were climbing up Angel's legs, and racing towards her thighs.

Peter ran towards her and felt crunching and stabs to his feet. All around here were scorpions, large, small, multi colored.

"Thousands of them! Coming from under the building." Peter wanted to tell them to go back, but they couldn't. The scorpions were climbing his legs. He swatted them away from Angel's waist. Her hand and his worked feverishly to stop the things, but others just climbed on top of them and seemed to multiply.

"Stinging! Oh!" Angel cried, tears in her eyes, and a frown on her face as she smacked one then another.

Peter felt the venomous attack of several of the beasts but ignored the burning pain as he swatted as many as he could from Angel. Screams and curses sounded behind him. Argia and the others must be fighting off attacks also.

Streams of them piled on Angel, climbing on top of each other, making it hard for him to remove them. The ones on him were intertwined, moving up his chest like a heavy weight of armor.

"Kick hard!" Peter shook Angel, hoping to jar some of them off her.

"Oh! I..It's not working." Angel twisted, hopped a bit, waved her arms; the things wouldn't fall.

Another scream behind him, he could swear that was Kyle yelling louder than Argia.

The itchy pincers on the scorpions were digging into Peter's neck. Then a stab, so painful, he stumbled, falling to his knees. "Ow!"

"Ah!" Angel yelled then stumbled and fell to the ground, her body crushing the rocky ground of beasties.

Peter scrambled toward her even as his legs, and arms grew numb, and the world went black.

CHAPTER 49

He ached everywhere. Peter groaned and struggled to sit up. He blinked at the high moon. They'd been out for hours. Jumping to stand, filled with a new burst of energy, Peter searched for Angel who was sitting.

His eyes narrowed. "Did you get taller?" and thicker, he wanted to say, but he didn't want her to get ticked at him for asking. He held out his hand for her.

"I feel like it, but I'll never be a giant like you." Angel grasped his hand and pulled herself up.

Peter widened his eyes as Kyle jogged over to them.

"About time you woke up." Kyle grinned at him. "Who'd thought hundreds of scorpion stings would make me feel better."

Peter rubbed his chin, the fine hairs of the beginnings of a beard he wished to have one day teased his fingers. Micah and Argia joined them with a new bounce to their step and a thicker, harsher appearance.

"I think being attacked is part of the process at the Sanctuaries and Strongholds."

Argia nodded. "Yes, it's part of the lock mechanism. Not only unlocking the Stronghold, but something within us. I studied it in the last Sanctuary. Each time we encounter a creature or are bitten, they somehow pass that genetic code to the main security instrument and secrete another change in us. I guess it's why we are a bit different than the other kids in the Sanctuaries guarded by the Elders. The kids aren't used to unlocking the barriers; the adults do it."

"The Sanctuaries I uncovered that had the clues to the Stronghold were uninhibited. I don't think the Elders know where these are."

"That's best, considering the corruption we know is part of the Decretum Venia," Kyle added. "The bastard we saw murder the Elder at the last orphanage was a mad man."

"Let's go. The mansion is ahead. We need to search for an entrance. Daylight is here, so it should be easier." Peter grasped Angel's hand and kissed it.

Angel smiled at him, and walked alongside him. "I was so scared."

"So was I, the scorpions wouldn't move no matter how I tried to get them off you."

"I know." Angel's eyes studied him. "You sacrificed yourself for me."

"I tried, and failed. Like usual, I guess." Peter raked his hands through his hair as he focused on the huge structure ahead. A mansion that went on forever. Encased in a silver shell that made you believe something in there was either being protected, or was keeping anyone out.

"Failing is not trying, right?" Angel squeezed his hand. "I promise your love won't be wasted on me. I am trying to get my thoughts and mind to focus on good instead of bad." Tears slipped from her eyes.

Peter pivoted around to hug her to his chest, he gently kissed her forehead. "You've done that and more. You are working on this with me. I am happy that you haven't given up on me or yourself. We had a rough time, but we will survive this." He tilted her chin with is finger and kissed her.

"Really! Now? Let's get in this monstrosity first." Kyle slapped Peter on the back of the neck. "If I'm not getting none, you're not going to either."

"Kyle, you suck." Peter jabbed Kyle's arm with his.

"Flattery will get you nowhere, now. I'm saying, we just walk up to where the front door should be and give it a kick."

"Not that simple." Peter slid his arm around Angel's shoulder.

Micah and Argia caught up with them.

"We should check all sides for symbols." Argia crossed her arms, moving her hips side to side as if agitated.

Micah scratched the dark thick hair on top of his head. The sides were close cut into a stylish mohawk. "What kind of symbols?"

Argia grabbed Peter's hand with a strength that belied her size. "Like this." Then she dropped Peter's hand and tugged Kyle's. "Or this."

"What?" Kyle moved his hand from hers and scratched the palm of his hand. The wiggly lines on his palm were a crisscross of thick keloid blood of veins. "Why is it that Peter and I are the only ones with marks?"

Argia frowned. "You aren't. Angel has scars too."

Angel shook her head. "Uh, mine weren't...they aren't like Peter's or Kyle's. Mine was from torture."

Argia shook her head. "Doesn't matter. I see them even though they are deep within your new skin. Naked eyes won't see the scars, but when your DNA activated, those scars meant something. Your ancestor had the same ones, in the same patterns. Your tormentor didn't realize it, but he was freeing you and doing the first step in 'activating' your angelic genes. It had to be Gavin because his demon likely gave the same scars to your angelic ancestor."

"Deep shit," Kyle muttered.

Micah nodded. "Everything has a purpose; even the things we believe are out of our control or cause us pain are almost pre-destined to teach us a lesson or take us to the next level of our capability of strength."

Angel rubbed her arms. "You really believe that? After being abused and held for months by the Order of the Dragon? How did that torture serve you when all mine caused me was pain?"

"It made me angry. I now treasure every moment. I am not easily shaken anymore since I know what real darkness in a soul can cause. Those followers and descendants in the Extraho of Obscurum have a way out of their torment and they don't even realize it. They enjoy and savor their pain with the hope of power and things they get here on this Earth without realizing the price they are paying is for an eternity with a creature that hates their existence. After the time I suffered with them, I realized there is one thing they can't take from me: my version of the reality I create within my mind and the soul I carry in me." He thumped his chest. "I decide who owns it."

"Wow." Angel bit her lip. "I never thought about it that way. I focused on the weakness."

"I only focus on it to fight it." Micah patted Angel's shoulder. "The things that cause you pain...you can make it your pleasure if you control the way you respond."

"True," Argia added. "That's how I kept going when I thought I would never find Rosa, or you, Peter."

Peter smiled. Micah was a good guy. He only hoped he could keep Micah as a friend and not lose Kyle as one. "Thanks for that, man."

"Yeah, thanks." Kyle held out a hand to shake Micah's.

Micah's eyes widened in shock, but he took Kyle's hand.

Argia smiled, dampness within her eyes.

"Okay, everyone take a corner? Yell if you find something." Peter snuck another quick kiss from Angel as they split up.

It didn't take long for Micah to signal them over to his corner of the structure. The statues, three of them at the base of the metal coated stairs, had their swords pointed down. The statue in the middle wore a fierce scowl. It had a shield in front of it that nearly touched the other two. One was female and the others were male, yet the female stood as tall and wide as her male warrior counterparts.

"I don't know how getting up the steps will feel." The steps were riddled with sharp metal shards that stabbed upwards in a zigzag pattern.

"I'm not doing it." Kyle crossed his arms.

Micah shook his head. "Where's the symbol you found?"

"The sword, behind the shield." Kyle pointed.

Peter stepped closer and studied the symbols. There were three of them. "We have a problem. There are three symbols, but only two of us have brands on us."

Micah coughed. "Not true."

Peter frowned and stood up. "Who then?"

Micah bowed his head. "Me. I have one, too."

"Who gave it to you?" Peter eyed Micah suspiciously.

"Rosa."

Argia gasped. "What? How?"

"The Finn guy took me to her at my request. She cut her finger and my forearm, then drew this on me and told me I'd use it when the time came."

Peter released a deep breath. "Well then, wonders never cease with you, Micah."

"It's not like that." Micah slid up the sleeve of his shirt.

"I know, let's do this. Place your brand on the symbol." Peter did his.

Micah and Kyle followed and both mumbled complaints.

"Hurts like a son of a—" Kyle swore.

Creaking and popping echoed in the air. The spikes on the stairs sank within. The statues groaned and moved.

Peter and the others jumped back as the swords rose; the sword slid to the side and revealed a hollowed inside with stairs leading below.

"Wicked. I never would've thought it would be the entrance." Micah shook his head in awe.

"Let's go, these places don't hold the doors open for us long."

"No kidding," Kyle mumbled

CHAPTER 50

The Stronghold was enormous. Peter and the others walked the stone paved hallway, and their mouths dropped open at the intricately designed statues placed on the walls. The features were clear and prominent. Almost lifelike, they stood over twelve feet tall.

Angel gasped and touched one of the statues. "This is Michael the 2nd. My ancestor."

"Your donor was a warrior angel?" Kyle rubbed the statue's sandaled feet.

"Yes, he was one of the most fierce of his line. With the exception of his brother Michael 1 who was a fallen angel."

"Makes me think my ancestor's brothers weren't as good. Luke 23 wasn't meant to be a warrior but had no choice since his brothers before him had died."

Micah frowned. "So they numbered themselves instead of making their own names?"

Peter smiled. "They had their own names, but when the oldest brother or sister died, they took on their name, and number themselves. Unlike us humans, they don't have the ability to live in any realm when they are destroyed. They become nothing, with no awareness of self."

Micah crossed his arms. "So that means the war ended with your ancestor Luke 23 and hers, Michael 2nd?"

Peter nodded. "It did. The angel that found the formula to destroy the Wall of Ash knew our ancestors. He essentially created the Decretum Venia."

"Where do we begin? This place is so big, we could get lost for months." Kyle stretched.

"We split up. Get food, weapons, until we find that last scroll."

Peter waited until the others disbursed but held Angel's wrist. "You can come with me."

"I'd like that." She laced her fingers with his. "You know the book will be hidden."

Peter smiled and shook his head. "I know where it is. I just wanted to get rid of them. When I was knocked out in that last Sanctuary, this place, how to get here, it all was imprinted in my memory by the recurring dream I've had every night since we left there."

"Then why did you send them away? We can finish this now." Confusion marred her features.

"We need rest to do this. The last book—it won't be a short time inside. All of us will have to touch it and if we want to recover. We have to be rested."

"Okay, then, what are we going to do?"

"Go find a quiet place to eat, talk, be together while they figure out how to work things out. Kyle will find us in the morning. He always does."

"You're right about that." Angel squeezed his hand.

The warmth in Peter's chest grew. This place was the only stronghold that had been committed to memory. He led her to the adjoining corridor where the embedded multi-colored rocks scattered on the walls lit up as they neared.

"Here, this room has a bed and a food pantry." Peter pushed the large wood door inward.

"Not more stone furniture," Angel groaned.

"I can be your pillow." Peter laughed. "Hungry?"

"Starving, I don't even care if there is old water and beef jerky bites with dry crackers."

"Glad you're not picky." Peter went to the wooden shelf on the wall. He opened the door, then grabbed the decorative jars of flat bread and dried meat. The place reminded him of the medieval castle rooms he's seen in his Humanities school book. He'd only liked staring at the pictures instead of reading the text.

"Yum. What about water?" Angel took the meat Peter offered and stuffed a few in her mouth. "Sorry, I didn't"—she mumbled through bites—"realize I was so hungry."

"There's a pump at the bottom of the shelf. I guess this place has an underground stream or something."

Peter took one of the clay cups from the built in stone shelf and grasped the metal handle to the pump as clear water spurted into the cup. He lifted it to his lips and tasted, surprised at how good it was.

"Is it alright?" Angel eagerly held out her hand.

"Better than..." Peter filled the cup and gave it to her. Then he filled another.

"Tastes like it's coming from a freshwater lake. I went to one before in Canada."

"You tasted the water on purpose?" Peter smiled and leaned back on the wall.

"Yes, I wanted to know if it tasted salty. It didn't, it was refreshing. No fishy taste, either."

"That's good." Peter tipped his up to take the last drop. "It's odd how all this is coming together."

Angel finished her water and dug in the jar for another piece of the dry bread like cracker. "I know. Rosa and Pastor Finn must have a lot of people involved."

Peter nodded. "Pastor Finn is well connected. He was a police chief and even had a private detective business with several retired police working for him before he started managing the orphanage. He probably didn't give the business up though."

"Did he tell you that?"

"No, people came around sometimes that weren't with the Decretum Venia. But they carried themselves like the law, you know."

"I think so. My parents didn't interact with many people in the Decretum Venia. I don't think my father wanted to reveal their connection."

"When this is over and we destroy Gavin or the demon, whatever he is, we have to make a decision."

Angel frowned, "What about?"

"There will still be people taking over the leadership of the Order of the Dragon. That won't stop because we kill Gavin. There will always be another person waiting to take his place."

"What can we do, Peter? We are barely able to take care of ourselves. We'll have to figure out where to live. How to—" Angel's gaze wandered from Peter's face.

"Be together. We won't have to figure that out. I could get a job. Go into the military. I'd do anything to take care of you. We'll be nineteen years old. I know Pastor Finn would help us. We could do want ever we want to do."

"I don't know what that is yet, Peter."

"I know what it is for me. I want to marry you one day. I want you to be my wife, have my children." He kissed her, nibbled gently at her lips.

Her hands came up and rested on his face as she deepened the kiss.

"Just the way you are," Peter whispered. "Scarred, beautiful, fierce and mine to love."

"Oh Peter, you make me feel so..." Angel slid her hands in Peter's hair, "Sorry I am so difficult."

Peter went still. Angel's hands grasped the bottom of his shirt. It took every bit of concentration he had to keep the pace of their kiss and remain still while he allowed her to take the lead. He didn't know whether to stop her or go with it. So he went with it. Lifting his arms, he waited while she tugged his shirt over his head and briefly broke their kiss.

His chest moved rapidly as air rushed in and out of his lungs while they stared at each other. "Angel," his hoarse call slipped through is kiss.

She placed her finger to his lips. "Shhh." She unbuckled his belt as her gaze held his.

Peter fisted his hands at his sides; he wanted to grab her and kiss her so bad. He stepped out of his pants, with his shorts remaining. Peter didn't hide from her. He waited for any sign of discomfort. Instead, he witnessed awe and love on her face. Angel kissed his chest. Her hands slowly followed. Peter wanted to sob at the pleasure of having her touch him without trembling from fear.

"Can I take off yours?" Peter's voice came out gruff and deep.

As if coming out of a daze, she smiled at him. "Yes, please."

This time his hands trembled as he stepped out of his pants, putting him one step closer to Angel. Peter swallowed and kissed her lips gently, then each cheek, back to her lips again. Slowly, while kissing her, Peter slid her shirt upward. He wouldn't rush, didn't want to scare her off. He did it excruciatingly slow.

"Peter, please hurry." Her lips fell apart further into their kiss. "I want you. All of you."

Peter held her bunched-up shirt, just under her bra, "Are you sure? We can ...God, we can wait, but if we go any further, I think I'd die if you change your mind."

"I won't. Micah was right. When I am with you, it's beautiful. I want my memory of my nakedness to be with what I see in your eyes. Pure pleasure and love."

He was actually tearing up. Peter blinked them back. Angel kissed him.

"Okay, I will be gentle. I will make sure you enjoy us." Peter's voice was smooth, humble.

"Being connected with you will be all the joy I need."

Peter grinned. "Good." He lifted her in his arms.

Angel laughed and wrapped her arms around him.

"I will love you forever, Angel Ramirez. Will you be my forever?"

"Yes." Angel kissed him.

This time, he knew she was ready. Angel's kiss was hungry, sure, and full of desperation. Peter would go into battle with Gavin complete.

CHAPTER 51

Peter and Angel woke early, despite the long night they'd spent exploring each other. He felt so elated and invigorated. Peter didn't think he could hide the change in them in front of the others. He would try though.

He made sure he took every precaution so Angel wouldn't deal with an unplanned pregnancy. But he had to admit that one day she would carry his child because they'd be good together. She was the only family he needed, and for the first time in a year, Peter didn't doubt she was with him to stay.

There was yelling and arguing coming from one of the corridors. Peter smiled at the constant touching, rubbing, and hugging Angel did with him now. He hoped he'd helped her close that barrier.

"Wait," Angel whispered.

Peter bent to kiss her. He couldn't help himself. "Are you ready?"

"I'd rather us stay in the room alone, but if we must, I'm ready."

Peter chuckled at that. "I'd rather be here, too. Those guys will tear each other apart if I don't stop them."

Breaking glass shattered and the shards bounced out of the room.

"Go in before they kill each other."

Peter waited in the doorway to assess the chaos. Vases were shattered on the floor, and Micah was choking Kyle on the huge stone table, while Argia was trying to pull him off.

"Apologize!" Micah screamed.

"It's okay, he was just hurt." Argie tugged on Micah's shoulder.

"Get-off-me! Bastard," Kyle yelled.

Peter grabbed Micah around the neck, pulling him off of Kyle, who kicked Micah in the stomach. Peter dug his feet into the floor to hold back a rearing Micah. Kyle punched Micah, and Peter twisted Micah out of the way to take the brunt of Kyle's punch.

"Kyle! Stop, dammit." Peter's jaw jerked from the blow. He growled and pushed Micah out of the way and caught Kyle's next punch.

"Get out of my way; I will tear him apart." Kyle had tears in his eyes, and his chest was heaving.

Peter held him back. "Micah, leave." There was some scrambling from behind him.

"Kyle, please, it's not his fault," Argia's small voice pleaded. "Forgive me. I love you. I do, but Micah and I... He and I just..."

Kyle's tortured gaze nailed Argia. "I don't care. I wanted to be your last. Me." Kyle pounded his chest. "I get that I was a prick when we met. I am sorry for treating you so bad. I never apologized for that. But please, I'm begging you, don't leave me."

Argia started crying. "I don't want to choose, Kyle. I am in love with you, but Micah's connection to me is different. It's more than just my love for him."

Kyle nodded. "Is it acceptance? I know I didn't give that to you.

But please..." Kyle reached for her. "Let me hold you. Just let me hold you." His voice came out in tortured brokenness.

Peter held back Kyle until he felt the guy relax. "You good, man? I'm not letting you go to her if I can't trust you to keep it together."

Kyle nodded. "Send Micah back in."

"No," Peter stated.

"Do it. He needs to see this." Kyle's arm stretched out to Argia who slowly walked closer.

Peter nodded to Angel who motioned for Micah.

Micah came back into the room. "Kyle, I am sorry."

Peter released Kyle who enveloped Argia into his arms. Peter's heart clenched in his chest as he watched his best friend sob into Argia's neck. Then he kissed her. Argia hesitantly returned the kiss, then pulled away.

Kyle's voice cracked. "Argia, this is it. The last time I will pursue you. I understand my mistakes. I see that your heart never really left Micah's." Kyle set Argia on the floor and pushed her away. "Micah, take care of her. When we are finished this path together, I'm done. Done." Kyle's head fell, and he turned to the corner of the room, shutting them out.

Micah started to say something, but Peter held up a hand and shook his head.

"Everyone, I know where the last book is. Follow me." Peter didn't wait for them, he grabbed Angel's hand. His heart steadied at her squeezing his hand in return. Peter led them deep within the mansion. The halls all looked the same. Tall statues with swords and jewels embedded within them. However, the jewels weren't on the swords; they were on the bodies of the warriors that lined the wall.

Several wood doors were on each side of the corridor. Peter

knew what the clue was to the room he sought, though none of the statues or doors gave it away.

"It seems like we are going in circles." Angel pivoted around.

Peter wiped his hand through his hair. "I know, but we went through all the corridors except this last one."

"I think there is something different about this one." Angel placed her hand on the wrought iron fence that blocked the hallway. "It's not lighting up like these others."

Peter studied the gate. There was a symbol matching his in the middle of the design. He pressed his hand to it. The prick of the needles was quick. Then it opened. The embedded rocks that provided light were a different hue from the blue ones in the previous corridors. These were red.

Angel slowed. "Red, I think it's a warning."

"They will all have warnings; it's too late for us to let them stop us."

"I know." Angel walked over to the stone wall and traced some of the markings with her fingers.

Argia came to stand next to Peter. "This is it. There will be answers here for all of us."

"Are you ready?" Peter crossed his arms. "We are here." The symbols were arranged in an artistic form that resembled a warrior screaming at them. On the chest plate of the statue's armor, that fit his body like a glove, was each one of their brands. There were also slender lines of scars on his body from neck to waist.

"Let's put our marks to the ones on him," Peter directed.

They followed silently; Peter suspected emotions were still raw from their fight earlier.

"It's not working." Argia bit her lip.

"We need Angel to release her scars." Peter placed his hand on Angel's shoulders. "Let it go, and put your marks on his."

Angel nodded then crossed her arms over her chest, closed her eyes. Slices of light formed on the burns and cuts that Gavin had placed on her skin. Long threads of light protruded from those scars and connected them to the warrior.

Peter moved to stand in front of Argia. "I need you to scream, not as loud as you did to lock Gavin within the Wall of Ash, but loud enough for your Angels to hear you. Stand in front of the statue and scream towards the mouth."

"Cover your ears." Argia took a deep breath and yelled.

It was so beautiful, and sounded like an opera singer. The hairs on Peter's arms jumped. The wall opened to reveal a room with more statues. Unlike the others that were silver or stone, these were gold. All surrounded a pedestal with a gold plated book on it.

"The Book of Truth." Peter led them through the ring of statues. The statues moved and shifted so that each sword closed off easy entry, as if in final warning. He'd remembered the names of the other books he'd open: The Book of Secrets, then The Book of Fire, now...The Book of Truth. Whose truth, Peter didn't know. Soon he would find his answer.

"There are no symbols on these." Kyle walked the perimeter of the circle of statues.

"Argia, sing." Peter stood in front of the book. "It's a failsafe. I'm not supposed to open this book alone.

They covered their ears and Argia started her song. Slowly, one by one, with each heightened key, a warrior lowered his sword in front of him.

Peter walked through the statues. The book was a work of art. It was encased in gold with a vine around his symbol in the middle. In the corners were Kyle's mark, Micah's, and the jagged lines and dots that were replicated on Angel's body.

"This is it. When I open this, we all will be transported to a slip of time during the Thousand Year War. Micah and Kyle, you will be in the bodies of your ancestors. You will have to make a decision to take their knowledge, but it comes with a price. I don't know what the price is, but it's never an easy one."

Micah held up a hand. "This is our last chance to walk away, right?"

"Yeah, but at this point, we can't. You know that if we leave here without our answers, Gavin will use the kids he has, bleed them dry, and have their bodies as shields to get to the heavenly realm. That act alone will affect us all."

"Just do it." Kyle stepped up. "Micah, we have our issues, but none of us is doing this for our own motives. Yeah, I want answers to what I am and why I was hidden, but that's not all. You are...one of this team now, whether I like it not, we do this — together."

Micah nodded at Peter.

Peter waited for Angel and Argia's affirmations. Then pressed his palm to the symbol on the Book of Truth.

∽

*T*he air was stale, heavy and void of moisture. The barren land was riddled with cracked sand and rocks. Peter's hand was now three times its normal size and white, a contrast to his former dark hue. He stretched and searched around. The land was riddled with groups of small, shorter humans and warrior angels devoid of their wings who were giants compared to their human comrades.

A dark skinned angel approached him, the smile reminded him of Kyle's.

"Hey, stop looking at me that way. I knew I was black."

Peter laughed. "Kyle?"

"Yep, it's me. I feel so different. Powerful and comfortable in this

body. I know what we have to do. Come, we have to witness the battle first."

Peter followed the towering form of the Kyle's ancestral angel.

"Where are the others?" Peter asked as they approached the battle; the Wall of Ash they'd combated in this Thousand Year War was straight ahead. A tornado of ash, fire, and small demonites, weaving in and out of the thunderbolts within the gray moving matter. A living creature of evil in itself.

"Fighting." Kyle crossed his arms.

"What?! Why are we standing here?" Peter drew his sword and started to charge ahead.

Kyle's hand reached and held him steady. "Wait for it. They need to experience this in order to know how to release the poison."

"The poison? I don't understand."

Kyle's angelic ancestor's smile was a big one, a sure one. "Your angel's DNA mixed with Michael 2nd is released by our two Seekers. One Seeker will numb the demons with her song, the other Seeker is strong enough to hold the stronger demons trapped on the other side of the portal while the poison does its work."

"What about you? Why was your human and angelic line hidden?"

"If they killed anyone in my angelic line, the secret of the serum would've been lost. The reason we used Michael 2nd's DNA is because his brother, the fallen angel Michael 1st, helped the king of fallen ones create the Wall of Ash. Your human ancestor was from a unique strain, one of the closest tied to the original humans placed on the Earthly plane. Luke 23rd is a peacemaker; the human we merged his essence with was of strong heart and a noble line of humans who constantly tried to live the life they were created to live. That gave them favor with our maker."

"How do you know it will work?" Peter's hands flexed into fists as the bloody battle unfolded in front of him. He couldn't believe Angel was the key to the potion. Since she was Michael 2nd descendent, and likely

Lucien, Michael 1ˢᵗ descendent too. Michael the 2nd gave of himself to save his brother. To right the mistake his brother had made by siding with the evil one.

"*Just wait for it.*"

Everything went dark.

CHAPTER 52

Gavin felt different. The pain intensified. The meeting with Mara, his fiancée and the head witch of his sect within the Extraho of Obscurum, was staring at him with a keen and hungry eye.

"Are you alright, darling?" Mara leaned toward him.

He raised his large form at the head of the circle of chairs in one of his meeting rooms. This room was more comfortable than the others and was fashioned with large chairs and a leather ottoman that had a wood surface on top which could be removed.

Gavin controlled his breathing and braced for another attack from within. Sharp, cutting agony crawled from his groin through his chest. It pounded through his legs and behind his eyes. He gritted his teeth to bear down on the inner strength he'd relied on to control his demon master, Balaal. His control was slipping, but Gavin wrestled it back.

Mara, the evil condescending woman, always questioned him in that sweet respectful manner that belied her true motive. Her demon mistress sought a connection to Balaal. The woman had been chanting something under her breath for the last few minutes of their meeting.

"I'm fine, Mara." He nailed her with a hard stare. She had the decency to squirm a bit in her seat as a show of respect.

"Can I get you something to drink, brother?" Lucien's casual countenance appeared bored. He sat next to Jack with his legs crossed and a smirk on his lips. His unruly blond hair was tied back in a ponytail, and he was wearing a black suit.

"No!" Gavin growled, not to intimidate Jack, but to fight off the attack Balaal relentlessly waged inside him. Where did the beast get this renewed energy? Sweat rolled from his forehead; he fought to hold in his scream. Straightening his back and cracking his neck to the side, he walked over to Jack.

"As I was trying to explain, my men were ambushed. They had the Peter boy, and two or three other kids that were with him, cornered."

"You lie!" Gavin roared.

Lucien smoothly moved to rest his arms on this legs. "I believe he does, brother. You see, Jack came to me offering a deal. He wanted you dead so his demon master would take your place — your glory."

"Wha-what are you doing, Lucien?" Jack sputtered and stood.

Chanting behind him grew louder, hypnotic even. Mara was summoning a spell. Gavin felt a burst of sharp hooks piercing his soul; he stumbled forward. He reached out with lightning speed to grab Jack's neck. Squeezing to a punishing degree, Gavin did so, also, to have something to support against the pounding, stabbing, fire that bubbled up within him.

"Brother, I can kill him for you. If you kill Jack, neither he nor his demon can take your moment. The victory you've waited for." Lucien stood and wiped Jack's dark hair back from his red and purple face.

"Balaal! Come forth! My mistress summons you." Mara's command bounced off the walls as she repeated it over and over between chanted incantations.

"Mara! Shut up." Gavin reared around and slapped her. Her slight form slammed against the wall. She fell; blood gushed from her mouth. She coughed out blood, but in her daze crawled towards his legs.

Gavin stiffened both hands around Jack's neck, this time face to face as he pounded down the demon within him. He didn't want to risk tapping into the demon's strength; it would reveal the beast and might allow Balaal to overtake him.

"Brother, if you kill him, you gain control of his house, his holdings...everything. The witch knows of his plans to overthrow you. We will all support your claim." Lucien went behind Jack's shoulder with a knife drawn.

Jack appeared accusatory through his struggle. "He's lying! I would never do that!"

Gavin smiled at him. "Jack, my friend, today is your lucky day. You and your master will be as one." Gavin twisted Jack's neck. At the satisfying crack and release of blood from the dead man's mouth, Gavin dropped him.

"Balaal! Dig deeper, my mistress calls you forth," Mara's hoarse call repeated over and over.

Gavin pivoted around to shut her up permanently when an annihilating fire and tearing from within poured through his body. He stumbled. Balaal, *no...no, he is empowered.* "Mara! What have you done? Stop at once."

Jaws of fire latched onto Gavin's soul, a torment so deep, so agonizing, that it seemed to go on forever. Rips in his skin revealed a gold and red reptile from within. Claws grew and forced themselves out from his fingers. The excruciating pain from bones breaking, shifting, and moving in his head, legs, and back forced

Gavin to his knees. Skin tore, blood stained the floor. Gavin howled.

"No! Not there again." And even as his soul was sucked deep within the hell bound home of his demon master, Gavin never stopped screaming. His conscious embodiment became locked in a cage of piercing knives that cut and lodged into every bone, muscle, and soft tissue of his body. He only had a moment to catch his breath between screams as his entire essence was dipped in the fire.

"Gavin? Gavin?" Mara asked. The witch came close to study him.

Balaal stretched this human body, raised to his feet, and smiled. "Gavin doesn't live here anymore. It is Balaal; bow to your intended master."

Balaal glanced at Jack's twisted body and lifted his chin. The human accomplished one less thing he'd have to do. He turned to Lucien, the groomed servant, and said, "It is time."

Lucien sank to the ground, eyes averted. "As you wish."

CHAPTER 53

Peter hugged Pastor Finn tight. That he was taller than the man he'd considered an adoptive dad didn't matter. His respect and determination to make him proud was never ceasing. Under the cover of trees on a hidden road where their cars were parked in caves, the kids reunited with Rosa, Pastor Finn, and Sam from the doomsday prepper's makeshift sanctuary.

"Son, a few months and you've grown taller and wider." Pastor Finn chuckled.

Peter frowned. Pastor Finn appeared haggard, his once-blond hair with a few sparse pieces of gray, was now full gray. His blue eyes, now paler, were tired around the edges. His tall, straight posture was now a bit bent. But Peter still saw a fire of strength within them that he latched onto.

"A lot blew up in our faces on the way. More than once, we almost got captured by Lucien."

Pastor Finn scratched his chin. "Well, he has a purpose to fill. Just hard to nail down what that is. My man on the inside is close to him and tells me that Lucien is complicated, whereas Gavin is pretty much a what you see is what you get guy."

"I need to get to the Wall of Ash; the machine is there."

"I know. We have fighters ready to go in. The final book gifted everyone in ways we didn't anticipate. I hope it's the advantage we need."

"It is. How close to it can you get me?"

"Up front and personal, but you have to go in through another entrance. We can create a diversion. My informant has a team working with him that provided us access at several locations. The one I'm sending you through is here." Pastor Finn pulled out a piece of paper. "It won't be easy to get in, and you may run into trouble. I hate to say this, son, but shoot to kill. It's a life or death situation."

Peter nodded. "What about the others?"

"Everyone has a purpose. Some will be helping get the captives held in the dungeons to freedom. Others will destroy the key players of the Extraho of Obscurum since many of them are here now for the ceremony going on."

"We will need help to fight. The demons will be released."

"I know, my informant told me, it's not Gavin the demon-man we were dealing with. It's Balaal, one of the right hand men to the kingpin of hell himself. That will be a difficult task. Rosa has gathered others with her ability to infiltrate. Unfortunately, a few of them have been labeled as sacrifices. So, once you breach the Wall of Ash, the fighters will destroy the machine, you just kill the demon. Once they are destroyed with the dagger, they cease to exist."

"Dagger?" Peter wiped down the side of his face. "We need one?"

Pastor Finn nodded. "I have one. Sam? Hand it to him."

Peter grasped the jeweled dagger. The symbol on it was an intertwined symbol where his was in the middle. "Is this the only way?"

"No, there are many of those daggers. We have them made and stashed in several sanctuaries. I even gave one to my inside man to tempt fate in our favor. We can only use it on the demons strong enough to fully materialize into flesh and breach the barrier."

"Do you have more?" Peter tucked the dagger into the loop of his jeans.

"Gave them to the fighters who'll force their way in when we give the signal. You only need one to kill him. "Last thing: my guy will be wearing a pin with a replica of the dagger in the design. Not obvious, but if you don't see it, don't go with the man who meets you. Follow the map; there are tunnels through the dungeons. It won't be pleasant, but drop the bombs in the bags we gave Kyle into the cells. The prisoners will do the rest."

"How do they know?"

"We have a plant who looks like a kid, but isn't. He organizes things on the inside for me. Everyone is primed and ready for this."

"I'm impressed. I thought my crew and I were doing something, but you, Pastor Finn, were moving stuff."

"Not alone. Years in law enforcement, detective work, and negotiating, taught me things. Also, the Decretum Venia has some pretty good talent."

Rosa came up to Peter and hugged him. "I will see you soon." She winked.

Peter didn't doubt it.

~

Peter led the others from the car; each wore belts holding satchels with miniature bombs no bigger than marbles. The backend of the property, where the Wall of Ash was erected, was fenced pretty well. The grass was a bit wild on the boundary. It came up to Peter's knees.

"Why aren't we going in with the others?" Kyle asked.

"This way will lead us right in front of the Wall of Ash. The others are spread out and will be breaking in, blowing up stuff, and making a diversion. The ceremony won't stop though. Once they start it, they only have one chance to finish. The moon is high and red. It's the only time they can summon enough demons through the portal to be able to win the war they plan on waging."

Micah pulled Peter's arm. "I was here before."

"So was I." Peter stopped.

"This place is evil. I-I don't know if I can do this." Micah rubbed his hand on the side of his face. "I escaped this place. I don't want to let you down, or Rosa, but I am feeling sick to my stomach."

"Look, we've all been here. This place nearly killed us before, but we can never run far enough. They won't go away, and it will get worse if we let them go through with what they are planning. Every person in the dungeons will die tonight."

"I understand, but I don't want to trip up and get everyone here killed. They know what I am and will go after me. I don't know who you think you have on your side in there, but trust me, none of them are what they seem. They will turn on you."

"The guy who got you out of there didn't turn on you. Did he?"

"No, he didn't. But he wasn't the first person who pretended to want to help me. Lucien told me he'd give me a way out. He called it 'sweet death'. Then I found out he got some high off of killing and torturing kids, male or female. So, you understand why I am unsure here?"

"I know, but we don't have a choice. If Pastor Finn said we can trust the guy wearing the pin, then we can. We have to. If things get bad, we kill on sight. We have bombs, we have guns, and we have our demon killing weapons within us. You are stronger now. You've been through a lot. So have we. Use that to take your fight to the next level. Got it?" Peter patted Micah's shoulders. "I trust you. Friend."

"Thank you. I'll get it together."

Argia touched Micah's arm. "I trust you too, Micah." She gave him a sanguine smile.

Peter smiled at her. "You ready?"

Argia nodded.

Peter pivoted around and led them to the water well. It was several feet high, made of rocks stacked upon each other in a circular mold. A broken wooden bucket hung on a rope wound tightly around a metal pulley with a handle.

Peter used a small flashlight to find the hidden entrance the map pointed out. "Let's climb down. I hope those metal stairs hold us. Girls, you go first, the guys and I will brace it."

"I'll go, then Argia." Angel adjusted the knife on her arm band.

Peter smiled at her. Angel had her long hair up in a messy bun, a headband made of leather, and a heated gaze of fire. She'd changed, and Peter loved it.

Angel gave him a quick kiss. "Let's kick their asses." Then, she gracefully climbed down into the well with her flashlight in her teeth.

CHAPTER 54

Peter hopped into the tunnel from the ladder. The dim beams of their flashlights lit the rock enclosure. It had to stay steady since the tunnel was circular and not easy to navigate as it dipped in some places where rocks were missing.

Peter led the way until they got to a metal door. He released the metal lock. The door was pushed open by someone on the other side.

A man stood there with darkness to his back. His eyes and face were covered with a black hood that sat on top of his black suit jacket. The only thing Peter saw was a beard that was long enough to poke from under his hooded disguise.

The man flicked his lapel to the side where a pocket wore the pin bearing the dagger.

"Be ready, this is going to get messy." The man turned around. "Follow me."

Vile scents hung heavy from the dungeon. The room had boxes, tools, and shelves of mechanical looking equipment.

"It's the storage room. They don't come to this one often. It's why we decided it would be the best way in. We have ten minutes to pass through the cellblock of prisoners. Do what you came to do, but quickly, we may have to run."

Peter frowned at the man's voice, it sounded familiar. "Do I know you?"

"Yes, I got you and that boy with you free. Now you will get me out. One way or another."

The man led them through a damp hallway. The noise of crying and screaming with banging thundered around them.

"They witnessed me killing the guards. They are excited as it marked the beginning of their planned escape."

"We're ready." Peter dipped his hand in the satchel of small bombs.

"Let's run!" The man picked up speed.

Peter sprinted after him. They burst through a door. Inside, the smell of despair hit him. It was putrid, foul, and heavy. The people in the cells were in several forms of dress; some were naked and bleeding. He held back the reflex to gag and tossed small bombs in each cell while Angel handed in lock picking tools from her backpack.

"Damn!" the guy in front of them yelled. "Guns ready!"

Two gunmen raced toward them. Peter pulled his gun from his belt, and their guide shot one of the gunmen in the head. Peter fired at the one behind and hit him in the shoulder.

The guide shot the man in the neck. "Kill them! We can't let them report back."

Peter nodded, his finger itchy, as he aimed at one then another man. This time he aimed true to their hearts. Angel's back-up shot landed in each of the men's heads to finish them off.

"Stop playing nice, they will end us." Angel elbowed Peter. "I know."

"Got it." Peter nailed each of the coming guards with head-shots. Their guide pushed through the brief onslaught.

They cleared the dungeon cell block and ran through a dark hallway of enclosed rooms that had medical supplies, and a lab. Several nurses and doctors lay on the floor, knocked out.

"I took care of the medical staff with some of my inside team. This is the experimentation center. The patients aren't all victims from the Decretum Venia, so we have to wait for Rosa to identify them. Then we can get everyone out, and destroy the place with the cleanup team."

Peter lifted an eyebrow. "Rosa and Pastor Finn are good."

"The best," the guide agreed.

They were led into a stairwell where a girl was asleep in a chair at the bottom of the steps, plump and appearing innocent. Another was behind her.

"Them?" Peter pointed with is gun.

"Witches in training. Traitorous creatures, they won't be waking up. I took care of them. The less of them, the better." The guide waved. "Once we hit the main room, I will leave you to blend in. It opens into Gavin's office. Go through the side door next to the desk and out the door to where the ceremony will be starting. You won't have much time before the bombs go off to get to the Wall of Ash, which is behind them."

"Got it."

The guide turned to Peter and lifted his hood. He had a scar down his cheek, a pirate patch over his eye, and a toothy smile. "I knew you were worth saving, Peter." With a flick of his wrist, the hood dropped in place.

CHAPTER 55

Peter burst through the door. The red moon was high in the sky with black clouds moving toward the Wall of Ash. A tornado of soot, fire, smoke, and fire demons swam in an out of the moving mass. Their tadpole bodies and crowded mouths filled with white teeth framed on their bodies that seemed to have moving lava within them. Lucien, Gavin and a woman, stood on a small stage in front of the crowd with the Wall of Ash behind them. Torches framed the stage with thick fire that jumped in the mild wind, which seemed strange for a tornado raging behind them that reached up towards the clouds. Gavin was not the human Peter remembered—this was Balaal, the demon he'd ripped out of Gavin. From where Peter stood, the beast appeared to be waiting for something. And whatever it was, he was angry about it.

Balaal was massive. His skin shimmered like a snake with scales of red and gold in the torchlights that littered the clearing. His oversized head and shoulders stood at least four feet taller than Lucien's 6ft 3inch frame. The horns on his head shifted and extended with each breath he took. He was naked with a chest that stretched as wide as two men. Brown hair fanned downward to cover his lower stomach and underside almost like a loincloth made of thick curling fur. Huge thighs, like a beast stood on feet with clawed nails.

Peter stood frozen as Balaal's dark gaze collided with his. Balaal's arms lifted, the ground shook, then grew stronger as the earth cracked and quaked. Fire licked through the crevices in the earth. Demons poured from the growing Wall of Ash from top to bottom.

Some of the beasts climbed out of the huge cracks in the barren land. Fire snaked through the dry grass where the cracks widened. Demons, with silver armor over their bodies, were covered in human skin stretched and clamped in places on their chest-like capes. Human skulls strung like necklaces adorned some of their necks. Female demons wore skull-strung bras covering their breasts. Some appeared animalistic with their overcrowded mouths of teeth, bestial heads, goat or snake bodies, and gold skin. Others had beautiful faces with upper bodies that were almost human but lower forms of gold scaled snakes with stingers on the ends. They had eyes of complete darkness or fire as they attacked warriors from the Decretum Venia who wielded glowing swords and weapons straight out of medieval times.

"Weapons ready!" Peter yelled. With a flash of his hand, a sword of blue light framed in white fire appeared. He placed his hand at his neck. "Put on armor!" And with a flick of his finger on his neck, his body was covered in a moving glowing light that would protect him from the weapons of the demons, and minimize the damage from manmade weapons as well. He swiped his other hand downward—a sword of light appeared.

Peter nodded to Angel who had her armor ready with her weapon of choice: a whip with jagged pins along one edge. The sides of her body had thin strings of light that, when she twisted, extended matching thorns like her whip.

"We're ready." Angel lifted her hand.

Kyle was behind her, several feet in the air, with wings of light that had razor feathers. He flung the feathered knives at some of the attacking demons and swiped a jagged sword downward. "This is ripped!"

A sequence of explosive blasts shook the ground. Chaos erupted. Men with guns poured into the clearing between Peter and the masses of demons attacking. They ran alongside the Wall of Ash towards the crowd participating in the ceremony. A mixture of men in jeans and women in leather fought them. More fighters from the Decretum Venia chopped their way through. The men in black defended the demons and the ceremony of the Extraho of Obscurum. Decretum Venia fighters. Teenagers, women, and men, flew on wings of light, and threw knives of blue fire at the servants of the dragon. Decretum Venia armed men felled the rush of guards with a mixture of manmade guns and bombs.

Peter charged through. A human-shaped demon blocked his path with a silver sword slicing down at him, he would have been considered beautiful if not for his red eyes and serpents tongue. Dropping to his knees, Peter cut upward between the small breast-plate and its skin. The creature screamed and sliced downward toward Peter's head.

"Ahhh!" Angel cut off the demon's head with her whip slinging above her. She jumped on its burnt neck to down the bull horned demon behind it.

Peter pushed the carcass of the demon out of the way as it popped, then disappeared into thin air.

Another demon with an axe swung at Peter's head. He ducked and shifted to one side. He kicked the beast in the chest, flexed his sword, then stabbed the thing through its one eye that covered the upper half of its face. One final push had him pivoting around to cut off the attacking arm of female demon with hair of snakes tipped in fire, and she had eyes of complete darkness. Her gold tongue slithered out with a screech at the loss of her arm.

Peter sliced downward as her arm re-animated itself, and she grabbed him with her other hand at the neck.

"Kill Peterrrrr," she lisped, her black eyes lit with flames.

"Not today." Angel's whip wrapped around the demon's neck.

Peter stabbed through her chest while Angel yanked her whip back to cut through the creature's neck.

Peter jumped over a fallen Order of the Dragon guard, and punched another in the neck. A piercing shot from behind staggered Peter forward. The pain vibrated through his invisible armor, causing a flicker at the lit necklace that controlled the suit.

"Peter, keep going!" Angel yelled.

A chain wrapped around his torso. He stumbled. The stage was just ahead. Balaal was walking down, heading to the Wall of Ash.

"He's going in." Peter struggled against the chains of the demon that was pulling him backward.

Kyle jumped on the demon's neck. He formed a two-handled saw and cut downward through its head. "I got this. Go! Argia and Micah are near the stage. The poison is around their necks."

Angel fought next to him.

They jabbed, kicked, elbowed, and ducked thrown weapons until they broke through the Order of Dragons' human followers. Many were fighting to complete their ceremony amidst the fighting and chaos. Several were hurt or dead from the onslaught; their circle had moved in to continue their handheld chanting and swaying.

Peter found Lucien standing off to the side, calmly watching the fight. Two strategically placed guards blocked anyone who tried to get close.

"Leave him." Kyle stabbed a charging demon in Peter's path.

"Going." Peter jabbed, side-kicked and punched charging demons. "They know us."

"Their master knows you, they smell your ancestor on you. Just go get him. He's going into the Wall."

Still more demons poured out from the Wall of Ash, directed at Peter and Angel.

"Where are Argia and Micah?" Peter wiped the sweat from his brow with his forearm while piercing a demon in the eye that cut at his shoulder. The blow hurt on impact but didn't bleed through his armor.

"They are protected by her song. Basically, invisible." Kyle flew over Peter to slice through the torso of an attacker.

"Angel?" Peter frantically searched around, and spotted her surrounded by demons. She was killing some, but they were pressing in on her. "I got to get her!"

"No! It's important you finish him or this won't end. I'll protect her. Just go!" Kyle flew to Angel's aid.

Peter hesitated a moment, and a blinding cutting pressure pounded his back. He faced the two demons with multiple arms, slicing their weapons in succession. Peter backed up, decided to leave the fight for Gavin; he turned and ran.

He pushed through, slid under fighters from both sides, and focused on getting to the Wall. Peter ran up the stairs, whirled about, and stabbed a beast in the neck. Then he jumped off the back of the stage. Argia and Micah fell in beside him with ease.

"Where are your weapons?" Peter lifted his shield to cover them from an attack. Then his mouth dropped as Argia motioned to her hand as though it was wrapped around the creature's neck and it started to choke: its black eyeballs bulged out of the sockets as though a huge hand was squeezing its neck. Black blood dribbled from its mouth. All at once, it disappeared.

"I am using mine." Argia smiled. "Micah taught me."

"Where are your suits?" Peter asked, noticing they didn't have the slight glow that indicated an activated suit of armor.

"Can't use them, we are part of the poison," Micah said.

"Well then." Peter jumped as more demons ran at them, but Micah slapped back and forth and they slammed into each other with such force their bones shattered and blood poured from them before they disappeared.

"It's clear now." Micah grabbed Argia's hand.

Peter followed, but hesitated at the huge tornado of death, the Wall of Ash. "The demons in the wall will try eat your soul."

Argia nodded. "We know, but your suit will protect you if we release the poison. When we do, don't be alarmed at what you see, just kill Gavin."

"On it! I'm ready."

Micah yelled, "Jump!"

Peter leaped with them into the moving tornado. He couldn't see them, he heard their screams. He fought to get to them, but the demonites started biting him. They didn't penetrate the suit, but the pressure from their teeth felt like someone poking him with knives. He fought them, hit them, but he couldn't get his weapons to materialize. He was choking. The soot and smoke seeped through his suit. Peter fought being suspended in the moving air. He punched at the small beasts that stabbed at every exposed part of his body. Tears leaked from his eyes, the pain threatened to cripple him as he protected them. Pounding inside his chest kept him focused, and he frantically hit at the creatures.

A loud song followed by a baritone chanting floated through the murky barrier. A flash of light, then a sizzle raged through the mass of gray matter, followed by a popping sound so loud Peter covered his ears.

He fell to the ground, hard.

The Wall of Ash was gone. Thick, dissipating smoke filled the air with dancing flames of fire burning out by an unknown source. In front of him stood Balaal and the machine that caused this rekindling of a war. Peter struggled to stand. He pulled all the strength he had and lifted his flickering sword of blue light.

"So, you sacrificed two of your kind to destroy my portal?" Balaal's clawed hand waved at Argia and Micah who lay on the charred ground, their bodies unmoving, staring at some unknown force.

Peter remained still. He'd come too far to fail them all. He let anger fuel him; it poured through is veins and revived him. His blade grew larger, stronger, filled with fire.

"That won't kill me. I'm not a minion like the others you destroyed of my kind. I'm one of the originals." Balaal's snake eyes were black with gold pupils. It charged.

Peter held his sword tall and strong. It glinted with an inner light source that glowed in the smoke-shadowed surroundings of the aftermath of the Wall's destruction.

Peter thrust the sword upward, slicing through the thick outer layer of the demon's torso. There was a cut, but no blood.

Balaal laughed. "Are you acquainted with pain, boy?" The demon charged Peter's sword that sliced through his arm. Balaal, ignoring the black blood flowing from the lodged sword, grabbed Peter by the neck.

Peter wrestled against the claws of the demon's hand, seeing stars while kicking and choking. He flicked his free hand, making the large sword disappear then yelped, willing small sharp pins of fire to blow from his mouth.

The darts of light struck Balaal in the eyes, face, and mouth, blinding the demon. Balaal staggered backwards. Pins of black blood seeped from his face. One eye was covered in them and he couldn't close the lid.

Balaal grunted.

"Ahhh!" Peter swiped both hands upward; a lighter, jagged sword appeared in his hands.

Balaal plucked the sharpened nails of light out of his eye socket. An eyeball came with it. He roared and charged Peter, smacking the sword out of Peter's hand.

Peter flicked his fingers. Spears of light formed on his fingertips. He scratched, cut, and jabbed them into Balaal's neck.

Balaal went for Peter's throat, slipped a talon deep, and dislodged Peter's protective transparent armor. "You will die this day, boy! I will devour your soul!"

Peter screamed as Balaal stabbed his stomach. Through the murkiness of his tears, he saw Lucien.

It is over.

Balaal's thrashing talons felt like they were ripping Peter's soul apart. Stars formed in his eyes. He swallowed the metallic taste of his own blood. Peter thrusted his chest, forming pins of light all over his body. They pierced through Balaal's claws and chest.

Lucien and one of his guards came to stand on each side of Balaal.

"I will finish what I started." Peter's hoarse threat met Bakaal's wicked laughter. He flicked his wrist and formed a small sword with one hand. His trembling hand reached into his belt to grab the dagger Pastor Finn gave him.

"No...no!" It was missing. *No dagger, no death to Balaal.* A tear slid from Peter's eye as his body went limp. Balaal raised a claw to swipe down at him again.

Peter gulped back blood-flavored vomit.

Lucien raised an eyebrow. "That's an impressive weapon, son." He smiled at Peter.

Balaal laughed. "We will finish you off, boy, and eat your remains for dinner!"

Lucien whipped around. Out of nowhere, a shining gold dagger appeared in Lucien's hand. He didn't waste a second to dig it into Balaal's chest.

Balaal bellowed, this time with the wounded cry of an animal. His taloned hand grabbed the guard. The guard stabbed him with another dagger in his back. The beast sunk his talons into the man's neck. Blood spurted on the ground as the man fell from Balaal's hand. Then the demon turned on Lucien, lifting him high in the air.

"How dare you defy me! I will devour you for eternity."

"I'm betting on it!" Lucien fought against the demon.

Balaal's jaws grew wide and he bit off Lucien's head, tossing the limp body to the ground. The beast's remaining eye stared at Peter's while he fought to rip the partially penetrated dagger from his chest.

Peter didn't hesitate. A strength born from a renewed fight flowed through him like fire. He formed wings and flew high into the air. With a flick of his wrist he turned the sword into a huge hammer and pounded the dagger deep into Balaal's chest. Black lines of the beast's veins darkened. Then he heard it, Argia's poetic song, followed by Micah's baritone.

Balaal's gaze collided with Peter's as he pounded the dagger deeper. The red hue of his skin turned pale pink, then gray, then black as soot. Cracks of fire ran though the creases in his scales.

"I will be back. Your children will never be safe, Peter Saints!" With that, Balaal exploded, the flying embers of his body disappearing.

Argia and Micah stumbled to Peter's side and with raised hands, closed the tear in the portal Balaal had left open.

Peter hugged them to him until he felt a gentle hand on his back. Pastor Finn pulled him into his arms. "You did it, son."

Peter sagged into his arms. "Did I?" All the strength in him was gone.

"For our lifetime, you did. And that's enough."

CHAPTER 56

Wildflowers were scattered in the thick grass. There was a stream at the edge of the expanse, and Peter held Angel tight on his lap. He winced a bit, from the healing sutures on his side, but snuggled her closer to him. The chair was comfortable and the gazebo was laced with roses. He picked one and gave it to her. Angel leaned back to kiss him.

"I love you." The smile Angel gave him glowed. It had been a long time since he witnessed the depth of joy that seemed to vibrate through her entire body.

"I love you, too. With everything I have. You know that?" Peter bit his lip; he felt a bit more relaxed. More than he had in as long as he could remember.

"What?"

"We can make our forever now."

"Yes, we can. I mean, we are officially graduated from high school."

"Thank you, Pastor Finn for graduating us based on life experiences. I've done enough reading, writing, math, and geography to last a lifetime." Peter laughed.

Angel frowned. "Do you think we'll see them again?"

"Pastor Finn and Rosa are part of the prosecution team that will put Dr. Phillips to death. The bastard needs to die for killing the elder at the orphanage and feeding information to the Order of Dragon. All the kids he'd handed over to them alone shows how insane he was." Peter stretched.

"He led the Extraho of Obscurum to Hanna and Argia, even Micah. I didn't realize a Seer could manipulate both sides that well. I hope there aren't more like him."

"If there are, Pastor Finn will find them. He put a task force together to protect those like Argia and Micah. Rosa is the one who will manage it. No one that is working both sides will get past her."

Angel sighed. "I can believe that. I did like it when Argia and Kyle were dating and we were together. Even though it wasn't fun, there were good times."

"Kyle is with the Doomsday prepper group, with Sam leading them. They will never be fully on board with the Decretum Venia. At least they'll be on our side. Sam was happy Kyle decided to go with him and be trained to create more of them. Kyle, well, he just needed to get over his break-up with Argia and create a new start. We'll see him again, when he's ready."

"It'll be easier to see Argia and Micah since Rosa will only be in Europe with them for a few months before taking over one of the new sanctuaries she's turning into a school."

"She's a tough lady. Sucks that she didn't graduate them yet."

"Well, they still have a lot to learn to take over her role in the Decretum Venia."

"What do you want to do now? We can go to college or move out on our own. Get a job."

"I don't know, Peter. I just... I'm happy we made it out, but I want to make a difference. There are still people being kidnapped by different sects of the Extraho of Obscurum. Killing Balaal didn't destroy them."

"You're right. I wanted to ask you something. It's been on my mind since that day. I want to do more. I think you and I can make a difference if we learn under Pastor Finn. We can take over his detective and bounty hunter company while continuing his work to save others who were captured. It amazes me the connections he had. When I first got out of Gavin's house, the man who pushed me out of there was named Mr. Cadman, same man who smuggled Micah out of there. Working with Pastor Finn would mean we could make a difference by directly infiltrating what's left of the Order of Dragon. Cadman died saving me, being a part of what he did would make me feel his life wasn't wasted."

Angel squealed and twisted to wrap her legs around Peter's hips. "Sounds perfect! I was thinking the same thing. I didn't want to tell you since we both wanted to forget what happened. I can't forget, Peter. I want to change the future for kids like us. Besides, we can go to college online. Faster and less hassle." She nodded. "Say okay." Angel giggled and littered his face with kisses.

"Anything, as long as you say yes." Peter placed his hands on her chin and kissed her deeply. She fell into it with everything she had, her arms wrapped around his neck.

Peter pulled a ring from his pocket. It was tiny, didn't have much of a diamond, but he was proud of it. "Will you marry me, Angel? Be my forever."

"Yes, to everything. To our forever," Angel whispered and kissed him between her murmurs of "I love you."

THE END

A NOTE FROM THE AUTHOR

Thank you for reading Fierce Tides, book 3 in the Purgatory Reign Series. If you have enjoyed it, please consider leaving a review. You can visit my Author page:

www.amazon.com/LM.-Preston/e/B002R7KUCC/

COMING SERIES

Insatiable Souls, Caged Fire Series novella 2018
Caged Fire, Book 1 of the Vigilant Series 2018
Purgatory Reign Manga Series 2018

To stay updated on upcoming books, sales and new releases sign up for her Newsletter or follow her:

Newsletter:
https://landing.mailerlite.com/webforms/landing/v6q7e4
Email: lm.preston@yahoo.com
Web: www.lmpreston.com
Blog: http://lmpreston.blogspot.com/

Goodreads:http://www.goodreads.com/author/show/3348681.L_M_
P
reston

Facebook: https://www.facebook.com/THE-PACK-by-LM-Preston-127604857259681/

Google+: https://plus.google.com/+LMPreston

Twitter: https://twitter.com/LM_Preston

Instagram: https://www.instagram.com/lm_preston/

DISCOVER THE NEXT FROM LM PRESTON
Bandits,
Bandits Series, book 1

Daniel's father has gotten himself killed and left another mess for Daniel to clean up. To save his world from destruction, he must fight off his father's killers while discovering a way to save his world. He wants to go it alone, but his cousin and his best friend's sister, Jade insists on tagging along. Jade is off limits to him, but she insists on changing his mind. He hasn't decided if loving her is worth the beating he'll get from her brother in order to have her. Retrieving the treasure is his only choice. But in order to get it, Daniel must choose to either walk in his father's footsteps or to re-invent himself into the one to save his world.

OTHER BOOKS BY LM. PRESTON

The Pack by LM Preston–

Teen, blind, vigilante on a mission to save the missing kids on mars. Shamira is considered an outcast by most, but little do they know that she is on a mission. Kids on Mars are disappearing, but Shamira decides to use the criminals' most unlikely weapons against them—the very kids who they have captured. In order to succeed, she is forced to trust another, something she is afraid to do. However, Valens, her connection to the underworld of her enemy, proves to be a useful ally. Time is slipping, and so is her control on the power that resides within her. But in order to save her brother's life, she is willing to risk it all.

Bandits by LM Preston –

Daniel's father has gotten himself killed and left another mess for Daniel to clean up. To save his world from destruction, he must fight off his father's killers while discovering a way to save his world. He wants to go it alone, but his cousin and his best friend's sister, Jade insists on tagging along. Jade is off limits to him, but she insist on changing his mind. He hasn't decided if loving her is worth the beating he'll get from her brother in order to have her. Retrieving the treasure is his only choice. But in order to get it, Daniel must choose to either walk in his father's footsteps or to re-invent himself into the one to save his world.

Wastelands – Bandits Series, by LM Preston – Daniel's doing the unthinkable. He's planning to break into a prison to prove to his dead father that he has changed, only problem is – he hasn't.

Flutter Of Luv by LM Preston–

Dawn, the neighborhood tomboy, is happy to be her best friend's shadow. Acceptance comes from playing football after school with the guys on the block while hiding safely behind her glasses, braces, and boyish ways. But Tony moves in, becomes the star running back on her school's football team, and changes her world and her view of herself forever.

Explorer X-Beta by LM Preston –

Barely escaping their captors, Aadi and Eirena are determined to save their dying friend. After their final confrontation with the species that tortured them, they've changed— unfortunately, not for the better. The changes caused by a terrible experiment force Aadi to accept the possibility that he may never be fit to go home, and that holding onto his sanity, or leading his friends to safety will end in failure and may rip his friendship with Eirena apart, forever. Time is slipping away and the possibility of losing his friend is not an option, but the foe that awaits them may be worse than the one they left.

ABOUT THE AUTHOR

LM. Preston is an avid reader. She loved to create poetry and short stories as a young girl. With a thirst for knowledge she attended college and worked in the IT field as a Techie and Educator for over sixteen years. She started writing science fiction under the encouragement of her husband who was a Sci-Fi buff and her four kids. Her first published novel, Explorer X - Alpha was the beginning of her obsessive desire to write and create stories of young people who overcome unbelievable odds. She loves to write while on the porch, watching her kids play, or when she is traveling, which is another passion that encouraged her writing.

For more information, please visit
www.lmpreston.com

THE PURGATORY REIGN SERIES